CONNELLY'S
EXPEDITION

*Also by Noel Loomis
in Large Print:*

Ferguson's Ferry
Above the Palo Duro
Heading West

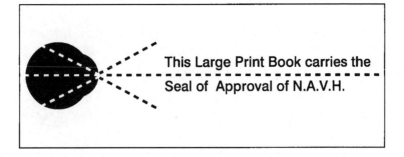

CONNELLY'S EXPEDITION

NOEL LOOMIS

Thorndike Press • Waterville, Maine

Published in 2003 by arrangement with
Golden West Literary Agency.

Thorndike Press® Large Print Paperback.

The tree indicium is a trademark of Thorndike Press.

The text of this Large Print edition is unabridged.
Other aspects of the book may vary from the original edition.

Set in 16 pt. Plantin.

Printed in the United States on permanent paper.

Library of Congress Cataloging-in-Publication Data

Loomis, Noel M., 1905–
    Connelly's expedition / Noel Loomis.
        p. cm.
    ISBN 0-7862-5984-1 (lg. print : sc : alk. paper)
    1. Mexican–American Border Region — Fiction.
2. Americans — Mexico — Fiction. 3. Trading companies
— Fiction. 4. Mexico — Fiction. 5. Large type books.
I. Title.
PS3523.O554C66 2003
813′.54—dc22   2003056728

CONNELLY'S
EXPEDITION

As the Founder/CEO of NAVH, the only national health agency solely devoted to those who, although not totally blind, have an eye disease which could lead to serious visual impairment, I am pleased to recognize Thorndike Press★ as one of the leading publishers in the large print field.

Founded in 1954 in San Francisco to prepare large print textbooks for partially seeing children, NAVH became the pioneer and standard setting agency in the preparation of large type.

Today, those publishers who meet our standards carry the prestigious "Seal of Approval" indicating high quality large print. We are delighted that Thorndike Press is one of the publishers whose titles meet these standards. We are also pleased to recognize the significant contribution Thorndike Press is making in this important and growing field.

Lorraine H. Marchi, L.H.D.
Founder/CEO
NAVH

★ Thorndike Press encompasses the following imprints: Thorndike, Wheeler, Walker and Large Pr int Press.

CHAPTER ONE

It was late afternoon in Chihuahua, and the warm sun of February was still high but had begun to yield to the night coolness flowing down the great slopes of the Sierra Madres.

It was deceptive, Ross Phillips thought as he let the great prancing black follow the other four along one street of the *plaza*. Those tremendous mountainsides that seemed to stretch softly up and up to the sky, were not what they seemed from a distance. In those slopes, now hidden by their own soft shadows, were mile-high cliffs that no man could ever climb, and great riven gashes washed out by the fury of Mexican cloudbursts until now they were deep, savage, almost impenetrable canyons.

Highly deceptive, like Mexican life to an uninformed observer. Here at the moment it was still and quiet in the middle of Chihuahua, and even the occasional yipping of a dog seemed peaceful enough. The masters of the whitewashed adobes were still occupied in their *siestas,* if they had not gone to the bullfight, and even the black-eyed children were quiescent for the moment. The only indication of activity was the occasional comforting sound of the slapping of *tortillas,* for, no matter what the occasion — bullfight or no, *fiesta* or funeral, this was the time of the afternoon when the *señoras* with their quick, competent, olive-skinned hands began to shape the *tortillas* for the evening meal, and presently the busy sound of their supper preparations would arise on all sides, like an evening vesper.

Ross grinned slightly as he thought of the simile. Luisa, down in Zacatecas, had often said he was a poet, but he had told her that in his kind of life there was no time for poetry and little inclination to indulge in it. Except, perhaps, for moments like these.

For a moment the clopping of the horses' hoofs against the background of slapping hands was the only sound, and then it was broken by the harsh *"Sangre! Sangre! Sangre!"* of a crow that flew out of the steeple of the cathedral. "Blood! Blood! Blood!" the Mexicans believed it said, and perhaps they were right, for Ross Phillips knew that this idyllic scene could erupt without warning into a volcanic tempest of violence, bloodshed, and death. This too would last but briefly and then suddenly the entire countryside would be still again, and there would be only the quiet wailing of the mourners, the masses to be said for death, the fees to be paid the priest — so many *reales* for ringing the small bells, more for ringing the big bell, still more for holy water.

Very often the *peon* shrugged and spent his copper *clacos* for *pulque* or *mescal* and got on a very fine drunk. This had its virtues and was far cheaper than a formal burial. Of course there was still the embarrassing presence of the body, but something would turn up. And then again the ancient cities of the *conquistadores* would lapse into their lovely lethargy, and nobody would hurry or worry, nobody would be concerned about anything. The only activity once again would be those flashing brown hands slapping the cornmeal dough to make the *tortillas* that were necessary for existence.

"*Por diós, señor. Por diós.*"

The four riders ahead pulled up their three great black horses and one chestnut, and Ross held back, watching.

The *pordiosera* was a hideous old woman

with a great open sore that covered the side of her face. She had sprung up from the shadows of the cathedral and scuttled crab-fashion into the dust of the street. She held up a wrinkled brown hand with fingers deformed by rheumatism, while she shaded her deep-set black eyes with the other hand. The joints of both hands were twisted and grotesquely large.

"*Señores?*"

The old voice was querulous but the black eyes darted from one to the other of the four, studying, weighing. She glanced once at Ross but passed him over.

Ross, with only half an eye on the four men ahead of him, gave most of his attention to the tiny wrought-iron balcony of a massive whitewashed house on the next corner. The three young Mexicans had come this way for the special purpose of leading him past the Sierra *casa.* He had not seen Valeria since she had left Durango two months before, and he was impatient to find out if she would still be as warmly attractive as she had been in Durango.

There was a swirl at the doors behind the balcony, and Valeria stepped out — floated, rather, it seemed to him. She was a pure Castilian blonde, a rare type in northern Mexico, and he had time to observe her as she scrutinised the men, and he saw her head raise as her eyes turned on him and he was sure she recognised him. He straightened in the saddle. She *was* as beautiful as he remembered her — perhaps more so, with the last sun on her golden hair, her dark eyes and white skin.

None of the others had seen her yet, and Ross alone watched her for a moment. Now, after two months, the sudden sight of her made him wish they did not have to go for the last round of brandy before each man would depart for his home in the mountains.

Apolinar Peralta, who was related to Governor Irigoyen, and at whose ranch Ross was staying until he finished his business in Chihuahua, was startled by the sudden appearance of the old beggar, and jerked his horse away by instinct.

Apolinar was tall, brown, handsome, bursting with life, resplendent in black trousers with flaring legs and green silk inserts set off by silver *conchas,* a red silk sash around his waist, a very white shirt, and the short, embroidered *chaqueta* worn in place of a coat by Mexican horsemen.

The other two Mexicans, Andrés Vigil and Hermenijildo Zamora, were likewise

11

young and in their full vigour, and, not least of all, gifted with a typical Latin love of showing off and the unconscious pride that made them graceful.

The fifth man, on the other hand, was dressed like the young *ricos* and his skin was as brown as theirs, and he tried to act like them, but his inherent self-consciousness and awkwardness were as obvious as his great striving. Mangum was, Ross noted, a good man to have in front, a dubious man to have behind — for Mangum had two opposing natures, and one would never know which way he would jump, whether he would be a young Mexican of the *gente fina* or just a rough-and-tumble, sharp-witted Yankee trader.

It was Mangum who rode the chestnut — one of José Cordero's horses.

Ross was glad in that moment that he had worn conventional *anglo* broadcloth and a beaver hat, for Mangum's clothing was out of place. Again Ross glanced at the balcony and the girl, who appeared to watch with interest.

"Por mis niños, señor, que no tienen leche." The *vieja* advanced a step towards Apolinar, with her crooked hand still held high.

Apolinar, having recovered his breath, could not seem to tear his eyes from her, and he kept a tight rein on the horse. The black walked sidewise, his head tossing. Then Apolinar partially recovered and tossed the woman a silver coin.

She picked it deftly out of the air. It was plain to see her crippled hands were no obstacle to that kind of work.

Ed Mangum, sitting his horse, said cynically, "She's too old to have babies. She's grey-haired. Anyway, neither she nor her descendants ever drank a cup of milk. She'll spend that money on *pulque*."

Apolinar, tall and a little more slender than the others, looked embarrassed to be caught by such an obvious trick, but Hermenijildo, who had married a niece of General Conde, said in reproof of Mangum, "As long as we have our brandy, there is no reason why the beggars should be deprived of *either* milk or *pulque*."

Andrés, who was a grandson of the customs collector at Matamoras, looked at Phillips as Phillips walked his horse up to them. "How is it in Boston or New Orleans, *señor!*"

"Not much different," Ross said thoughtfully.

"It is a great problem in all of Méjico," said Andrés. He alone, of the three young Mexicans, had a very neat black moustache, waxed at the ends, and it might be noticed, with the three of them together, that he was a little heavier than the others though he was the youngest. "There are so many beggars, all we can do is toss the *limosneros* when they hold up their hands. It is sad, but" — he shrugged — "*es cosa de Méjico.* It is a thing of Mexico." And with that, Andrés seemed to dismiss it from his mind.

The *pordiosera* was looking the five men over shrewdly from under her misshapen hand to see if there might be more alms from this group of *gran caballeros,* then apparently decided there would not, and went back to her inconspicuous sitting-place alongside the entrance of the cathedral.

Apolinar swung his horse around and led the way onward, and in a few steps the group had recovered its poise. For the Mexicans were very wise in these matters, both in performance and in discernment, and this was Chihuahau in the spring of 1839, and there was little for the *ricos* to do but eat, sleep, go to the *corridas* or the cockfights, inspect their estates, and make love — which latter was after all the only really worth-while occupation.

Phillips's horse was the kind to hang

back about a length from the others, but this did not bother him, for it gave him a chance to observe the four.

Phillips was brown but his colouring was not like theirs. He was taller and whipcord slender. His hair was brown, and he wore long, well-trimmed sideburns. From his obvious *anglo* colouring he was known to the Mexicans as a *güero*. Such light-complected ones were extremely popular among Mexican women — a fact which had led him into two duels in Durango the summer before. His dress was in keeping, rather plain and severe save for a white brocaded waistcoat.

He never would be a good Mexican, for he was too self-conscious to make a peacock of himself. The black stallions suited him because he liked good horses, but the red and green silk, the silver buttons and embroidered jackets, the gold-and-silver-mounted harness and embroidered saddles, black velveteen pants with blue silk inserts in the flapping legs — those were a little gaudy for his Yankee blood.

The patting of hands on *tortilla* dough now came from all directions, and somewhere off to the right a chicken squawked suddenly as a busy *señora* kicked it out of the living-room. Otherwise it was still peaceful and warm.

"Qué bonita dia!" exclaimed Andrés, who was immediately in front of Ross. "And what a lovely selection of bulls!"

"The fourth fight," said Hermenijildo fervently, "was beautiful."

Apolinar checked his horse and looked back at Ross. "I felt sorry for Arellano on his last bull. Nine swords! *Qué lástima!*"

"Why pity him?" Mangum said sourly. "He got paid for it."

"Oh, but the disgrace!"

Andrés, now facing a division of feeling, said dubiously, "Perhaps he did look clumsy."

"I don't think so," said Phillips, riding up. "I've seen Arellano fight in Querétaro, and he is an artist." He went on thoughtfully, "There was something wrong with that bull to-day. I dare say they have found a deformed shoulder blade to keep the sword from slipping through."

"I say he's clumsy!" Mangum said sharply.

Phillips looked into Mangum's face and was astonished at the belligerence there. He thought about it for a moment, watching Mangum's hostile grey-blue eyes, and then looked away. He was not too interested in Mangum and didn't intend to be, for their meeting that day had been a chance one and was not likely to be repeated.

A pig scurried frantically across the street, and after it came four small, black-eyed, barefooted children, shouting shrilly. They crossed in front of the horses and left a cloud of dust. For a moment the dust hung close to the ground, and Apolinar guided his black through it. All around them was the steady clapping of hands over *tortillas.*

They passed through the dust cloud and now were near the corner of the *plaza* and the Sierra home. The four men ahead slowed down, and Ross automatically pulled back on the reins — rather gingerly, for he visualised the action of that spade bit against the tender roof of the stallion's mouth.

Again, in spite of himself he wondered idly about Mangum and the curious sequence of events that had brought the man into such mismatched company. Ross, who was staying at Apolinar's father's ranch, had got along with the three Mexicans like brothers, and Don Fidel Peralta, Apolinar's father, had suggested they take in the bullfight to see the great Arellano perform. The four had ridden in from Los

Saucillos and found General Conde in a carriage with a broken wheel. They had given him a lift; he had insisted they go to his home for a glass of brandy; José Cordero had been there and introduced Mangum as his friend; Cordero, an older man, had suggested the four younger ones take Mangum with them to the fight, since he was new in Chihuahua and had no acquaintances — and there had been no polite way to decline.

To a certain extent Mangum had dampened the party. He seemed ready to argue about every point that came up and to disagree with anybody — especially Ross. However, it had been otherwise a nice day, and now if they could dispose of Mangum courteously they might yet end the affair with a fitting celebration. Ross assumed there would be a party somewhere in town — perhaps several of them — and he intended to be sure they would go to the one at which the *Señorita* Sierra also would be pres—

"I said — raise your hat, you *burro!*"

Ross focused his attention on Mangum, and realised with a start the words were addressed to him. Mangum glared, but it was a moment before Ross came out of his reverie and fully estimated the man's unaccountable hostility. Almost simultaneously his mind went back over the happenings of the last few moments, and he recalled that Mangum had called him a jackass. He looked at Mangum more closely, and this time he did not notice the man's face but saw instead the cold grey-blue eyes intent on showing him up.

Ross looked around. The three Mexican bloods were curvetting their stallions, their great black hats in their hands. Alone of the three, Apolinar must have heard Mangum's words, for he was watching Ross from the corner of his eye.

Ross looked up at Valeria on the balcony. Her golden-blonde hair shone through the white lace *mantilla,* and he was very conscious of the deep brown eyes even at that distance.

Without apparent notice of Mangum, Ross stood up in his stirrups and raised his heavy beaver hat towards the girl. He swept it low before him in a great arc, and then turned abruptly towards Mangum and swung the hat back-handed with all his strength.

It crashed against the right side of Mangum's head, and for an instant Mangum seemed to be stunned. His big, square hand went to his face and he shook his head briefly. Then his eyes cleared. They turned hard as he glared at Phillips.

"You know I'll have to kill you for that," he said coldly.

"It's a matter of opinion." Ross spun his crushed hat into the street. "And the ability," he added.

He saw Mangum stiffen, but when the man's words came they were controlled. "My seconds will call on you this evening."

Ross, his hands resting on the big Spanish saddlehorn, said, "It isn't necessary to go through with such rigmarole. We're both *anglos*. We can settle it now."

The three young Mexicans drew around them silently, apprehensively. Ross glanced up at the balcony. Valeria was watching, but when she saw his eyes on her she turned quickly and went inside, her full skirt swirling. Almost immediately, however, her face reappeared, partly hidden, behind one of the tiny window-panes.

"We shall fight as gentlemen — not as ruffians," Mangum said harshly.

Ross looked at him. The pig ran back into the street from the other side, with eight or ten children now after it, all shouting, and they stirred up a tunnel of dust as the frightened pig darted across the *plaza* in a course that veered unpredictably.

Ross, his eyes half closed, looked again at Mangum. "Fighting is fighting," he said. "It's up to you."

"My seconds will choose the time and place. You will have the choice."

"I know the rules," Ross said sharply.

Whatever else he was, Mangum wasn't a bluffer. "Very well," he said stiffly, and without a word or a look for any of them he wheeled the chestnut and rode off at a gallop.

Ross raised his eyebrows. "He took his leave without ceremony, it seems."

Apolinar said quickly, "*Señor,* allow me to offer my earnest regrets. I personally am devastated, and I know the governor will be distressed to learn that a man who is practically a guest of the State has been challenged to a duel on his third day in Chihuahua."

Ross said, "It's obvious the man has been looking for trouble ever since we met him. But why?" He looked sharply at the three. "Did any of you know him before to-day?"

They all shook their heads solemnly.

"Then why did *Señor* Cordero ask you to take him with us?"

"Don José is my godfather," said Andrés.

Ross raised his head. "Why did Mangum

concentrate his ill-humour on me? It could not have been personal, so it must have been — of course, it was business!"

"But you've never had dealings with him," said Hermenijildo.

"No. No, I haven't — but I have a feeling I shall have in the future."

Andrés said with some anxiety, "He is said to have killed a number of duellers at Acapulco."

Apolinar said sharply to Andrés, "Watch out for the heels of the black. That stud has marked up every horse that was ever pastured with him."

Andrés moved around.

"He seems to feel the need of practice," said Ross. "What does he fight best with?"

"Pistols, they say."

"Very well, I shall choose six-shooters. Would one of you care to be my second?"

All three spoke together.

"One is enough," said Ross. He looked at them. Hermenijildo was a year or two older than the others and looked reliable. "If it isn't too much trouble," Ross said apologetically.

Hermenijildo's voice was grave. "*Me da tanto gusto.* It will be an honour."

Almost as one man the four wheeled the blacks to the south in the direction of Los

Saucillos. But a woman's voice stopped them as they leaned forward in their huge old Spanish saddles:

"*Señores! El sombrero fino!*"

Ross stopped the black on its haunches, turned it and looked down. A young Mexican woman stood with his big beaver in one hand. She was not shading her eyes and not frowning or squinting into the sun even though it was not far over Ross's shoulder. She wore the usual low-necked white blouse — spotlessly clean, for no matter what the circumstances, a Mexican woman always managed to have a clean blouse. She was in her early twenties, bare-legged, and wore home-made moccasins. Her glossy black hair was drawn neatly to the back of her neck, and somehow, in spite of a heavy baby in one arm, she managed to look graceful and pretty, though she wasn't over five feet tall.

Three more children of stair-step ages hung to her red skirt, and a little behind her, leading a *burro* piled with some mysterious cargo (though it was hard to believe these people could have accumulated anything), was her husband, about the same age and also pleasantly clean.

Ross noted the ragged condition of their clothing and reached in his pocket for a silver *tostón,* but the woman said quickly, "We are not *pordioseros, señor.*"

Ross was momentarily undecided. He looked at the man, who was hardly older than Apolinar but who wore a handsome moustache — more notable because the left side was glossy black, the right side snow white. "We are happy to be of service to you, *señor.*"

"How are you called?" asked Ross.

"Diego Olivarez, *señor,* but I am sometimes called" — the *peon* smiled broadly — "*Bigote Doblado* — Double Moustache."

Ross bowed slightly, "I would like —"

"No, *señor.*" Diego was pleasant but firm, and Ross liked his look of capability and self-assurance — pride, perhaps, that was too often lacking in the *peones.*

The woman moved nearer and held the hat up. He took it, noting that already she had brushed it for him. "*Mil gracias, señora. What is your name?*"

"I am Carlota, wife of Diego."

"I know him," Apolinar said in a low voice. "He worked for Olivarez until he paid off his father's debt."

"He's not a relative of Olivarez, then?"

"Not legally." Apolinar shrugged. "He might be so by blood. Who knows? Sometimes the Indian slave girls had babies without husbands — this was before slavery was abolished — and they usually adopted the name of the owner. Now of course there is no slavery —"

"Only legal bondage," said Ross.

Apolinar shrugged again. "It is the law."

"Where do you live?" asked Ross.

She pointed north-east.

"In the desert?" he asked.

"Across the desert."

"It is a long way to come to trade."

"We don't come often — twice a year."

He held out a gold coin. "Please take this for the *niños.*"

Her answer was dignified. "No, *señor.* We have all we need — a place to live, the *niños*" — she glanced down at them proudly — "plenty of game to eat, sunshine to keep us warm, the stars at night."

"You could buy coffee with this."

"We will buy coffee with the skins Diego has on the jack."

"Sugar, then."

"There is wild honey for the gathering." She backed away two or three steps.

Ross put the hat on firmly. "I am under great obligation to you, *señora,*" he said.

"It is nothing," she answered.

"I will burn a candle for you both," he said, and turned the black.

They rode in silence through the town. Gradually the tension left Ross, and he became aware of the steady plopping of the hoofs, the ubiquitous and comforting domesticity of hands shaping *tortillas*, the sudden and almost disconcerting squawk of a chicken, the intermittent yapping of dogs, the cries of children racing in the dusty streets.

The sun was lower, nearing the ridge of the Sierra Madres. The sudden explosion had come and gone and there was now only the reaction. The edge was gone from the sauciness of the three *caballeros*. Hermenijildo had become very sober as befitted the second of a man who might well be dead within twelve hours. Andrés seemed frightened; Apolinar appeared concerned, for Ross was the guest of his uncle the governor — not to mention the fact, well known to them all, that Ross's mission was semi-diplomatic and very important economically to the state and city of Chihuahua and its merchants.

Ross rode along easily, allowing his body to move with the horse. Now that the first impact of the challenge was over, he found himself thoughtful but quite calm. Fighting duels seemed always to be a part of his business.

They rode in silence, crossing the aqueduct that brought water to Chihuahua. The adobes were very scattered. A donkey looked out of a front door and stretched his neck upwards in a raucous bray.

They left the town with its dusty streets, its church bells and irrigation canals, and struck out across the prairie, following a trail well beaten into the sparse grass of the dry soil. The shadows down the mountains were very long, and left the great slopes hidden in a twilight haze.

"Fine horses," Ross said casually.

Andrés nodded. "Don Fidel has bred nothing but black horses for thirty years."

Apolinar nodded. "*Papá* has thousands — all beautiful."

A mile past the aqueduct Andrés turned off. "I am expected at home before the *baile* to-night," he said, and added half-humorously, half-wryly, "No doubt *papá* will have some instructions for my proper conduct."

Apolinar laughed shortly. "Is his concern for you or for the *señoritas?*"

Andrés lifted his eyebrows. With his moustache he was a very handsome and also a very engaging young man. "I think his chief worry is for the foreigners." He glanced at Ross.

"With the Magoffins and Connelly, and Doctor Jennison, and Adolf Speyer, and *Señor* Mangum and *Señor* Phillips —" He shrugged. "The commerce of Chihuahua is being overrun with *anglos,* to hear him tell it."

Ross studied his horse's ears. "There *are* a lot of us." He looked up. "But most of the money is put up by Mexican merchants."

"*Papá* says men like Magoffin and Wiley are becoming much too well intrenched. However, that isn't his real concern."

Apolinar leaned over to rub his horse's neck. "To tell the truth, Don Mauricio is worried about the younger generation," he said. "The *mejicanos* stay home and do the bookkeeping while the *anglos* get in the saddle and take the caravans through Indian country, and Don Mauricio has a dire feeling that the Mexican race is losing its vigour." He laughed. "You wouldn't think so, from the squadrons of *niños* that spring up each year."

Andrés raised a hand. "I'll see you to-night," he said, and put the black into a far-ranging lope, for the Vigil *ranchería* was three leagues into the mountains.

Hermenijildo, sitting back quietly, said with gravity, "If you don't mind, Apolinar,

I'll stay at your place until the duel is over — since I am Don Ross's second."

"By all means." Apolinar saw that Ross was looking back at the town, and turned his horse alongside. Hermenijildo noted their movements, but his eyes were cloudy and he did not join them.

The sun was over the western range of the mountains, seemingly balanced on the exact top of the ridge, sending long streamers of yellow light across the wild, rugged slopes, lighting up the pine-covered ridges but leaving the valleys dark and mysterious like Mexico herself. This last sunlight lit up the town of Chihuahua — now to their north-east, lying in a crescent-shaped flat in the mountains.

Beyond the town, to the south, a spur of the Sierra Madres rose high and jagged and forbidding. The mountains there looked impassable, but the road to Durango wound somewhere through those precipitous canyons and forbidding passes. To the north, mule trains and ox-cart caravans, as well as the heavy-laden wagons of the far-travelling, hard-booted men from Independence, came with merchandise that tripled and quadrupled in value by virtue of making the 2,000-mile trip from Independence in creaky wagons pulled by oxen, across plains swept by savage Comanches, through mountains infested with deadly Apaches.

All these things Ross Phillips thought as he watched the sun play on the peaks beyond the town. With luck, he thought, that profitable trade would soon be travelling a different road, and new fortunes would be made on the turn of a single trip.

Ross turned finally to Apolinar. "Nice town," he commented.

Apolinar turned his horse. "I like it except when the Apaches come."

Ross glanced back at Hermenijildo as they rode off. Young Zamora was taking his duties as second very seriously; he hadn't smiled since the affair in the street.

Two hours later they turned in at the big gate of the Peralta Ranch, Los Saucillos, about dark. The brand was burned in the gate-posts, but Ross hadn't figured out yet what it was; he suspected it had started out as a capital P with flourishes, but somewhere a cross or two had been added and perhaps a royal crest, and now it was truly a *"Quien Sabe?"* — "Who Knows?" — brand.

The usual pack of dogs came to meet them. Apolinar ordered them back to the house; Ross said nothing; Hermenijildo maintained an aloof silence.

A man rode from a clump of willows along the creek, followed by a servant on a mule.

"Don Fidel," said Ross.

"Señor!" Don Fidel Peralta looked at them keenly. He glanced at his son Apolinar, then scrutinised Hermenijildo's sober face. "So! There is trouble, no? *Señoritas,* yes?"

Apolinar did not reply immediately, so Ross offered information. "It is hard to say, Don Fidel, what exactly *is* at the bottom of it."

Peralta's black eyes narrowed. He was a fierce-looking man with swarthy, pock-marked skin and a black moustache at least a foot wide. "Then it wasn't one of these *muchachos.* It must have been you, Don Ross." His eyes narrowed. "From the tragic look on Hermenijildo's face, you have been challenged and he is your second."

Ross rested his hands on the saucer-sized saddlehorn and looked up. "Maybe you can tell me who has challenged."

Peralta paused. "You haven't been here long enough to get involved in politics. I would judge it was economic."

"Señor Mangum," Apolinar said shortly,

31

unable longer to restrain himself.

There was a quick raise of Peralta's heavy black eyebrows. "So? *Señor* Mangum."

Apolinar explained. "We were before the *Señorita* Sierra's house, and —"

"With the *señorita* on the balcony, of course."

"*Por supuesto,*" said Ross.

Peralta smiled and nodded to Apolinar to continue.

"Unaccountably the *Señor* Mangum seemed to take offence because Don Ross did not take off his hat as soon as the rest of us."

"I was thinking," Ross said, "about the *señorita* when she was in Durango."

Peralta nodded wisely.

"He insulted Don Ross, and —"

"I very nearly unseated him with my hat," said Ross, and added speculatively, "I'd always wondered if it could be done."

"And the answer is no?"

Ross bowed apologetically. "I tried very hard."

Peralta nodded absently. "It is perhaps no surprise, but one wonders why he chose that particular time and place."

"To appear important in the eyes of the *señorita,*" said Apolinar quickly.

Peralta's glance was sharp. "Perhaps you *muchachos* know more about life than Don Mauricio suspects. You are most likely right. Does *Señor* Mangum then, have calf's eyes at the *señorita* — and, if so, for herself or for her fortune?"

"*Doña* Valeria's father and *papá* were brothers," Apolinar explained. "They were in partnership, and half of Los Saucillos still belongs to her."

"It doesn't matter," Peralta said. "There's enough for all. There are millions of *varas* and forty-five thousand horses."

Ross observed, "A man marrying into the family might force a division."

Peralta considered. "Whatever it is, you may be sure that Mangum is deadly serious about it, as he is about everything."

Ross leaned over and straightened the brow-band of the bridle. "What is he doing in Chihuahua?"

"I am told that Cordero sent for him."

"For what purpose?" asked Ross.

"Mangum is well experienced at moving goods over difficult trails. He has worked all over Mexico and South America."

Ross looked up sharply. "Connelly and Magoffin and a dozen others know every league of the Santa Fé Trail."

"They do," said Don Fidel, "and so it is

fairly obvious that Cordero is not spending a large amount of money to have Mangum find the way to Independence."

"That leaves —"

"Exactly what it seems to leave, Don Ross. Cordero has heard of our plans — actually there has been no secret about them — and he has employed Mangum to be sure we are not successful in establishing the trail across Texas."

"Why is that necessary?" asked Ross. "There is room for all."

"Not if you are already committed in Independence or St. Louis, *señor*. It may even be that Cordero's operating money comes from that end of the Santa Fé Trail, and if he were to change his route he might lose that backing."

Ross smiled. "I thought all Chihuahua merchants were wealthy."

"Since the panic," Don Fidel said, "we never know who's broke and who's well fixed. It's worth noting that Cordero has not offered to come in with us on the Texas venture."

"That argues that he can't afford to lose."

"Exactly. I know he has a caravan leaving Independence in May, and the goods for that are already bought, so —"

Ross said thoughtfully, "Then the verdict is that Mangum has been brought here to stop the Texas expedition, and he has already taken the first step by challenging me to a duel."

"With obvious assurance that he will win it," said Don Fidel.

Ross smiled. "If he loses, he won't collect his fee."

Don Fidel looked worried. "You are not afraid, *señor?*"

Ross took off his heavy beaver, examined it carefully. One edge was bent in where it had struck Mangum's face. He brushed the hat with his sleeve as the horse broke into a lope. "It rather seems to me," he said, raising his voice over the rhythmic swish of the horse's hoofs in the deep grass of the meadow, "that I am pretty well armed." He put the hat back on his head and looked at Peralta and smiled.

CHAPTER TWO

Since the only trees were cottonwoods and willows down by the creek, the open meadow was still fairly light and gave a good view of the Los Saucillos head-quarters, which was like a small town. Don Fidel's home was a large abode of two stories, built as a hollow square, with the centre, the *placita,* used to protect the animals, and various rooms around the outside arranged for fighting off an attack. Around this main building and out to a distance of three hundred yards, were scattered at random the one-room adobe huts of the *peones.* Prominent among these was a small church, square and flat like the other buildings but distinguished by a cross on top.

The four men rode into the scattered cluster of huts. A fifteen-year-old mother with a baby on her hip was shooing two scrawny chickens into the hut for the night, and she paused to stare at them. One of the black stallions, Ross knew, was worth many times the entire value of such a family's possessions, including their hut and their clothing and whatever assorted barn-yard animals they might claim. Dogs ran out yapping in droves, but retreated when they heard Peralta's voice. A bare-footed young man of eighteen, wearing the *peon*'s big straw hat and a soiled white shirt with a collar-band, fingered a beaten-up guitar and sang a sad song of love and passion unrequited:

> *O my chiquita, have pity on me,*
> *A poor vaquero*
> *Whose heart is at your feet.*

Apolinar said briefly, "He's at it again."

"He sounds heartbroken," Ross observed.

Peralta snorted. "That's Plácido's special talent. He's the most persuasive lover between Chihuahua and Durango — and only a billy-goat is more democratic in his taste." He added: "He's also one of the best mule-men in northern Mexico."

"Who is the girl this time?"

"Anita — a servant girl of *papá*'s. She must be working in the kitchen just now."

Near the church a Franciscan priest was watering nasturtiums, bright with an abundance of yellow, orange, and red blossoms.

He straightened, bare-headed, brown-

37

robed, and with only sandals on his feet.

"Good evening, Father Ramón," said Peralta.

The priest smiled. *"Buenas noches."* He noted Hermenijildo. "How is your wife, my son?"

"Very good, Father."

"No *niños* yet?"

Hermenijildo said, rather shortly, "Not yet."

The priest observed the note of tension in Hermenijildo's voice, and said, "There is time," and went back to his watering.

They rode through a large opening in the big house, past massive gates tied back with rawhide, into a large courtyard. Peralta dismounted, and servants ran forward to take the horses.

The patio was enclosed on all four sides by the building, and within the square were stables, blacksmithing equipment, two wagons, a great clumsy coach for the ladies on state occasions, and a well with stone sides and a bucket hanging from a rope. They were well fortified against attack.

"Let the horses roll," Peralta told the *mozos.* "Give them some old corn and turn them into the meadow. Remember — *old corn.*" He spoke to Ross as they walked across the yard to the left side of the building. "Last week," he said with disgust, "one of the fools fed new corn to a three-year-old mare, and when I took her out for a ride into the mountains next day she died fifteen miles from home and left me afoot!"

There was no more to be said. A man afoot was no man at all in this country of great distances.

"Now," said Peralta, stopping at the hand-hewed cottonwood door of Ross's room, "Connelly and Magoffin will be here presently to look you over and see if they want to risk a quarter of a million dollars in gold and silver to your care."

Ross nodded. "Naturally."

"We'll have dinner when you're ready." Peralta turned abruptly to Hermenijildo. "And you — since you are acting as the *señor*'s second, you'd better room with him to-night — though he probably can take care of himself." He turned to Ross with a twinkle in his eye. "From Hermenijildo's manner, one would think this a serious business."

Ross looked at Hermenijildo and knew how the young man felt. "It may be that," he said quietly.

"*Caray!*" Peralta was impatient. "With

such an important venture ahead of us, we have no time for play. The welfare of the entire northern half of Mexico depends on the outcome of this expedition."

Apolinar spoke from behind them. "*Papá,* this *is* serious. He has been challenged by *Señor* Mangum."

Peralta snorted. "Well — pleasure before business, I suppose." He glanced at them all and said thoughtfully, "This is a big event in a young man's life. A challenge, a duel." He lifted his black eyebrows. "Life or death. I was young myself," he said reminiscently, and then his eyes narrowed. "But remember, all of you — you most of all, *Señor* Ross: a duel can be fought every day in the week, but a chance to make a fortune comes once in a lifetime."

He stamped off, obviously annoyed at the whole situation. Apolinar smiled stiffly at Ross. "Don't mind *papá.* He believes in making money — but in the next breath he, like Don Mauricio, will be moaning because the younger generation is not man enough to stand on its own feet."

Ross started into his room but heard Peralta's boots as the man turned. "It's not that we lack vigour in our own race," he told Ross, "but our young men do their riding inspecting their estates, and they do their fighting behind a guitar."

Ross looked full at him. "I find it difficult to believe, Don Fidel, that your vigour has not been passed on to your sons."

Peralta glared at him. "So you're a diplomat as well!" He turned on his heel and strode away.

Apolinar chuckled weakly. "Another speech like that and *papá* will adopt you."

Ross grinned. "I would not wish to further complicate my life," he said, and pushed through the door.

He threw his heavy hat on the pallet in one corner, hung his coat and waistcoat on pegs, and prepared to wash in the silver bowl. But he swung to Hermenijildo. "Don't stand there like Hidalgo's monument. Aren't you hungry?"

"*Señor,* I cannot take this lightly."

"Is this your first time as a second?"

"*Sí.*"

Ross plunged his face into the tepid water. "You have full authority," he said through dripping water. "Receive the challenge, name the weapons — six-shooters, and agree on a time and place." He looked around, shaking the water out of his eyes. "Now get ready for dinner!"

They gathered around a massive table in a room lighted by candles. There were none but men at the table, for Mexican women did not eat with the men, and Ross got set for the endless *platicando* that accompanied any sort of Mexican transaction.

For food there were not the omnipresent *guisado* or stew of the *pobres*, but a first course of wine, and later chicken, pork, and beef, followed by sweet cakes and coffee. At that point the faint chorus of barking dogs came to them through the night air.

Peralta, dropping a piece of brown sugar in his coffee, looked up. "Confounded dogs! I can always tell when we have friendly company, for the dogs are bold. Let an Apache show his head over yonder hill and the dogs slink into hiding."

"It's not the dogs' fault, *papá*," said Apolinar. "They are not trained."

Peralta glared at him. "What do you suggest — a full-time dog trainer?"

Apolinar flushed and looked down at the table. Obviously the canine birth rate precluded any thought of training. "It has to be endured," Peralta growled, "but not liked."

He arose and went into the courtyard and to the big cottonwood gates, which now were closed and barred. Ross,

Apolinar, and Hermenijildo went with him. Peralta swung a peephole cover up and looked out. *"Quién es?"* he called in a ringing voice.

Above the dogs' yapping came an unruffled answer: "Santiago Magoffin and Enrique Connelly!"

It was now thoroughly dark, and two servants hurried up with blazing torches of *sotol* stalks. They slid the three log bars out of their keepers and swung the gates wide. A tall man on a dun mule rode into view. In the sputtering yellow light his sloping shoulders gave the impression of great strength. He had large ears, a high forehead, a generous, well-formed nose, and a straight, firm mouth. His grey eyes singled out Ross Phillips at once, and for a moment he scrutinised him. Ross felt that he had been examined minutely, but he did not know the man's conclusion. Then Magoffin swung down from the saddle of his mule and said, "Don Fidel, it is good to see you."

They embraced. Magoffin was not dressed like a Mexican, but wore the long, sombre-hued coat of an *anglo*, a shirt collar that stood up around his neck, and a wide black tie in a large bow.

Doctor Connelly dismounted — a man

similarly dressed but a different man in appearance — stocky build, square shoulders, rather deep lines alongside his nose, and his eyelids pulled down at the outer corners as if he had been much in the wind and sand.

Peralta took them both into the *sala* and Ross and the boys followed. Peralta got the visitors seated and poured brandy. "Cigars?"

"Later," said Connelly.

"Thanks," Magoffin said. "My years on the trail taught me to prefer a chew."

"Well, gentlemen!" Peralta looked around at the three young men, who stood patiently near the door. Peralta was in a high good humour. "*Señores*, here is the man you have been waiting to see. It is my pleasure to introduce *Señor* Ross Felip, and I am assured by the Mexican consulate of New Orleans that if any man can take a caravan through the Texas Comanches, this man can."

Connelly studied him over his brandy. "Looks young to me."

Magoffin chuckled. "That's why you and I aren't trying it on our own. We're too old."

"I'm barely forty," Connelly said argumentatively.

Magoffin was fingering a plug of

tobacco. "That's too old for a trading expedition through unknown country — and you and I have been sleeping on *anglo* mattresses too long."

Connelly looked again at Ross and suddenly arose, seemingly without effort, and held out his hand with a smile. "Welcome to Chihuahua, Phillips. Been in Mexico before?"

Ross shook hands. "All my life — off and on."

"Trail experience?"

"Three or four years on the Santa Fé Trail," Ross said casually.

"I never ran into you," Magoffin said, and it was not an idle remark.

"I can think of no good reason why you should, sir." Ross looked into the penetrating eyes. "I know *your* name, though."

"At that," Magoffin went on thoughtfully, "the cut of your jib has a familiar look."

"You may place it later," Ross said quietly.

"What did you do on the Trail?"

"Everything — teamster, scout, bullwhacker."

"Why?" asked Connelly.

"I liked it. Open country, fresh air, adventure — what more does a man need?"

"Money," said Connelly quickly.

Ross sighed. "I found that out. I put my money into a cargo from China. I thought I was going to make a fortune — but the ship sank in a typhoon near the Philippine Islands."

"How long ago was this?" asked Magoffin.

"Thirty days ago I got the news." Ross faced them squarely. "Gentlemen, you may as well know that I am penniless. If I don't make a deal with you I'll have to borrow money to get to Paso or else get a job with one of the wagon trains going through."

There was silence for a moment. Connelly cleared his throat. Don Fidel reached abruptly for the brandy. The two younger men studied their glasses.

"Sorry," said Magoffin. "I wasn't trying to pry."

"You had a right," said Ross. "But don't misunderstand one thing. In spite of being broke, I know what my services are worth on this expedition, and I'll get my price or find a job skinning mules."

Magoffin muttered, "He's an independent cuss for a man without money." He went on, "I'll be honest. A man who has been unable to make any money on his own is not too appealing to me."

Ross did not answer.

"Had any experience with Indians?" asked Connelly.

"Took my first scalp on the Apishapa — a Ropihue, Old Bill Williams said."

"You knew Bill Williams?" It was a quick question.

Ross shook his head. "*Nobody* knew him. It happened I was trapping castor in the Shining Mountains that summer, and my two pardners got done in by redskins crazy for hair. I lit out for the Napestle, and rode into the valley of the Apishapa with four Injuns at my heels. Ran right over Bill Williams's fire, and he cursed me for two days for leading them to him."

"And you got one?" Connelly asked presently.

Ross took the brandy offered by Peralta and tossed it off. "Four. Matter of honour. They made me lose two bales of beaver plews."

Magoffin's keen eyes were on him. "What did Old Bill say?"

Ross looked at the floor for a moment. "It was my first scalp. Old Bill looked them all over and said, '*Sacre, enfant,* must be a goddamned dull knife you sawed them off with.' "

Magoffin roared and hit the table with a

huge hand. "He was with Bill, all right!"

Connelly nodded. "He talks like a mountain man when he wipes off that veneer, right enough. Sit down, everybody." He poured another brandy. "The story isn't long but it's damned important." He looked at Ross. "You know that most of the goods that reaches northern Mexico comes by way of St. Louis and Santa Fé or from England through Guaymas. Either way is expensive."

"We sell the stuff and we get our price," Magoffin said, "but we have a lot of competition — Adolf Speyer, José Cordero, John Kelly, Olivarez, Solomon, Macmanus, Anderson — a dozen others."

"It's a long haul," Connelly said. "Nearly two thousand miles and dangerous every *vara* of the way — from Indians, cyclones, cloudbursts, desert, outlaws — everything in the book."

"Even taking the gold and silver out is risky," said Magoffin. "Since the Government prohibits the export of precious metals without a permit — and such a permit would cost more than the metal — then the specie or bullion we take to pay for goods is all contraband and subject to confiscation by Mexican officials. It is getting so it takes a pretty penny in bribery to get the stuff out of Mexico, and now there are so many on the Trail the prices we get for goods drop every season. The risks being what they are, we've had to devise a way to cut the costs."

"In other words, a shorter haul," said Ross.

Connelly unrolled a large sheet of heavy paper with wavy edges. "See here?"

Ross stood up beside him. Ross, taller and more slender, had no trouble seeing over Connelly's muscular arm, a printed and tinted map of Louisiana and Texas.

"Only about a fourth of Texas has been explored," said Connelly. "The north-west frontier is on a line running from Austin to San Antonio. The rest" — he swept the north and west portions of the state with a quick movement of his thick arm. "Unexplored. Inhabited by Kiowas and Comanches. Water is scarce or not fit to drink."

"So I've heard," murmured Ross.

"Ever been in that country?" asked Magoffin.

"No."

Connelly went on. "Precipitous ranges, fast and deep rivers, swamps and bogs, mosquitoes and flies, and the Cross Timbers, which is said to be impenetrable."

Ross, having seen the map, settled down

in his chair with a glass of brandy. "You don't think it will be easy?"

Connelly seemed slightly disgusted. "I *know* it won't be easy."

Ross looked at him. "I understood that before I came to Chihuahua. If it were easy, you'd send someone of your own."

"Very good," said Magoffin, nodding approval.

"It is not commonly realised," said Connelly, "but Presidio del Norte is a legal port of entry. It was made so four years ago, just before the Texas revolution, but for obvious reasons it never has been used as such. All goods for Chihuahua comes through Mexico City on the south, Guaymas on the Pacific coast, Taos in the north, or Matamoras on the east coast. Matamoras is an important point but it's twelve hundred miles from Chihuahua across the Bolsón de Mapimí and might as well be in another world. The key to this entire project is the fact that goods can legally enter through Presidio del Norte. Since it is a very tiny post and the commander is no higher than a lieutenant, he will be agreeable to whatever the governor suggests. Thus we can get a customs certificate for our goods, and once we have accomplished a legal entry we can take the stuff anywhere in Mexico."

Peralta poured more brandy. The two young Mexicans, Apolinar and Hermenijildo, sat stiffly against the wall, eyes wide.

Connelly sat down and fixed his droopy-lidded eyes on Ross. "From St. Louis it is 2,000 expensive miles; from Jonesborough or Pecan Point or whatever port we can reach on the Red River of Natchitoches — somewhere in Arkansas or Louisiana —"

Peralta said, "I thought the Great Raft —"

"The raft was cleaned out of the river last year," said Ross, looking up. "The Red is navigable to Fort Towson. Steamboats run all the way from New Orleans."

"I dare say you know it," Connelly told Ross, "but I want us to understand each other. The expensive part of any trip to Chihuahua is cross-country by ox-teams that make 12 miles a day. The ox-team part of the trip would be shortened to 1,300 miles by this proposed route." He paused. "It would give us an edge on competition for at least a couple of years."

Ross nodded.

"Since you know this will be a very dangerous trip," said Connelly, "why did you answer my letter?"

"Because I want to make a lot of money

51

in a hurry," said Ross, "and the only way I know to do that is to engage in something dangerous — something that most men would think over twice and then reject."

"For our part," Connelly said, "of course we're pleased to get your answer. There aren't three or four men in Mexico capable of conducting this expedition successfully."

"There is Mangum."

"Whom we would not trust. Besides, it was essential for a trip like this, knowing there would be many levels of opposition, that we have a capable fighter — one who knows all the tricks and can use them."

"What do you mean by levels of opposition?"

"You have lived a dangerous life on the Trail," said Connelly, "but you know little of business affairs as they are conducted in Mexico. Here's what will happen: Cordero will hire Mangum to oppose you; Mangum will hire somebody else to try to incapacitate you without risking his own neck, and probably Cordero will hire still another to work independently of Mangum. The man who conducts this first expedition across Texas will have to fight — and whip — all of these lower levels."

"And Cordero too?"

"Doubtful. If you ever work up to

Cordero, he will concede gracefully. That," he said, "is the way it is done here."

Ross shrugged. "I can fight," he said, "if it's necessary — or if it's interesting."

"I'm curious," said Magoffin, "why do you want to make some money fast? You've apparently taken your time for years."

Ross smiled. "Recently I have come to think money a useful commodity. I would like to have a good deal of it."

"To buy a ranch?" asked Magoffin.

"Yes."

"Got one picked out?"

"No — but I have selected the place where I want it — Chihuahua."

"Why would a man want a ranch in this country?" asked Connelly.

Magoffin shrugged. "Some men like champagne — others drink tequila. How do I know?"

"You haven't told me," said Peralta to Connelly, "how you interested the Merchants' Bank of New Orleans in this project?"

Connelly turned to him. "Gold bullion sent from here to New Orleans clears ten and a half per cent over gold coin of the United States. Isn't that inducement enough to any man interested in a profit?"

"It's illegal to ship bullion."

"It's illegal to raise tobacco in Chihuahua too," Connelly said sharply, "but I saw a patch of young plants along the road."

Peralta raised his eyebrows, twisted one end of his moustache, and returned to his brandy. "I'm no business man," he said. "I'm a rancher."

"Just before I wrote you," Connelly said to Ross, "I was in New Orleans, and the Mexican consul there recommended you as honest. Why?"

"He's a friend of my father," said Ross, "and I have a suspicion that for the last ten or twelve years, while I have been making myself familiar with the Western Country, that my father has related some of my exploits, and perhaps those have impressed the consul."

"What does your father do?" asked Connelly.

"He is interested in the Merchants' Bank."

"How?"

Ross looked at him without change of expression. "He owns it."

"That explains a number of things," said Magoffin. "It offers a reason why the Merchants' Bank was willing to put up some of the money for this venture."

"I don't think so," said Connelly. "I dealt with another man."

"The cashier," said Ross. "I said my father owns it — not that he runs it."

Connelly said, "How is it, then, that you have spent so much time out here?"

"Frankly," said Ross, "because I don't give a damn about banking." He looked at Connelly.

"I could ask — but I won't — why you came to Chihuahua. Who knows? A man does what he does, doesn't he?"

"There ought to be a reason," Connelly insisted, but Ross did not take it up.

"When do you expect to start?" Ross asked.

"Within two weeks — about the first of April."

"If *you* are going, why do you need me?"

"That's not hard to answer. I'm not too old to go, but I don't feel up to things that will be encountered in the active management of a hundred and fifty men and several hundred mules. I need somebody who knows the country to take over that."

"You could have hired anybody who can handle men and horses."

"No. I don't want to have to make the dozens of decisions that come up every day on a trip like this. If you get involved, I'll be there to put in my two cents' worth, but mostly I expect you to handle things on your own."

Ross considered. "We can do it that way if you don't try to take over."

Magoffin was watching them closely, and now he nodded approval. "Well said." He pointed at Connelly. "You need have no fear of the doctor. He has made a career out of hiring men to do the hard work."

"What is the Republic of Texas going to say to this?" asked Ross.

"We don't look for any trouble. Houston and Lamar are fighting each other, but they both know the establishment of this trade route would be a great thing for Texas. Anyway, we're keeping in the wilderness areas and not going through any settled portion of the republic. We're going to stay north and west of San Antonio and Austin and even Nacogdoches. We'll hit the Red and follow it down to Arkansas."

"A lot of unexplored country in there," Ross suggested.

"As far as white men are concerned — yes."

"It ought to be interesting. How about the United States?"

"No trouble there. The merchants favour it; the Government encourages it."

"There remains," Peralta noted, "the slight problem of getting bullion out of Mexico and getting goods back in without exorbitant duties."

Connelly said with assurance, "Our friendship with Governor Irigoyen will ease the way. He has promised to halve the import duties at Presidio del Norte so as to encourage the building up of trade. It's a good thing for Chihuahua, since this would naturally be the wholesale centre for northern and western Mexico."

Ross set down his glass. "Will we get an open fight out of anybody besides Cordero?"

"Probably not. The stakes are high, but most of these men are in a position to turn their eyes east if the profit lies there. Kelly will watch us carefully. Olivarez will follow Kelly. Adolf Speyer is a man well able to take care of himself, and besides, he is backed by Armijo in Santa Fé. Mangum is the man to watch, for I suspect that he has money of his own on the Trail."

"That was his train pulled in yesterday from San Juan," said Peralta, looking up.

"A rough crew they had," said Magoffin. "They spent to-day in the *juzgado* sobering up."

"So I heard," said Ross.

"Wagon foreman name of Link Habersham. Know him?"

Ross looked up. "I know him."

"A one-eyed man," said Magoffin.

Ross nodded.

"Had a run-in with him?" asked Connelly.

"A slight one."

"Maybe," said Magoffin, "he'll be your first lever to clear out."

"Perhaps," said Peralta, "you'd better not go into town to-night."

Apolinar said quickly, "The *Yanquí* freighters never bother the *bailes, papá.* The *fandangos* — yes, of course, but not the *bailes.*"

Ross looked at them both absently. "If there is to be a fight, let's get it over with. Besides — you have forgotten — I have a duel to take care of in the morning. If there is anything unscheduled, we'd better handle it to-night."

"A duel!" said Connelly. "You're not serious."

Hermenijildo said stiffly, "I am his second."

Magoffin's eyes narrowed. "Who's your opponent?"

"Mangum."

Magoffin shook his head. "This could

lead to international complications. He's a British subject. He took out citizenship to get the protection of a British passport."

Ross said indifferently, "Perhaps he will have it with him to-morrow morning."

Connelly was on his feet. "You can't fight a duel. It would cancel the whole project if you were killed."

Ross looked at him and reached for the brandy glass. Peralta sank back with contentment on his face and in every line of his body. "If you ask me, *señores*, I would say Don Felip is looking forward to this duel with pleasurable anticipation. And I will admit that I plan to be there myself. But what an unholy hour to get up!"

"Papá," said Apolinar, "you don't know when the time will be."

"Oh, yes," Peralta grumbled. "Anyone as deadly serious as Mangum could not possibly choose any time but sunrise."

CHAPTER THREE

Ross got up, stretching. "You gentlemen will want to talk it over. Meantime, we'll get dressed for the *baile*."

He led the way to his room. Apolinar left them and went to his own. He was just pushing in the door when it opened and a Mexican girl gasped. "O *señores!* I am sorry. I was just leaving Don Ross's clean shirt for the *baile*."

"All right," said Ross. *"Gracias."*

He found the white shirt laid out on the bed, beautifully laundered. "Nice looking girl," he observed.

"Anita?" said Hermenijildo, taking off his jacket. "She's a beauty. Already she has three children and no husband."

"Who's the father?"

Hermenijildo shrugged. "Nobody knows — least of all Anita. She's pleasant, a good servant — but she'd sleep with the devil himself for a silver peso."

"Maybe she has to have a man."

"It's more than that." Hermenijildo

frowned. "She gives one the feeling that she is completely without awareness of any principles whatever."

Ross shrugged. "Perhaps that is why the Lord made so many girls — so a man could choose."

Hermenijildo stopped to look at him. "*Señor,* there is one thing I should say."

"Say it."

"Your business is your own, but as your second I may have the temerity to advise you."

Ross poured warm water out of the crockery pitcher into the heavy basin. "Go ahead."

"I observed your fencing with the men to-night over the reason for wanting to buy a ranch near Chihuahua."

Ross stopped in the course of plunging his hands into the water. "I was not aware I said exactly that — but go ahead."

"I have been with you on three occasions now," said Hermenijildo seriously. "Once at Jennison's *baile* night before last, at the *corrida* to-day, and again coming home this evening — and on all occasions, *señor,* I observed your conduct in the presence of the *Doña* Valeria."

Ross paused, then plunged his face into the warm water.

"I recall," said Hermenijildo, "that *Doña* Valeria was visiting in Durango a month or so ago."

"Coincidence," said Ross, wiping water from his face with his hands.

"And you asked us this morning to take you by her house."

Ross grunted.

"You wish to have a ranch near Chihuahua," Hermenijildo said inexorably, "and it is very easy to understand why: because you, being an honourable man, would not ask the hand of *Doña* Valeria unless you had some goods of your own to offer."

To avoid answering, Ross plunged his face into the water again. Finally he lifted it and said, "You're a romanticist in the largest sense, Hermenijildo."

"I am not old, *señor.* I —"

"Age has nothing to do with it." Ross reached for a linen towel.

"Then perhaps you will leave me a message to be delivered to her in case of your — after the duel to-morrow morning."

Ross chuckled. "If I'm dead, it won't do much good. If I'm alive, I'll deliver it myself. Now, then!"

"*Señor?*"

"I don't mind your noticing things, and I

don't mind your saying them to me — but no further."

Hermenijildo bowed. "*Sí, señor,* it shall be as you wish."

They left for town about 9 o'clock that night, and on the way Connelly and Magoffin began to talk terms, apparently having got over the misgivings that resulted from learning of Ross's having nothing.

Ross agreed on a cash fee of $10,000 and a split of 10 per cent of the net profit for his own work in taking the contraband bullion through the wilderness of Texas and bringing back the goods. Connelly and Magoffin, along with some other American traders and a number of Mexican merchants, would pool their resources and make up a train of some $300,000. This huge sum should be at least doubled on the expedition's return.

Magoffin was dubious about one man in the chain: General Conde. "I don't know how he will feel towards this project," he said. "He might have some money in the St. Louis trade, or he might sincerely oppose the contrabanding of bullion. Whatever stand he takes, he will wield a strong influence."

"Can't he be reasoned with?" asked Ross.

"It is difficult. He and Irigoyen often do not see eye to eye. There lies the risk."

"Irigoyen will be governor long enough for us to return."

Magoffin idly slapped his mule's withers with the ends of the reins. "You might be delayed, and Irigoyen might die." He shrugged in the starlight. "A thousand things might happen, but we can only speculate, the same as we speculated when we first went to Santa Fé."

The *baile* was at the Cordero *casa,* not far from the *plaza.* They rode in through the ornate *portal,* illuminated by smoking wicks in bear oil, and turned their horses over to uniformed servants in the *placita.* The house was similar to Peralta's, as were all Mexican homes when the owners could afford them.

Magoffin and Connelly followed Peralta off to the dining-room, where the older men would talk business, while Ross followed Apolinar to the dance, in a large, high-ceilinged room with a rug laid on a dirt floor. The orchestra was a violin, a guitar, and a bass viol, played by swarthy Mexicans dressed in black pants, red sashes, and white silk shirts with wide, flowing sleeves. They played and sang plaintive songs about love and death and disappointment.

There were twenty-five or so ladies in the room, all well-dressed in silk and lace, all black-haired but one — Valeria Sierra. Ross touched Hermenijildo's arm. "She is here!" he said.

Hermenijildo sighed. "I do not have to look, *señor.*"

Ross went to her immediately, and she studied him over her fan. She was eighteen and the kind that made a man want to reach. She let him touch her fingers. "I understand," she said, her head tilted a little to one side and her dark eyes filled with humour, "that in New Orleans they have the curious custom of fighting with hats."

Ross bowed. "*Señorita,* New Orleans is a town of many curious customs, but of one thing it has never been accused: failure to appreciate the loveliness of an exquisite lady."

She smiled. "For a *yanquí* you are very well-mannered — *muy simpático.*"

"I talk better when I am moving," he said. "Will your *dueña* mind if we dance?"

She glanced to one side, where a chunky little brown-skinned woman, sitting in one of the few chairs in the room — a massive thing made of cottonwood — was nodding.

"Probably not, since she is asleep," said Valeria.

The next tune was the Spanish version of a waltz, and the couples began gliding over the rug with astonishing gracefulness, the lace *mantillas* of the ladies floating and swaying gracefully. Valeria raised her arms and Ross moved in closer and put his left hand, fingers wide-spread, against her side. She did not wear a corset — few Spanish ladies did — and he realised she had no need for one. They moved out on the floor, maintaining a discreet six inches between them. "*Señorita,*" he said after a moment, "I cannot remember when I have felt such lovely ribs."

There was a smile in her eyes. "The Chihuahuans talk of the moon and the stars. You speak of ribs as if you were buying a haunch of mutton."

He kept time with the music and looked down at her. The floor, though large for a private home, was getting crowded, and he had to watch. "It is not quite that simple," he said without embarrassment, "nor is any reference intended to food. My theory is that you can tell a great deal about a girl by the way she feels when she dances. Some girls are stiff and unyielding; one might as well dance with the statue of Hidalgo."

She danced very lightly, and now she was resting her right arm on his left, and watched him over the edge of her fan. "You would have quite a struggle with the *padre*'s likeness. I'm sure it would be amusing."

"You are jesting, *señorita*." He chided her gently. "I am trying, in my clumsy way, to pay you a high compliment."

Her eyes changed instantly to contrition. "A thousand apologies. I was only fencing."

"You thrust with a sharp sword and a persistence that comes from long practice."

"To be unmarried and unbetrothed at my age is phenomenal. It is almost a disgrace."

They went by the orchestra, and at that moment Ross felt a draft of cool mountain air. "Are you opposed to marriage, then?"

"By no means! It is merely that I have not found a man who suits me."

"I thought these things were arranged by parents."

"My parents were killed in the revolutions. Don Fidel Peralta is my legal guardian, but I am afraid he has given up breaking me to the plough."

67

He shook his head slowly, holding her eyes with his own. "Well he might. You are hardly suited for anything so ordinary."

She smiled. "And you, *señor,* you are married, no doubt, with many *niños?*"

He laughed. "A woman is always direct when it comes to that subject." He looked at her gravely. "As a matter of fact, *señorita* — no. Not yet. However," he said, still looking into her eyes, "in Durango this past winter I saw a girl who changed all my ideas on marriage, and upon my return from Arkansas I shall be in position to discuss the matter with her."

She did not move her eyes from his. "How long will that be, *señor?*"

"Ninety days — a little more, perhaps a little less. Too long in any case."

"Perhaps," she said after a moment, and that half-smile was in her brown eyes again, "you do not hear well."

He was puzzled. "You said you were not betrothed."

"Yes. But I should tell you now the music has stopped."

He looked around and laughed. "The musicians need a drink of brandy."

He did not offer to take his hand from her side, and she did not try to move away, but stood at the distance at which they had danced and continued to look up at him. Then he sensed something wrong.

He glanced at the wall and saw the girls with their various *dueñas* — mostly short, fat and elderly. He saw the young bloods in group, handsome with their brown skins and white teeth, beautifully dressed. But they were not talking and laughing together. Without a single exception they faced the door that opened on the court-yard. Hermenijildo stood apart, his eyes unchanged, and with only that gravity of demeanour that since this afternoon had overshadowed everything else. Apolinar stood rigid, his face turned a little ashen.

Ross swung, putting the girl behind him, and faced the entrance. A big man stood inside the door. The top of his limp-brimmed hat was even with the top of the door-mantel. His red flannel shirt was greasy and torn; his buckskin pants, hardly big enough to hold him, laced at the front with a buckskin thong; his knee-high boots were wrinkled, worn and dusty. His face was covered with an untrimmed red beard, and he wore a dirty buckskin patch over one eye.

Apolinar stepped forward quickly, but Ross was in front of him more quickly. "No," he said, pushing him off balance.

"This is my meat."

He had a moment of tightness, and drew a deep breath as he faced the big man. "This is a private dance," he said.

The big man fixed his one eye on him. He said, "They told me I'd find you here."

Up to that point Ross had thought the appearance of the freighter to be a mistake, but at the big man's words he knew that trouble was planned. He took a step forward, still trying to side-track the violence that he knew would be very destructive not only to life but also to property. "This is no *fandango*, Habersham. This is a private home."

Habersham took one giant step into the room. "Fancy clothes you got on. Fancier than what you had the last time I seen you, up at Bent's Fort." He turned to the four rough-looking men behind him. They had come inside and ranged themselves in a line. "You like that fufarraw, gents?"

"I like it," said a small fat man whose boot-loops seemed too big for him. "That fancy ruffled shirt really shines in my book."

Ross, watching the gleam in Habersham's eyes, warned, "You remember what happened the last time you tried to rawhide me — when we were crossing the

Cimarron desert."

Habersham didn't grin. "It won't happen this time — no matter how many friends you got here."

Ross saw the girls and their *dueñas* crowding together at one side, and vaguely he was aware of their sparkling eyes and held breaths; they loved violence as much as the men. On the other side, the young men were moving restlessly, but Ross held a warning hand towards the floor.

Habersham grinned. "I'm gonna pluck out your eye and feed it to the crows."

A whisper came from behind Ross. "This is a matter for the *alcalde*."

"The *alcalde* isn't here," said Ross, keeping his eyes on Habersham. A 14-inch bowie-knife stuck out of the bullwhacker's waistband. "Give me a knife," he said, holding one hand behind him.

He felt the haft of a knife pressed into his hand, but he did not look around. Bringing his arm to the front, he knew the blade was small and light but he liked the balance of it, and it could be taken for granted it was good steel, for any Spanish knife invariably had a fine blade if it was made for personal use.

"Tell your friends," said Ross tightly, "to keep out, or they'll be mowed down with balls." That was strictly a bluff, but he thought it might keep the freighters at bay long enough for him to take care of Habersham and thus avoid a general fight.

Ross said to Habersham, "This time I'll take an ear." He added calculatingly, "Your ears are too big anyway. They flop."

They began to circle each other warily, Habersham bent-kneed, not too sure now of his procedure. He was sober, and that in itself was unusual. The man should have been roaring drunk. Therefore this invasion was entirely premeditated, and most likely with money behind it. This, then, was the first level he had to dispose of. They were wasting no time.

One thing about it puzzled Ross. Mangum not only wanted to block the Arkansas expedition; he also had that feverishly intense desire to establish himself as a gentleman, and so why wasn't he content to go through with the duel? The circumstances argued that Cordero, not interested in Mangum's personal ambition, was intent on confronting Ross with every possible obstacle, feeling reasonably sure that Ross would not surmount them all.

The flat slap of Habersham's boots as he shuffled sidewise, the tense breathing of the young men behind Ross, the sputtering of a candle in the draught, for a moment were the only sounds. The three men of the orchestra, Ross noted, were standing quite still, waiting to see which way the battle would go before they decided to take part or stick to their fiddling.

Ross moved towards a corner to avoid presenting his back to Habersham's friends. He saw the gleam grow in Habersham's eyes and knew that Habersham anticipated smothering him in the corner.

Habersham's eyes left Ross's only once — to glance at the tiny knife; then Habersham, with a sardonic smile, drew the bowie-knife with his right hand, and a gasp went up from one of the *dueñas* as the huge blade gleamed in the candlelight. From the fresh scratch marks Ross knew it had been honed very recently.

Habersham held it wide, moving his hand in a small circle, swinging his arm a few inches back and forth to loosen up the muscles. They were about six feet apart, and Ross, close enough to the walls for protection but not too close for freedom of movement, stopped and waited, balanced on the balls of his feet, moving a little to keep facing the bullwhacker.

The four men at the door spread out. Each had a knife, and each looked deadly with it, for these men were products of the Trail — the longest, most difficult, and most violent trail in all history. A man with years behind him on the Trail had not survived by his wits alone. These men were accustomed to violence and death-fights, and they expected them and were always ready for them. Opposed to the explosive temperament of the Mexicans, it was a dangerous combination, for though the Mexicans could hold their own at their own kind of fighting, they hadn't been brought up in the deadly school of the Trail.

One thing was in Ross's favour: he too had spent years on the Trail — and it never had been easy, for men like Habersham always had distrusted and disliked his speech, learned in a private boys' school, and his manners likewise. On the Trail, what a man distrusted he sooner or later tried to destroy.

Past Habersham's shoulder Ross saw that Valeria's *dueña* had got up and was standing on the chair, her eyes wide in her round face. Then Habersham lunged.

Ross moved aside and the big blade went past him. Habersham moved with such force that it seemed he would bury the knife in the *yeso* — whitened wall. Ross turned in his tracks and made a quick, hard cut with his small dagger in the direction of the man's kidneys.

He drew blood, and he knew from the drag on the blade that he had laid open at least half an inch of flesh, but the big man had not thrown himself completely into the thrust, for at the bite of the steel he twisted, using the bowie-knife like an axe, slashing and hacking.

Ross stepped back, weaving to keep away from the blade. He felt the point bite through the top of his forearm, and leaped to his right to get Habersham off balance.

Habersham stopped, bent over, glaring, his knife dripping blood. "I'll sink this in your gizzard up to the Green River," he said, holding the blade before him.

Ross taunted him. "You'd better do it soon or you'll spill enough blood to grow cactus on a rock."

Habersham growled. He lunged again, but this time more cautiously and consequently less dangerously. Ross moved aside. He had taught Habersham respect for the small blade, and now he could afford to wait him out. In that kind of contest he would win, for the man wasn't particularly adept with the knife. He was big and strong, and his bull-like rushes usually won for him. But for work with the blade —

Habersham fooled him. He left his side unguarded for a moment, and Ross stabbed at it with a sidewise cutting action to do the greatest possible damage. But Habersham had known what he was doing. He moved as Ross lunged, and Ross, so sure of his target, found nothing there and could not regain his balance. He tripped over Habersham's out-thrust leg and sprawled on the dirt floor.

He rolled instantly, and Habersham's big boots landed where the small of his back had been. Blood splashed to the floor when Habersham's feet came down.

Ross was close to the four men spread out inside the door. He rolled back as Habersham swung a big booted foot on his throat. He got the blow on the shoulder, and that was better than on the Adam's-apple. He sliced the dagger down the calf of Habersham's extended leg and bounded to his feet.

Habersham roared. He whirled as Ross kicked him behind one knee and leaped up. He went half-way down, and Ross leaped behind him and took a slash at one ear. The knife only grazed it. Habersham, standing spread-legged, his back still to

Ross as if he was confused, shook his head in rage. Ross jumped on his back. He put his bloody forearm under Habersham's chin to force his head back. He slid his right arm in front of Habersham's biceps and immobilised the bowie-knife. Then he bared his teeth and went to work on Habersham's ear.

Habersham roared in uncontrolled rage, but he was helpless. Ross gathered the top of the man's right ear between his teeth and bit into it. . . . Afterwards he leaped from Habersham's back and faced him. Habersham's head was bloody but the light of combat was undimmed in his eyes. Nothing but unconsciousness or death would stop him, now.

Ross caught movement. The men at the door were starting to close in with murder in their faces. It was time to change tactics. A three-inch dagger against a fourteen-inch bowie-knife was good for just so long. He snatched a lighted candle and threw it in Habersham's face, then leaped towards Valeria's *dueña*. The women scattered like chickens before a weasel. He grabbed the chair and raised it above his head. The attackers momentarily paused. Ross brought the heavy chair down on the floor and smashed it. He snatched a leg and brandished it before him. He jerked off a table runner of heavy velvet, upsetting three more candles, and wound it around his left forearm by swinging his arm in a circular motion while he kept the five men at a distance with the chair-leg.

He held the padded forearm before him and began to advance. The chair-leg crunched against a skull, and it sounded like the caving in of a ripe pumpkin.

Now there was activity behind him. The young Mexicans were getting the idea.

The four remaining freighters saw that too, and started to rush him, but he swung the chair-leg viciously. He smashed Habersham's right hand and heard the man grunt, saw the knife drop to the floor from paralysed fingers. Then Apolinar and Hermenijildo were beside him, and they drove the attackers back. The four men broke and fled. One man lay sprawled on his side, and didn't move.

Ross heard the dogs bark as the freighters ran through the yard. The girls and the *dueñas* fluttered back into the room, and picked up the candles. One stooped by the man on the floor. Ross looked at the pool of blood. "He's dead," he said, tossing away the chair-leg and taking a deep breath. "Haul him out." He picked up Habersham's knife, wiped the blade with the velvet runner, and slipped it under his wide belt.

"A very good fight," said a resonant voice.

Ross turned to see James Wiley Magoffin standing in the door. "Why didn't you help?" Ross demanded.

Magoffin shook his head. "I'm not in it with you younger fellows. Anyway, I wanted Connelly here to see what kind of man he had picked."

Ross said shortly, "He might have seen him laid out on a cooling-board."

"Not a chance." Magoffin patted his hip. "I had a six-shooter."

Connelly was nodding his head, his lips tight. "You're still fighting a duel in the morning."

"Perhaps."

"I sincerely hope you will get this fighting out of your system and get down to business. With two weeks to go."

Ross said, a little impatiently, "You *told* me I'd have to work up through several levels before I'd lay hands on the real enemy."

Don José Cordero appeared with glasses and a bottle of brandy. He was a tall man, very thin, with a black imperial goatee. "Gentlemen!" he said. "If you will all come this way." He glanced at Ross. "I'm sure the *anglo* feels the need of refreshment."

Ross heard an odd intonation in the word *"anglo"* and wondered what it meant.

They went into the dining-room. Cordero, wearing a black waistcoat embroidered in gold, poured brandy for all and offered one to Ross. *"Salud, señor!"*

"A very interesting fight," Cordero went on. "I have not seen that trick of the chair-leg before. There's a little too much — brutality — about it for our countrymen, I'm afraid."

"I learned it from a master," said Ross, and bowed to Magoffin. "He and I and two other freighters stood together at a *fandango* in Santa Fé and beat off a small army of jealous lovers."

Magoffin slapped the table. "That's right! That's where it was. And you said you'd never run into me."

Ross smiled. *"You* said that. *I* said nothing."

Magoffin compressed his lips with pleasure, his eyes alight.

"I remember that fight," said Connelly. "It was the first time I ever saw you, Wiley. I had been in Santa Fé for six months and I was watching from the Mexican side." He looked at Ross. "There was a boy in the fight — not over fifteen. Was that you?"

Ross nodded. "It was as good a time to start as any."

"That was about ten years ago," Connelly said, speculating.

"Well, gentlemen," said Cordero, "it's a reunion, eh? Shall we drink to it?"

They drank. The musicians were tuning up again.

"You still have the dagger in your hand," said Magoffin. Ross looked down. The dagger was so light he hardly felt its weight. He must have changed it to his left hand without being aware of it. The handle was of chased gold and inlaid silver, with a ruby on one side and a diamond on the other. "It's a good blade," said Ross. He got up suddenly. "If you will excuse me —" He bowed slightly to Cordero.

Ross went back to the dance. The musicians were playing again, and the floor was filled. Ross looked over their heads, not knowing whom to look for but expecting to be seen. Valeria was not in sight.

"May I have the knife now?" asked a soft voice, and Ross turned to look into her brown eyes.

"*Señorita*," he said warmly, "the quality of the blade is exceeded only by the great beauty and the gracious thoughtfulness of the owner."

She was not flustered. "It is a historic weapon," she said. "I am satisfied that it has been well used."

He wiped the blade on his coat sleeve, took it by the point, and handed it to her. "My great thanks, *señorita*."

Her deep brown eyes, fixed on his, were inscrutable. *"No hay nada para que me las da, señor."*

Two servants had picked up the dead man by the feet and shoulders and were carrying him through the door. Cordero, very suave and very fashionably dressed in the striking attire of the *gente fina*, went to the door to watch the disposal of the body.

Valeria was still looking up at Ross, puzzlement in her clear brown eyes. "I am curious what kind of man it is who would chew off a man's ear. It was one of the most savage things I have ever seen."

"He is no different from any other man," he assured her. "When he is with men who chew ears, he chews ears."

"I don't agree with all of that statement, *señor*. I would say he is much different — because he has not only the ability but the courage to do such a thing — and yet I do not think he is a brutal man."

"Thank you." He was very pleased. "I would not fight that way if it were not necessary."

"From what you said, you fight this man before?"

"He forced a fight about as he did tonight — and I gouged out his eye because he was after mine."

She shuddered. "And what will it be next?"

He backed out of the way of Apolinar, who was dancing with a very short but enticing black-haired girl. "There can be no more mayhem," he assured. "One of us will have to kill the other."

"And you do not intend it to be this man who does the killing?"

"*Naturalmente!*"

"I don't know," she said. "I am not sure."

"You're not sure whether I'm always that brutal?"

"Yes."

"It is a hard thing to say," he told her. "Will you excuse me for a moment?"

He went back to the dining-room. Connelly was standing in the door and took him to the kitchen to get cleaned up. Ross said, "Do you really think Cordero was behind this attack on me in his own house?"

Connelly shrugged and looked at Magoffin, who had followed them.

"The stakes are high in Chihuahua," Magoffin said. "And business methods are somewhat primitive even though on the surface we are very genteel. It is a *cosa de Méjico*."

"He doesn't have to be in such a hurry," Ross argued. "Next year he himself could have a caravan through Texas."

Connelly and Magoffin looked at each other. Magoffin spoke finally to Ross. "Freighting down the trail is a gamble," he said. "Last fall Cordero sent a mule train of bullion to St. Louis to buy goods and on the way lost half of it to Indians; his wagonmaster ran off with the other half — and there's no insurance on the Trail."

"For all we know," said Magoffin, "he may have millions left. On the other hand, he may have every penny he owns between here and St. Louis. In any case, if he has sent a couple of hundred thousand dollars East, he sure won't want to take a licking on that — which he would do if his man bought goods in St. Louis and freighted them 2,000 miles while we make a quick trip to Pecan Point and returned with goods to be sold at half his price. Men have gone broke in a hurry through things like that."

"And," said Connelly with finality, "he has offered to put up no money on this expedition. Draw your own conclusions."

"You will excuse me, gentlemen," said Ross. "A waltz is starting, and I have an unfinished dance." He left them and reached Valeria just ahead of four splendidly dressed young Mexicans who were converging on her but who fell back at Ross's approach.

He turned to smile at them. *"Les doy las gracias á todos,"* he said, and took her arm.

CHAPTER FOUR

Before the dance was over he saw Hermeni-jildo standing in the inner doorway, very sober. When the dance was finished, he took Valeria back to her *dueña* and thanked her in his most flowery Spanish. "And I hope this will be only the first of many such occasions," he said.

She looked at him over her fan. "It may be — if you are in Chihuahua."

"I'm leaving in a few days," he told her, "but I'll be back."

She said slowly, "It is not advisable to wait too long, *señor.*"

"And yet one does not buy the most beautiful race horse without a chance to observe it — as you have already demon-strated." He looked at her, and wished he could speak then. "You will be as beautiful all your life as you are at this moment, *señorita.* A few weeks longer will only make you more desirable. And I'll be back."

He thought she blushed behind the fan. She nodded slightly, her creamy lace *man-*

tilla, suspended on a very high comb in the back of her blonde hair, moving only a couple of inches.

He went to Hermenijildo, still standing like a statue in the doorway. "You need a drink, *amigo,*" said Ross. "Follow me."

He found the older men pleasantly settled around a black walnut table with massive carved legs. Cordero was pouring brandy, and looked questioningly at Ross.

Ross nodded.

Cordero observed, "After such an affair, I would think so." He took two glasses from a servant. "I understand it was a tremendous battle. I'm sorry I did not reach the — arena — before it was over." Ross stiffened. "However" — Cordero held out one glass — "I hope for better luck next time." He held out the second glass.

Ross took his and tossed it down. He eyed Cordero fully. "The next time," he said, "I may not be so lenient."

There was abrupt silence in the room as the other men realised what fencing was going on.

Cordero raised one eyebrow. "Lenient!" he repeated. "I understand you murdered a man just now."

"You are under a misimpression, *Señor* Cordero. The man attacked me with a deadly weapon. The killing was in self-defence."

Cordero looked down at his glass. "Well, I presume the *alcalde* will understand all that."

"If he does not," Ross said hotly, "there will be a revision of the judicial system in Chihuahua."

Cordero raised both eyebrows. "You would question the authority of the law, *señor?*"

Ross got control of himself. "I do not question the law, I question your interpretation of it."

Cordero shrugged as if it were a matter of no moment.

Ross slammed his glass on the table. "I apologise for having disgraced your house with my presence, *señor.* You will be kind enough to excuse me."

He stalked out, followed by Hermenijildo, who still held his glass. "Don Ross," he whispered when they were in the courtyard, "you insult a very powerful man. Don José will some day be Governor of Chihuahua."

"He isn't governor now," said Ross. "And he insulted me first. Come on, let's get out of here."

Andrés Vigil came hurrying after them

with a girl. His dark eyes were luminous. "*Señor,* I wish to go on the expedition with you. You are a great fighter, *señor,* and I would consider it an honour to load your rifle."

Ross was touched by that, for the sons of wealthy Mexican *rancheros* usually considered anything short of racing and bull-tailing, attending cockfights and *bailes,* as far beneath them. "Very good," he said. "You shall go, but it will not be necessary for you to load my rifle. You will be too busy loading your own." He looked at the young man. With his brown, almost golden skin and his dark hair and his neat moustache, he was truly, as the Mexicans said, pretty. As they used it, this did not necessarily mean feminine, and certainly it did not in the case of Andrés. Ross glanced at the lovely girl around whose waist Andrés's arm still lingered — intentionally, no doubt — and Ross said, "We'll be a long time on the road. You'd better take care of your social duties now."

Andrés smiled dazzlingly. "*Gracias, señor!*"

Ross watched them sweep away, the girl looking up into Andrés's face with adoration in her eyes.

"Mexican girls," Ross noted, "are very

easy to hold in the arms, aren't they?"

"*Señor?*" Hermenijildo sounded puzzled.

"I have observed the same to be true," Ross noted, "with English girls and Dutch girls and Italian girls — to mention some nationalities off-hand, and I have no doubt that a more intensive study would reveal that girls are, most of all, girls."

"*Señor,* I do not think —"

Ross nodded. "It is confusing, *amigo,* is it not, for I am in high dudgeon against *Señor* Cordero. Very well, let us resume our indignant exit." He turned on his heel. Head high, unsmiling, he led the way out of the courtyard.

Out on the street, Ross stopped for a moment. "From the sad look on your face," he said, "I assume Ed Mangum's second got in touch with you."

Hermenijildo nodded. "It is so. He delivered the challenge and I accepted in your name. He asked me to name the weapons, and I said six-shooters. He thought I was making a joke, but I assured him that was your choice. He was horrified. He said somebody might get killed."

"Isn't that the general idea?" asked Ross.

"Perhaps not so, *señor.*" Hermenijildo sounded thoughtful. "There is of course always the possibility, but it is above all an affair of honour. Many times both men survive and become fast friends."

"That is one custom of yours I don't approve. When an *anglo* fights a duel, he fights to kill — and why not?"

Hermenijildo shrugged. "I do not know. It is a *cosa de Méjico*. However, the second felt affronted, as I have said, that you named six-shooters. He wanted to know where such weapons might be purchased in Chihuahua."

"Who is his second?"

"One *Capitán* Esquibel of the Chihuahua Dragoons."

"Do you know him?"

"By reputation," said Hermenijildo.

"I take it his reputation is not flattering."

Hermenijildo considered. "It is said he has a price."

"Very well, you may tell Captain Esquibel that I have two such pistols with me. If the deeply aggrieved Mr. Mangum wishes, he may choose either of mine. And if he wishes, he may load it himself. What about the time — sunrise?"

"*Sí, señor.*"

Ross shuddered. "There's not much point in going to bed."

"But rest, *señor* —"

Ross stopped in the middle of the dusty

91

street on the cathedral side of the *plaza.* "This is not a target match, Hermenijildo. There is much more to a duel than skill with arms. The greatest skill is in knowing your opponent and outflanking him."

"Nevertheless, *señor,* this is a serious affair. Much more so now that I have learned your intention is to kill. And I earnestly —"

"Hermenijildo," Ross said suddenly, "isn't there a party we can invite ourselves to besides the one we have just left?"

"But Cordero —"

"Cordero is disgruntled that I didn't get my skull split open, and the fact that he did not hide his antagonism means that he had counted on it. No, if I have any further fighting to do to-night, it won't be under Cordero's roof."

Hermenijildo said obediently, *"Sí, señor."*

"Then where —"

Hermenijildo considered the question soberly. "The social event of the evening is the *baile* at Cordero's —"

Ross asked sharply, "Are Habersham and his men, then, highly placed in Chihuahua society?"

Hermenijildo said in reproof, "You jest, *señor.* The Governor and perhaps General Conde will be there later. It is a shame that

92

you could not —"

"Yes, a shame." Ross walked on. "A shame they didn't come earlier. By the way, Hermenijildo. You're married, didn't you say?"

"*Sí, señor.*"

"You like your wife?"

Hermenijildo nodded with great assurance. "She is Chonita, sister of Apolinar. We have been married five months."

"Where is she to-night?" Ross asked abruptly.

"I have sent word to her that I am acting as your second and I shall not be home until it is over."

"You live close to Los Saucillos?"

"Just over the mountains, *señor.* My grandfather had a silver mine, and now he's getting old and I look after things for him. My father raised mules, and I am taking care of that business for my mother."

"What happened to your father — if you don't mind."

"He was killed in the revolution."

"I'm sorry."

"I was very small then."

"Your ranch — is it big or little?"

"About half as big as Don Fidel's."

Ross grunted. "High-priced help I

got for a second."

Hermenijildo's voice sounded puzzled in the darkness. *"Perdóneme, señor?"*

"I said, since we don't want to go back to Cordero's, what's left?"

"There are always *fandangos* when the wagon trains come."

"There always were — but if I know which way the stick floats, somebody would have to die if I tipped my flag in there to-night."

"The *Señor* Habersham is in an ugly mood, *no?"*

Ross stopped and stared at him. "A bald eagle spittin' bile would be as calm as a horny toad settin' in the sun compared to Habersham when he gets soaked in *mescal* about an hour from now."

"Then I take it," Hermenijildo said, still somewhat mystified, "that we shall not attend the *fandango.*"

"That's right." Ross resumed walking. They had been around the *plaza* twice now, and were passing the cathedral. "I like the night air in Chihuahua," said Ross. "It cools the blood — if you let it."

"Sí, señor."

"By the way, where is the duel to take place?"

"In the hospital yard at the prison —

94

where Hidalgo was executed."

"By the rope?"

"By shooting, *señor.*"

Most of the huts within sight were dark and the dogs were still. Few of the *peones* could afford candles, and it occurred to Ross that the great physical shortage of goods — and consequently of course their high price — was a major factor in the poverty of the *peones.* "Hermenijildo," he said, "do you suppose if we shortened the trade route by half and brought in goods at a much lower price than now, these people could afford candles at night?"

Hermenijildo asked, "Why do they need candles, *señor?*"

Ross considered. "Then let us say milk."

"Milk? When they have beer?"

Ross slapped his thigh. "That's it, of course. They could have more beer."

"But —"

"Don't you think there would be fewer beggars if there were more goods?"

"The old *pordiosera,*" Hermenijildo said, "would be a beggar no matter if she had a thousand black stallions and mares. She would not be as happy at anything else."

"It does, however," Ross said with considerable satisfaction, "give this expedition the flavour of a crusade."

They turned into a cross street, and Hermenijildo led the way through a narrow, dusty lane towards a door that showed yellow light behind its single dirty pane. "*The Nueve Gatos* — Nine Cats," said Hermenijildo. "It is not likely to be visited by the freighters, and here we may have a glass of that refreshing beverage while we compose ourselves for the ordeal ahead."

CHAPTER FIVE

It was a cold morning in Chihuahua, with the night wind sweeping down through the black canyons of the Sierra Madres. It was hard waking up, even with Apolinar shaking him by the shoulder, but presently Ross grumbled and got up, stood shivering in his shirt for a moment, yawned, and got into his broadcloth pants.

"It feels like winter up here," he complained.

"It will be warm as soon as the sun comes up," Apolinar said cheerfully.

Ross washed in the icy water, and shaved carefully by candlelight.

"I see why poor people never duel." He spoke without turning his head. "You can't fight a proper duel without a fresh shave, and you can't shave without a light."

"*Cómo?*" asked Hermenijildo.

"I'm trying to shock myself into waking up."

Hermenijildo looked concerned. "Perhaps the cold air will freshen you."

There was a faint knock at the door, and Ross pulled it open. "Come —"

He stopped. The girl Anita was there with a wooden pail full of hot water. "If the *señor* will forgive me, I did not see the light until just now."

"It's all right." Ross took the bucket and thanked her. "She goes lingeringly," he told Hermenijildo. "She wonders what a man looks like who is about to die."

"Or she is choosing a father for her next child," said Hermenijildo.

Ross chuckled. "One might do worse." He poured hot water into the basin. "What time is it?"

Hermenijildo shrugged. "I don't know. I think it's time the sheepherders get up." He yawned. "You didn't stay out as late as you said."

"I changed my mind," said Ross. "I remembered that daylight comes early."

They went to the dining-room and found Don Fidel, fully dressed in his formal clothing of the night before, sipping steaming coffee poured from a pot over a fireplace in the corner of the room. He greeted them and poured coffee for all. Ross sipped his gratefully.

Don Fidel looked up. "The confounded dogs yapping again. It must be friends!"

He went into the patio. The servants were up by that time, and Ross heard faint talking through the heavy cottonwood door. Then Don Fidel came back, followed by the neatly moustached Andrés and his father Don Mauricio, a very short, round little man with black moustache and goatee.

"How did you know about this event?" asked Don Fidel, pouring more coffee.

"It's all over Chihuahua. It's the first real killing duel that I can remember."

"But the time and the place —"

"Captain Esquibel of the Chihuahua Dragoons, who is second for the *Yanquí — perdóneme, Señor* Felip. It is thus we think of foreigners of *Señor* Mangum's calibre."

Ross looked up from his coffee. "You don't like him?"

"Who does?" asked Don Mauricio. "He's a *coyote* trying to be a *toro* — or is he a *toro* trying to be a *coyote?* It doesn't matter. He ends up being neither, but in the process he has made many persons miserable."

Ross dropped a piece of brown-sugar *piloncillo* into his coffee. Its fragrance began to clear his brain. "Hermenijildo, you got my revolvers as I told you?"

"*Sí, señor* — likewise the powder flask,

extra bullets, percussion caps, bullet patches —"

"Then let's be about our work." He tossed off the last of his coffee. "Since I was forced to get up at such an unholy hour, I'd like to make some use of it, and I can think of no better way to spend the time than taking a shot at the man who caused it."

The men had been quiet but now they turned sombre as they went to their horses. The servants had them saddled, and immediately put on the bridles and led them out of their stalls.

It was still black; the stars were brilliant; a *coyote* was singing on a hill west of the *rancho*. The spicy sweet smell of burning juniper enveloped them for a moment and then gave way to the aromatic fragrance of sage, borne down the *cañon* on the night wind of the mountain.

Hermenijildo led, as was his right, carrying the six-shooters and equipment, and they followed in a scattered group, saying little. Ross listened to the soft clop of unshod horses' hoofs in the dusty trail, the good creak of saddle leather in the early morning. Presently the sky began to lighten a little over the eastern plains, far across the trackless desert of the Bolsón de

100

Mapimí, and Ross yawned briefly and then shivered and shook his head against the morning chill.

"How do you feel?" asked Don Fidel.

"Good enough."

"I don't see how you go through Indian country when you wake up so slow."

Ross looked at him from under heavy lids. "I don't wake up slow in Indian country."

The sky was half lighted when they trotted through the dusty streets of Chihuahua to the old prison and entered a narrow gate at the back.

The hospital courtyard was about sixty feet long — just right for a duel at point-blank range, Ross saw, and enclosed all around by thick adobe walls. Near the centre of the outer wall was a huge old pine tree, and under it were a dozen men.

Magoffin strode out to the gate to meet them; Connelly was at his side, stocky, energetic, quick-moving.

They all shook hands silently. The *anglos* were dressed in black broadcloth, as formal as if they were going to the opera; the Mexicans were resplendent in black velvet with red, blue, and green silk, and many huge silver *conchas*.

Magoffin introduced a man Ross had

not seen: Doctor Jennison, tall, spare, florid, director of the mint of Chihuahua.

"He has consented to act as official physician," said Connelly. "At least you'll have medical attention."

"Glad to see an American," said Ross.

"Do my best to patch you up if you get hit," said Jennison.

Hermenijildo walked stiffly towards the group under the tree on the opposite side.

"We've brought the pharmacist too," said Connelly. "Von Brauch."

Von Brauch was a big, blond German of military erectness. He snapped his heels together and bowed from the waist. "I am at your service in this hour," he declared.

Hermenijildo came back across the open ground followed by a Mexican officer in the red-and-blue uniform of the Chihuahua dragoons. "*Capitán* Esquibel," Hermenijildo said, and Ross bowed very briefly.

"He would like to see the pistols," said Hermenijildo.

"Why don't you show them to him, then?"

"*Con permiso.*" Hermenijildo somewhat gingerly handed the two six-shooters to Captain Esquibel, whose dark eyes took them in with professional air.

"He may choose, of course," said Ross.

Esquibel tried both weapons in his hand, first for balance, then for sighting.

"He wishes to show them to his principal," said Hermenijildo.

Ross nodded. He still wasn't nervous and he was trying to keep from becoming so. He watched Hermenijildo and Esquibel walk back across the yard, and turned his attention to Magoffin and Connelly.

At last Hermenijildo returned. "*Señor,* the other principal wishes to load his own weapon."

Ross snapped, "Let him do whatever he wants. Just keep one of those six-shooters in your hand. I loaded them both yesterday, and I don't want to do it again."

"*Sí, señor.*"

Don Mauricio observed, "Hermenijildo is taking his duties very seriously. His father was a great duellist before the revolution."

Presently Hermenijildo came back, followed by Esquibel, and held out one of the six-shooters. "He will use this one, *señor.*"

Ross glanced at it. "Cap it," he said.

Hermenijildo put caps on all six nipples and handed it, butt first, to Ross. Ross fitted the butt into his palm and pointed it upwards. He pulled the trigger six times so fast the shots, crashing upon one another, sounded like the distant roll of artillery fire.

"Very good," Connelly said in a loud voice, to talk over the temporary deafness. "All cylinders fired."

"Of course they did." Ross gave the pistol back to Hermenijildo, who gave it to Esquibel.

"Does he wish powder and balls?" asked Ross.

Esquibel shook his head and started back, with a faint spiral of smoke curling from the muzzle of the pistol. Magoffin moved out of the cloud of smoke, and the entire group reformed some ten feet away. Two doves sitting on the wall went *"Cú, cú, cú,"* and a crow flapped up heavily from the pine tree and called harshly, *"Sangre! sangre! sangre!"* "Blood! blood! blood!"

A rooster crowed, and dogs began to bark. The distant echoes of the shots were still rolling among the mountains.

Ross took six caps from a tin box hanging from the powder-flask, pinched them a little, and pushed them on the nipples of his six-shooter.

"You're sure he didn't tamper with the loads?" asked Connelly.

"No, *señor*," said Hermenijildo. "I held it

in my hand all the time."

Ross looked across at the knot of men under the tree. "No telling what they've done to the one they're using — but that's none of my business." He balanced the six-shooter in his hand. "I'm ready when —"

"*Señores!*" A cry rang out through the courtyard.

Don Mauricio looked. "A *peon*," he said, dismissing the interruption.

"*Señores!*" The cry was closer and almost anguished, Ross thought. He looked towards the gate.

A bare-footed, straw-hatted *peon* ran across the dusty yard. Ross saw the black and white moustache and said, "Diego!"

"Why do you interrupt?" Don Fidel demanded sternly.

"*Señor,*" said Diego, "it is a matter of life and death."

"I know him," said Ross. "He worked for Olivarez. Let him talk."

"*Señor!*" Diego pleaded. "You will believe me?"

Ross glanced at the group under the pine tree. They were watching. He said sincerely, "I will believe anything you say, Diego."

"*Señor.*" The man was almost wringing his hands. "My wife — Carlota — she has a sister works for Don Fidel."

Peralta nodded, his eyes narrow.

"She has told me the *yanquí burro* hired someone to injure the *pistola* so it will not fire. Please believe me, *señor.*"

"Who did the tampering?" demanded Peralta.

"I do not know, *señor.* She would not tell."

"She never would, either," said Peralta. "These *peones* can't be forced to talk if they don't want to."

"It's a job," said Connelly, "to throw you off your balance."

Ross looked at Diego. "It is not impossible," he said, thinking, "that some servant could have been bribed to plug the touch-holes with soap."

Abruptly he raised the pistol and pulled the trigger. There was a soft click. Ross snorted but made no sound with his lips. He pulled the trigger five more times and met five misfires. He looked at Don Fidel's ashen face. "It would seem," he said, "that Diego knew what he was talking about."

"*Señor,*" said Peralta, speaking with difficulty, "this is an unforgivable disgrace on my house. I can — I shall never get over it."

Ross said calmly, "You'd better keep an

eye out for the traitor." He turned to Diego. He started to reach into his pocket, then remembered. He slapped Diego hard on the shoulder. *"Gracias, hombre, mil gracias."*

Diego beamed with pleasure and backed away.

"Un momento!" said Ross.

"Señor?"

Ross took half a dozen steps towards Diego. "Why did you do this?" he asked. "You knew it might be dangerous to interfere."

Diego shrugged. "One does not refuse to do a thing just because it is dangerous, *señor* — if one knows it is right."

"How did you know that?"

Diego shook his head wisely. "A man does not shoot a pistol that will not fire. Besides, my Carlota said you had a kind face. She said, 'That one may be a very great fighter, but he has a good face, and he looked on us as *méjicanos,* not as *pelados.'* "

"True enough," said Ross. "Give Carlota my sincere greetings, and for yourself — if you ever need help, *hombre,* I shall feel hurt if you do not let me know."

Diego smiled and started to leave.

"Don't you want to watch the duel?" asked Ross.

Diego shook his head. "I am sorry, *señor*. We must get an early start this morning across the desert. It is slow with a *burro* and four children."

Ross nodded. *"Vaya con Diós, hombre."*

He went back to Hermenijildo and held out his hand for the powder flask. "There's a hatpin in there to clean out the holes," he said. "Otherwise we'll be here all day trying to draw the loads."

"Señor," said Peralta, trying to recover his voice, "this is the greatest shame in my life."

Ross felt sorry for him. "We were warned," he said. "No harm has been done."

I will find out who did it," Peralta threatened, "if it takes the rest of my days."

Ross picked at the holes with the pin while Connelly fumed. "That would have been murder."

"Rather," said Magoffin, "it looks like the act of a man desperately trying to be a gentleman but determined above all to win."

Don Fidel's face now held the look of a thundercloud. "I shall find out who did this," he said, "and stake him out on the Bolsón for the buzzards to feed on."

"I would say, rather, you'd better send

him to work for my opponent. A traitor is always handy if you know who he is."

Ross held the pistol in the air once more and tried it. Five cylinders fired, again filling the morning air with a crescendo of shattering explosions. He moved out of the smoke cloud and worked once more on the sixth cylinder, finally got it cleared and fired it. Then he examined all nipples carefully, and finally called for powder and ball.

He measured the charge of coarse powder, set the ball on a linen swatch, and drove it home with the loading lever. When all were loaded, once again he capped the nipples, pulled the trigger to half-cock and turned the cylinder and inspected each chamber thoroughly. He didn't like to admit it, but now for the first time he was getting nervous. He had almost walked into a death-trap, for the other man, filled with the knowledge that he would not be in the way of hot lead, could have taken his time and made the first shot good. Ross handed the pistol to Hermenijildo.

Heads were looking in at the gate, and Mexicans — all *peones* — began to file in to watch this strange satisfaction of honour, as formal to them as a dinner with linen and silver and fine wines.

"Quite a crowd here," observed Doctor Jennison.

Wolfgang von Brauch sized up the street wall. "At least forty witnesses," he noted.

Esquibel was coming back across the yard, and Hermenijildo went to meet him, then reported to Ross. "He notes that the sun soon will be up, and requests that the duel take place as soon as possible."

Ross said acidulously, "We are waiting for him."

"Then let us begin," said Esquibel.

The two groups of men drew together. Ross noted that Cordero was not on the grounds. He would not be, of course. But Ross saw a priest left behind by the men.

"He seems to have observed every custom," he said, staring. "That might have been expected if he wanted to marry a Mexican girl, but for a duel —"

Connelly said, "A very strange man."

The two groups came together. Von Brauch was to direct the duel. "You will stand back to back in the centre. I will call, 'One, two, one, two,' and you will march forward. I will call 'three, four' in the same cadence, and at the word 'four' you will turn and commence firing. You will continue until your loads are exhausted or one man is down. Is it agreed?"

110

"Yes," said Ross, for the first time looking at Mangum, and again wondering at the deadly intensity on the man's square face — a hunger, almost.

"Take your places," said von Brauch.

Ross walked to the centre of the yard, aware that Mangum was slightly behind him. Hermenijildo handed him his six-shooter, and he glanced to see that all caps were still in place.

A man ran in at the gate and in a high-pitched voice cried, *"Señores!"*

Magoffin groaned. *"Anaya* — the *alcalde*'s coyote."*

Anaya waved a small piece of stiff paper in his hand, sputtering Spanish.

"It's a summons," said Magoffin, "to answer for the death in Cordero's house last night."

"I don't know anything about it," said Ross. "Let's go ahead with the duel and take care of the summons later."

Von Brauch fixed his cold grey eyes on the *coyote* and said sternly, "This is an affair of honour. You will wait?"

Anaya looked perplexed but said, *"Sí, señor."*

"Ja wohl!" Von Brauch said, "I am ready to count. One, two, one, two —"

Ross marched out, listening for the

"three, four." The doves had arisen from the wall after the last round of shots, but the crow was still swooping and wheeling over the yard and calling its raucous *"Sangre!"*

"One, two, one, two —"

He was marching towards the east, and the sky was well lighted although the sun would not be above the wall for some time. He no longer smelled the pungent powder smoke but rather the fragrance of apple blossoms, and it was a mild surprise to him, because he had supposed they would be much later so high in the mountains.

"One, two, three, four."

His right foot was forward, and he swung to the left.

Mangum fired, and almost immediately was obscured by a cloud of white smoke. Ross fired — more to hide himself than anything, and then waited.

Mangum stood where he was, for Ross could watch his feet. A yellow explosion blossomed from within the smoke, and Ross fired at it.

Mangum answered twice before Ross fired again. Mangum fired a fifth time, and now of course they had to judge position entirely by their feet. The shots echoed loud and crashingly from the walls of the prison yard, and Ross thought the rifle shots must have sounded much like that to Hidalgo in the instant before he died.

Mangum fired his sixth shot, and Ross answered.

Mangum stepped from the cloud, and Ross aimed at him deliberately.

Esquibel shouted suddenly, and Mangum for an instant looked blank and then started back into the smoke cloud.

Ross could at least have winged him then, but he held his fire. He had no wish to shoot an unarmed man and certainly none to kill him even though he disliked him. The shot would have been entirely legal and justified since Mangum had taken his six shots, but Ross hesitated. Almost immediately he realised that he was in an embarrassing position, for he was still entitled to a shot, and the Mexicans, meticulous in such things, would wonder why he did not use it. As a matter of honour, of course, Mangum should march out of the smoke and demand that Ross take his shot. But Mangum stayed in the slowly thinning smoke cloud while Ross stood, his elbow bent and the pistol pointing at the sky, trying to think of some way out without shooting at the man. Mangum, of course, had already disgraced himself by taking refuge.

While he hesitated, a mounted man galloped through the gate and shouted. "*Señores! No más!* A paper from the Governor!"

He rode up to von Brauch and stopped his horse with a great flourish befitting the occasion.

Von Brauch stepped up and took the paper and glanced through it. Ross stood his ground.

Von Brauch looked up. "Gentlemen! This is an order from Governor Irigoyen prohibiting a duel between any subject of Her Britannic Majesty and a citizen of the United States under pain of a heavy fine and prison sentence." He looked at Ross and then at Mangum, from whom the smoke had arisen to reveal him as a perfect target. "I am forced to say, gentlemen, that this order comes too late. One principal has fired six times, the other five; therefore I take the responsibility of ordering the duel continued until the twelfth shot is fired."

Ross aimed. Mangum was now a clear target, his arms at his sides, the empty six-shooter in one hand. Ross lowered his pistol and said, "Herr von Brauch, it is not my wish to cause you difficulty with the

Governor. I therefore reserve my shot until the next meeting."

Von Brauch bowed. "As you wish, Herr Phillips." He waved one arm. "Gentlemen, the duel is over. Do the principals wish to shake hands?"

Ross glanced at Mangum. Ross had no great desire to make any sort of peace with Mangum, but he did not want to be rude. But Mangum turned his back and stalked away.

Ross's arm dropped. Connelly took the pistol. Magoffin said, "I thought I saw a bullet tick your coat, but there was so much smoke I must have been mistaken."

Connelly had walked around behind Ross, and exclaimed, "It went through his coat!" He stared at Ross. "How did it get there?"

Ross felt his eyelids drooping in spite of himself. The pistol dropped from his fingers. "How the hell do you think?" he asked. "It went through my guts!"

CHAPTER SIX

The wound was painful but healed well in the next few days. Doctor Jennison and Doctor Connelly both attended him, and were of the opinion that the ball had missed the intestine and gone through the fatty part of the abdomen. Short of infection, it would heal well and soon, though Connelly thought they had better put off the start of the expedition.

But Ross was back on his feet within a week, and would not hear of it.

"I'll be able to ride without losing blood," he said, "in another week — and time is important. There will be grass for the animals by 1st April, and with good luck we can make the trip to Pecan Point, take care of our business in New Orleans, and return to Chihuahua before the northers set in."

Doctor Jennison shook his head, but Magoffin and Connelly had been long on the Trail, and they agreed that if there was no infection, the wound was but an incident. Magoffin explained it to Jennison:

"If we had stopped for every bullet and arrow wound it would have taken us ten years to make a round trip — and then we would have gotten still more of those things."

"Most of the time," said Connelly, "a man is pampered too much when he gets hurt."

Jennison shook his head. "I admit I am but an ordinary frontier practitioner, and most of my practice is limited to those who more or less enjoy a moderate spell of sickness."

Ross was hospitalised in a large bed in a cool room of Connelly's home in Chihuahua. The *alcalde*, a small, very slight Mexican with grey hair and moustache, came to hold a hearing over the killing of the freighter.

Cordero was not present.

The hearing was held in Spanish, with the *alcalde* asking questions. "You knew this man Link Habersham?"

"Yes," said Ross.

"And those with him?"

"One of them."

"You knew the one you killed — Kerlérec?"

"Not at all."

117

"You did not?" The *alcalde* seemed astonished.

"Never saw him before."

"Then why did you kill him?"

"Because he attacked me with a bowie-knife."

"You have the marks?"

Ross bared his forearm, where the welt was eight inches long.

"This was made by the man you killed?"

"No. By Habersham."

"But I do not understand. Why was Habersham fighting?"

"He started it."

"For what reason?"

"I don't know." Ross grinned suddenly. "Maybe because I gouged out his eye up on the Cimarron."

"Is it true that you bit off his ear?"

Ross nodded. "It sure is."

"That is a crime also."

"Is it — when it's self-defence?"

"But, *señor*, you can hardly plead that biting off an ear is self-defence."

Ross drew a deep breath and looked at the old man. *"Señor,"* he said solemnly, "picture me on the back of a man who is trying to disembowel me with a fourteen-inch knife. He is a man with big ears, and I cannot see past his head because of them.

118

Would you consider it wrong for me to chew off an ear to improve my vision?"

The old Mexican studied him absently, obviously trying to visualise this situation. "Perhaps not," he said at last. "But there is one more question. You know it is against the law to have a weapon in Chihuahua?"

"Never heard of it."

"I am informed that you attacked these four men with a dagger for which you have no permit."

Ross lowered his eyes significantly. "Have you been told it was a small blade with jewels on it — such as might have belonged to a woman?"

"*Si.*"

"Then," said Ross, "I can only testify that it is an affair of honour, and I feel sure the gallantry of a Mexican gentleman will not require me to name the lady involved."

The *alcalde*'s eyebrows raised; this of course was a new aspect of the matter and one which he could well understand.

Connelly moved forward and shook hands with the *alcalde,* thanking him for his courtesy and suggesting that the patient was weary and should not be questioned further. The *alcalde* bowed out.

"Well," said Ross, "that was easier than I expected."

"You showed an astonishing under-standing of Mexican law and custom," said Magoffin.

Ross chuckled. "The best knowledge was exhibited by Doctor Connelly when he slipped the gold doubloon into the *alcalde*'s palm."

Connelly waved it away. "Sixteen dollars well spent. Now! Let's get on with our plans. I've been looking at mules and I've got fifty dragoons promised as a guard."

"Dragoons!"

Connelly chuckled. "If the governor sends them, I don't have to pay them."

"Dragoons," said Ross, "to guard con-traband bullion that is going out of the country."

"It is better for you to stick to the prac-tical matters," said Connelly. "I will admit you handled the *alcalde* admirably, but I suggest you should not question govern-mental affairs too closely as they affect Irigoyen."

Ross nodded. He felt tired, and sank back on the bed. Magoffin saw the motion. "Sleepy?" he asked.

"No. A little tired — but not too tired to think."

"Don Fidel is coming," said Connelly.

Ross brightened. "How about the

brandy, Doctor? Don't you have some brandy for special guests?"

Connelly muttered. "I don't mind the brandy, but every occasion requires the best."

"Don't mind," said Magoffin to Ross. "He brought a whole wagon load from St. Louis."

"Don Fidel!"

Don Fidel strode in, sweeping moustache and all, and embraced Connelly and Magoffin in turn, shook hands with Ross. Apolinar stood back quietly.

Connelly called loudly for a servant to bring the brandy.

"*Qué novedades hay?*" asked Magoffin.

"Nothing new," said Don Fidel. "I've been trying to locate mules around Durango, and not having much success. It seems there is a threat of a Texas invasion of New Mexico, and the Government is putting its hands on all the mules possible."

Connelly snorted. "That threat comes every year."

"This time it's supposed to be true. Anyway, my man returned to-day with a hundred and thirty-five animals that I would not feed to the buzzards. Also two dozen jackasses!"

"Donkeys might be all right," said Ross. "They'll carry a big load and they can forage on the Bolsón and come out fat."

"Too slow," said Connelly. "They would take forever."

The brandy came, and Connelly poured glasses for all.

"To your health, *Señor* Felip," said Don Fidel.

"Gracias."

"Now, when is this young rooster going to be out of bed?"

"In two days," said Ross.

"Good. You know of course he is released on bond?"

Magoffin spluttered. Connelly swore softly.

"Ten thousand dollars," Don Fidel said, licking the brandy from his lips.

"Ten thou— !"

Connelly swore softly.

"It is of course an attempt to embarrass the backers of the expedition — but naturally a little thing like ten thousand pesos is not going to stop us."

"Naturally not," said Connelly, "but it doesn't help any."

"Likewise it is sort of a parole. I strongly suspect that if *Señor* Felip does anything the other side objects to, the bond will be forfeited."

"In other words," said Ross, "it's blackmail."

"A nasty word," Don Fidel observed.

"Well, there's nothing for it but to sign the bond and have it over with," said Magoffin. "It may be the *alcalde*'s way of getting more than a doubloon."

"The doubloon was well spent," Connelly said. "It gets him out of here. The bond was decided on two days ago and would have been set anyway. The only way of avoiding that was by putting Phillips under arrest — and the doubloon let them out of that one. You forget one thing: a man in jail is no man at all."

"All right. We better get down and take care of it."

"No, hurry," Don Fidel said cheerfully. "Your property will undoubtedly be held as surety whether you sign the bond or not. Besides, this is good brandy. The brandy we've gotten from Paso lately," he said, "is too green."

"I haven't seen Hermenijildo since the day of the duel," said Ross.

"Hermenijildo is occupied," said Don Fidel. "The *padre* has chided him for not producing *niños*, and Hermenijildo is, as you know, a man who takes his responsibilities very seriously. He has had much work in the silver mine recently also," he added.

Ross asked no further. He realised the bullion he was to take to Arkansas had to come from somewhere, and probably Hermenijildo was buying it at the mine and getting it ready for shipment. Five or six tons of illegal silver were not to be taken lightly.

CHAPTER SEVEN

Ross was soon about again and the next several days were very busy. Ross hired a cart but did most of his business sitting down. He felt fine but wanted to save himself. There must be no failure, with Mangum now publicly courting Valeria. What a shame a marriage like that would be, Ross told himself — like hitching an oxen to a race horse. And it was worse because everybody in Chihuahua except Valeria made no secret of their belief that Mangum was after Valeria's inheritance.

But if he *were* favourably looked upon by Valeria — and at that point there was little Ross could do about it — there would of course be considerable delay, and certainly nothing in the nature of a marriage could take place before fall. By that time, Ross was determined, he would be back with money of his own — at least enough so that he would not be empty-handed. And then, he promised silently, the race would be a fast one, and *Señor* Mangum, the

Mexican *Yanquí,* who was neither the one nor the other, should find out what real competition was like.

And so he drove about the country, usually with Apolinar or Don Fidel or Connelly, and looked at mules, bought mules, begged mules for the monstrous caravan, for Connelly said they were sure now of $300,000 in silver and gold bullion. Hermenijildo worked day and night, and the stores were piling up in Connelly's warehouse. He purchased seven good wagons from traders out of Independence, and both he and Ross began to hire men, for they would need at least fifty in addition to the fifty dragoons.

Likewise there was the problem of a *mayor domo* to boss the *arrieros* — the mule drivers, and all in all the entire city of Chihuahua was filled with great excitement, for this *atajo* would be one of the greatest caravans ever seen in northern Mexico — seven hundred mules, no less. And to take such a giant caravan through an Indian wilderness — it would require a man of great courage and resourcefulness to invade the land of the Comanches under their very noses. *Caray,* yes, for the Comanches, as everyone knew, were the scourge of all northern Mexico. Very few

Mexican families had not suffered the loss of a husband or son scalped or a mother or daughter taken captive and carried up on the vast Llano Estacado to be sold as a slave. And everyone knew too that captive women meant only two things to a Comanche: one was drudgery and the other was unspeakable, for the Comanches were truly savages, and no girl of ten years or more had ever come back alive without a tale of repeated and brutal rape, sometimes going on for months.

This was the country the caravan was going into, and the Mexicans took a fine delight in thinking that it would penetrate the very heart of Comanche-land. No matter that it was not a war party; the Chihuahueños had been under the rifles and arrows of the Comanches so long, and had feared them so abjectly, that even a gesture of defiance was heartening.

Ross felt dejected over his inability to pursue his courtship of Valeria — which by now seemed taken for granted not only by himself but by the *Señora* Magoffin and Mrs. Connelly. There almost seemed to be a rivalry among the women of Chihuahua with Ed Mangum for Valeria's hand.

That was some satisfaction, but it was quite apparent to Ross that it would not win the girl. He remembered those brief moments when he had danced with her, and he recalled the instant when he had looked around to see Habersham, and he remembered that Valeria had pressed against him for a moment, and he recalled her firm softness and her warmth and the fragrance of her perfume, and it was hard to keep his mind on buying mules.

Five days before the departure he said to Connelly, "We have not yet a *mayor domo* for the *arrieros*."

Connelly's eyes widened. "I guess I took it for granted that you knew. Plácido is the man for that job."

"Plácido!"

"He is one of the best."

"Can he take care of the mules?"

Connelly shrugged. "If you make him. If you don't, he'll drive them until their shoulder blades stick through their hides."

"Can he handle men?"

"He will get more out of the mules and men, and cheat you out of more money for feed when you reach Arkansas, than any *arriero* in Mexico."

"That's good news," said Ross. "It takes care of one problem — but how can Plácido leave Josefina?"

Connelly shrugged his heavy shoulders

again. "That is one problem I cannot pretend to answer. Perhaps you will be able to tell me when you get back." He stared across the *plaza*. "A much more pressing problem to the Chihuahueños is: how is Josefina going to get along with out Plácido?" He shrugged. "I have no doubt somebody will come to her rescue. Somebody always does."

Ross dismissed it from his mind. They now had title to 650 mules, all of which were pastured on Don Fidel's ranch. Don Fidel himself had picked out a beautiful black gelding for Ross to ride on the trip, noting that ease of riding should be a consideration on such a long trip, and that stability and endurance were vital. "This horse," he told Ross, "is no race-horse and no show horse. The boys wanted to get rid of it last fall, but I predicted it would be useful."

Ross took in the glossy coat, the strong legs and short barrel, the deep chest and strong neck, the wide head and intelligent eyes. "It looks like my kind of horse," he said, rubbing the muscular withers. "I can see why he would not appeal to Mexican riders, but for this trip I think we will go a long way together."

The horse's head swung around to

inspect him, and Don Fidel said approvingly, "A good sign."

It was settled almost from the beginning that Apolinar would go with the expedition, not merely to keep an eye on his father's interest but also to gain some valuable knowledge, his father said, of something besides bullfights and cotillions. But Ross got his first big shock that afternoon when Hermenijildo came over to make arrangements for the loading of the bullion.

Hermenijildo came on horseback, accompanied by his wife, and three servants on mules. The serious young man was very attentive as he helped her down from her box-like sidesaddle, and Ross noted that his hands lingered affectionately wherever they touched her. Nor did he greatly blame the young man, for Chonita, though a full head shorter than him, had sparkling black eyes and quick movements and awareness of everything about her.

Ross said, "*Señora,* I have long wanted to meet the wife of the man who assisted me so ably."

She smiled up at him and said simply, "*Gracias.*"

He went on easily, "I had built up quite a picture in my mind of a very beautiful and charming creature who alone would be worthy the devotion of such a staunch one as Hermenijildo, but now I find I must revise my wondering to speculate on how Hermenijildo could merit the faithfulness and devotion of such an extremely attractive woman as you are."

She smiled as if it was a great secret between them. "And I in turn have wondered, *señor,* what kind of man could be so pretty" — she meant "handsome" — "and at the same time make such lovely speeches."

He raised his eyebrows. "I have been making other such speeches?"

Laugh crinkles formed around her eyes. "You have said to her, 'I cannot remember when I have felt such lovely ribs.' And the *señorita* answered, 'You speak as if you were buying a haunch of mutton.' Shall I go on, *señor?*"

For a moment he was astounded; then he smiled. "Perhaps it will not be necessary, *señora,* for I am sure your husband has heard it many times already." He looked at Hermenijildo, whose face did not change. "Is there nothing sacred in Chihuahua?"

"In a courtship," she told him mysteriously, "many curious things may happen.

It is a *cosa de Méjico.*"

"Thank you for warning me."

"But, *señor,* you must not think of that when you are dancing with the *señorita.*"

"This — mind-reading — might be useful in other ways," he noted.

"Yes, *señor?*"

"For instance, what does the *Señor* Mangum say to the *Señorita* Sierra?"

"Ooh! Very dull things." Her face suddenly became as sober as Hermenijildo's; the twinkle went out of her eyes and for a moment her face looked very plain.

" '*Señora,*' " she mimicked, " 'do you think Santa Anna will again be President of Mexico? What is your opinion of the right of Texas to claim her boundary to the Río Grande? What of the state of trade? Do you not think Mexico's future lies west, towards China?' "

This was so absurdly un-Mexican that Ross could not restrain a smile. "And what did the *señorita* answer?"

Chonita shrugged expressively. "Who needs to answer a man like that? He answers himself."

A servant took away her black horse.

"Then I take it his courtship of her is not very serious."

Her eyes opened wide. "On the contrary,

señor! It is very serious. For one thing, it is different. For another, no person is as completely ignorant of what she should do as a girl in love."

"In love?"

"But of course, *señor.* All Chihuahua knows that she is in love with you. It is simple, *verdad?*"

"I confess I find it not only not simple but actually not understandable."

"She is much taken with you, *señor,* and you have only to say the word and she is yours. But in the meantime, you do not expect her to sit home and make *tortillas* while you debate your mind — especially when a man is ardently pursuing her."

Ross drew a deep breath. "I — she —"

"Perhaps you are not a man who wants to marry, *señor.*"

"On the contrary," he said, "I have been thinking about it very seriously for the last several months."

"Then, *señor,* are you afraid to speak — you who are not afraid of bullets?"

"No," he said earnestly. "No, I — you see, *señora,* it is hardly fair that a man setting off on a dangerous mission from which he may not return should —"

"What is to be lost?" she asked.

He floundered. Obviously those men

who knew he was without funds had kept it to themselves, and he could not under any circumstances reveal it to the women, for in such a case it would be the same as asking Valeria to marry him but confessing his condition. It wasn't just that Valeria would be repelled by his poverty, for she had plenty of money, and she was the kind of woman who would share it — but Mexican custom positively would not allow it. There was only one answer: he must have money before he asked her to marry him.

Chonita held Hermenijildo's hand for a moment. "Don't take too long, *señor*. A girl in love is most vulnerable — not only to the man she loves but to others — if the first does not exercise his rights."

He drew a deep breath and looked away at the rocky peaks of the Sierra Madres, unknown, unknowable. A woman's ways (beyond ever-present flirtation or the ever-common temporary love affair) were like the distant mountains — unknown and unknowable except to other women. "*Señora*," he said finally, "I am greatly indebted for your interest. I cannot believe she would marry such a dull man."

"It must go further than that," she warned him.

He hesitated. "Yes, of course it must.

Thank you again, *señora.*"

He watched Father Ramón in his garden some distance away while Hermenijildo took Chonita into the house. The sun out there was warm and invigorating, and he climbed into the seat of one of the wagons they had bought and sat there to soak up the warmth. Don Fidel was to furnish four thousand pounds of corn, and this would be loaded in this wagon the next day.

Hermenijildo returned. *"Señor,"* he said looking up and shading his eyes with his hand, "I hope you do not take it amiss that my Chonita has advised you in your relations with *Doña* Valeria."

"Not at all."

"A Mexican woman — as, perhaps, do all women everywhere — relives her own experiences in love when she observes a couple going through the machinations, and I think she derives an unusual satisfaction when she has a chance to advise the man involved. This is a woman's privilege, *señor.*"

Ross looked down at him. "You may put me on record, Hermenijildo. Your wife certainly is a woman in every possible respect."

"Gracias — and now I have a question, *señor.*"

"All right."

"You have not assigned me my post."

"Post? You're busy eighteen hours a day, aren't you?"

"On the expedition, *señor.*"

Ross frowned. "I didn't know you were going."

"But *seguro.*"

"You're just newly married."

"Chonita will wait for me."

"But —"

"Señor," Hermenijildo said earnestly, "I am young and have good health, and this is a project that means much to the entire state of Chihuahua and perhaps all of northern Mexico. It is not too much that some of us forgo the comforts of a warm bed for a little while to help assure the success of an enterprise that means so much to Chihuahua and my people."

"Very well," said Ross, getting down. "You go along as my assistant." He pulled up his belt. To tell the truth, he rather liked the idea, for Hermenijildo was one of the most dependable young men he had known. And although he did not say so he knew there were other factors that impelled Hermenijildo: a love of adventure — for Hermenijildo had been pretty close to home all his life; and, not the least by any means, a desire to prove himself in the eyes of his wife.

"Can your grandfather take care of the mine, then?"

"Yes. He is not old — sixty, maybe."

"And he is there by himself?"

"Yes."

"And Chonita will stay at your place?"

"No, it's too isolated. Sometimes the Apaches sneak down from the mountains — and Chonita is *enceinte*."

Ross nodded wisely. "In that case she will want to be with her mother while you are gone. Is there anybody there with your grandfather?"

"Oh, yes, my grandfather's two brothers."

"Two?"

"Twin brothers."

"Older?"

"They are all twins."

"You mean triplets?"

Hermenijildo shrugged. "You want to go to the mine, *señor?*"

Ross got into the saddle for the first time and went up into the mountains, where small, heavy sacks of pure silver were stored one on top of another to the ceiling of a room dug out of the rock like a cave. This was well within the mountain and guarded by two fierce-looking men with rifles.

"How much is in here, Hermenijildo?"

"About a hundred and twenty *arrobas*."

Ross did some multiplying in his head. "About three thousand pounds," he noted. "This is short of the goal, isn't it?"

"Doctor Jennison at the mint has been buying, and *Señor* Connelly said yesterday he had enough silver and gold to make up the total."

"We'd better bring enough mules Tuesday morning to haul this stuff into town."

"Sí, señor."

He found Magoffin and Connelly at Los Saucillos when he returned, and they went into a discussion of plans. "We can load 150 pounds to a mule," Connelly said, "so we'll need two hundred mules to get the silver from the mine."

"And don't forget men to handle the mules," said Ross.

"That's right."

"You'll know where to find Plácido," said Don Fidel, pouring brandy.

"That's the virtue of inconstancy," said Magoffin.

"The mint," said Connelly, "is close in. We can load Jennison's part Wednesday morning."

"Will you be able to get the guards to

watch the silver in the *plaza* overnight?" asked Don Fidel.

Magoffin said, "Irigoyen has promised — and the rest of us will watch the guards."

"We've bought the flour and coffee and sugar and bacon and salt. That's stored in my warehouse. All the harness is ready — we've been working on that for months — and we have got the best firearms we could find. Not like your six-shooters," he told Ross. "We have only single-shot rifles and pistols."

"That will be sufficient — if they know how to use them."

"And if they remember to use them properly," warned Magoffin.

"If they don't," Ross said firmly, "they will find themselves flat on their backs. I will have no men along who do not obey orders."

They heard the dogs barking, and Apolinar looked from a tiny window deep-set in the massively thick adobe walls. "It's Andrés!" he said. "Something must have happened!"

Magoffin and Connelly rushed to the courtyard. Andrés had galloped through the big gate and now dropped his reins and came towards them. He seemed oblivious to all but Ross Phillips. *"Señor!"* he cried. "A very sad thing has happened. My father will not permit me to accompany you on the expedition!"

Ross thought quickly. "Perhaps he needs you at home."

"I do not know. He says that I may not go."

This was completely unprecedented — that a well-bred young Mexican should so impulsively report his parental injunction to somebody outside of the family — and indicated to Ross how overwhelming was the boy's desire to go and how complete his confidence in Ross.

"Perhaps he will change his mind."

"I have hoped, *señor,* that you will speak to him, and show him the importance of this expedition to our country. Perhaps then —"

"To-morrow night," Ross said, "I'll see him at the Governor's reception, and I'll try to broach it to him."

"Thank you, *señor!*"

Don Fidel revealed that he too understood that Andrés was very upset. He said, "You need a glass of brandy, Andrés. The sun is hot, and that bay has a ragged gallop that would jar juice out of a mesquite root."

Andrés began to recover his control. *"Gracias,"* he said, with a slight bow.

When he was gone, Magoffin said to Don Fidel, "That's a sample of what you Mexican fathers are doing to your sons. No wonder they don't engage in daring adventures. You won't let them!"

Don Fidel chuckled as he pulled the cork from the brandy bottle. "Fortunately I can overlook that, because Apolinar of course is going. However, you are right, *señor.* We build up great estates and we have a son and we want him to fill our shoes, and we expect him to do it without training or experience because we are afraid he might get hurt." He lifted the bottle. "It is so all over the world, is it not?"

Connelly agreed. "Too bad. Andrés is nearly twenty. When I was twenty I had been on the trail five years."

Don Fidel sighed. "True — and a lot of others were on the trail with you at that age." He added soberly. "Most of them have been dead a long time."

"Those who are left are good men," said Magoffin.

"Some," said Don Fidel, filling the glasses. "Some are no better than *pordioseros* and some have married Indian squaws and raised big families to do their hunting for them in their old age. You gentlemen" — he handed them glasses — "survived by a combination of ability and luck, and you have entered on a new life. I doubt that anything makes much difference, gentlemen. If you are destined to live, you will live. If not, you may ride across the mountain and your horse may fall in a badger hole and break your neck and you die under a hot sun, and the buzzards will pluck out your eyes with no less relish and no more relish than if you were a *pastor* — a sheep herder."

Connelly looked at Ross. "I'm really most worried about the Comanches. I've been on the Trail for twenty-five years, but I haven't done much freighting in unexplored territory. What's your idea, Ross?"

Ross considered. "At the moment I'm not worried about the Indians. The best protection against Indians is other Indians, so I've always found, and this morning I engaged four Tonkawas as spies. The Tonks hate the Comanches anyway."

Magoffin nodded. "That will take care of the Comanches. *I'm* more worried about the Texans."

Connelly said, "I talked to President Lamar when I was in Austin last winter.

Everybody in Texas is as much interested as we are. The only thing is, as far as Texas is concerned it has to be unofficial to avoid starting a ruckus with the Houston camp. That's why we're skirting the Texas towns and keeping to the wilderness."

Ross put down his glass. "What if we *do* run into Texas people?"

"If you are unlucky enough to encounter them," said Connelly, "you apologise profusely, remind them you're an *anglo*, elaborate on the subject of the great benefit Texas is bound to derive, and in general —"

"Talk my way out of it?"

"Yes."

Ross said reflectively, "A very curious condition has developed in the last couple of minutes." He looked at Connelly directly. "You said repeatedly that if so-and-so happened, 'you' should do so-and-so. Why not 'we' would do so-and-so?"

"Because," said Connelly softly, "you are going by yourself. I am not going with you."

Ross stared at him. "You aren't going!"

"I never intended to unless I felt I had to. I could make the trip, but it would take me months to get over it. Besides, I will have plenty of business to take care of. As soon as you leave, I am going to New Orleans, and it will be my job to explore all possible avenues of making a profit. It may be that we can persuade the United States Government to allow us a drawback on goods exported to Chihuahua, to get the trade established."

"And," said Magoffin, "you may have to smooth the Mexican consul's sense of duty so he will neglect to report that a merchant from Chihuahua is buying a third of a million dollars' worth of goods — for if news of this gets to Mexico City, there is no telling where it will stop."

"But" — Ross stuck to the point — "you are not going on the trip, Mr. Connelly."

"No. You will be in complete charge."

Ross held his glass while Don Fidel filled it.

"What do you think of that?" asked Magoffin.

Ross took a deep breath and looked over the edge of his glass. "I don't think I'm getting enough money," he said.

CHAPTER EIGHT

Irigoyen's reception was given for Magoffin and Connelly, the Mexican merchants who were backing the expedition, for Captain Esquibel, who would command the dragoons, for Ross Phillips, for the two young men, Apolinar Peralta and Hermenijildo Zamora, who were going with it.

Esquibel's appointment had caused some consternation, and Connelly had spoken to Irigoyen about it, but he reported that Irigoyen seemed set on Esquibel, and they'd have to accept him or forgo the guards.

The Governor's house was not a palace but a big *hacienda* on Irigoyen's ranch near town. Ross rode out with Don Fidel and Apolinar, and they passed a line of massive, awkward Spanish-built coaches pulled by five or seven mules, all postillion-style, with the driver mounted on one of the near mules. The coaches were heavily curtained, and only occasionally would a curtain be surreptitiously drawn back and an olive-brown face peer out for a moment.

In the great *sala* of the Irigoyen house, with its massive hand-hewed ceiling beams and its smooth adobe-plastered walls whitened with *yeso* or gypsum, and the big fireplace in the corner, were gathered the great men of the entire state of Chihuahua and all the most dazzlingly beautiful ladies. Some of the more elderly women were fat, and this sometimes created a ludicrous effect, for nearly all Mexican women were very short, but nevertheless the roly-poly ones were as flirtatious as the younger ones. That was one art a Mexican woman never quite forgot.

Ross had got a pair of dove-coloured trousers for the occasion, but even so he was sombrely dressed against the velvet and silver and the red and green and blue silk of the *caballeros*.

Governor Irigoyen was a tall, thin man, rather more plainly dressed than most of his compatriots. He took Ross into his study and offered him a cigar.

"You are informed, I suppose, as to the nature of the bullion you are to take?"

Ross nodded.

"It is not, of course, strictly legal to look the other way while this is going on, and yet it is being done all over Mexico by the simple process of giving certain officials a percentage of the gain. That ten and a half per cent is enticing."

"As I understand it," said Ross, "you are closing your eyes to this project officially because you feel it will mean a great deal to the area as a whole."

"Yes. If there is money to be made, let it go into all pockets instead of one pocket."

Ross struck a match and held it to Irigoyen's cigar.

"It is a source of some concern to me that General Conde, whom you will meet presently, does not seem to be much in sympathy with this expedition."

"For what reason?"

"Probably because he feels that the *anglos* are obtaining too strong a hold on the business of Chihuahua. I have tried to point out that Connelly is responsible chiefly for the idea, that the bulk of the money is put up by Mexicans, but Conde is not easy to persuade. However, I don't think he will go so far as to call this expedition to the attention of officials in Mexico City."

"Let's hope not," Ross murmured.

"Business in Mexico is always conducted on two levels: one official, the other practical. The President himself is well aware of that, having grown up with it, but he too can ignore a great many things as long as they are not put down in official reports. The newspapers might be full of it, and it might be freely talked in official circles, but it is not a matter for governmental action until it turns up in a report."

"I think I understand."

"I want to be sure you understand more." Irigoyen's eyes, in the light of the candle, looked intently into his. "It is possible I could be forced to do something I would not want to do. In such a case, I ask you to remember my position and not hold it too strongly against me."

"In other words, if somebody reported that the expedition is carrying ten thousand pounds of bullion, you might be compelled to try and stop it."

"Something like that."

"We shall not worry about that until it happens," Ross said firmly.

Irigoyen got up. "I'd better see my guests. I hope you will make yourself at home. My house is yours, you know."

"Thank you."

To tell the truth, Ross was somewhat weary of all the business details and endless *platicando* that went on in any Mexican affair, and he was quite familiar with the practices of Mexican officialdom. Nevertheless he acknowledged the rather unusual courtesy of Irigoyen in openly telling him the situation in advance.

But now, at the other end of the long room he saw, past the embroidered frockcoats and the creamy lace *mantillas*, the golden head of *Doña* Valeria, who was just within the door, and he started that way.

"Ah, *Señor* Felip, I have the great honour of presenting you to his Excellency, the General Conde."

Ross stopped and looked around. José Cordero, smiling stiffly, was at his side, and Ross controlled his impatience and bowed. "It will be a pleasure," he said finally.

He managed to keep an eye on Valeria as she made her way through the far end of the room, and then she disappeared and Cordero was introducing him to Conde, a large, portly, florid man, probably with a lot of Irish blood in him, Ross thought, but with a very watchful and cynical eye.

"I have heard a great deal about you," said Conde. "They say you whipped four or five men from the wagon trains one night."

Ross resigned himself. "One, actually."

"I heard you bit off one man's ear and

killed another with a chair-leg."

"The second man should not have got in the way. The fight was already over."

"It seems good that such a man is leading the expedition to Arkansas."

"A great deal is involved besides fighting ability," said Ross.

"I do not doubt that. Nevertheless, our young men will get a taste of something besides drawing-rooms and receptions."

"It is my feeling," said Ross, "that this will suit the young men very well. Perhaps it is the fathers who will object."

Conde's eyes were narrow. "You're observant, *señor*." He changed the conversation. "I understand your home is in New Orleans."

"Yes, sir."

"I have been in New Orleans. A fine city."

"Yes."

"I was there for surgical attention during the Texan revolution." His eyes were watchful. "You are not a Texan, *señor?*"

Ross sensed an unusual feeling. "No, my family came from Connecticut."

"I am glad to hear that. My experiences with Texans have been very unpleasant."

Ross was noncommittal. "Yes?"

Conde's face seemed to become a little

more red. "In my mind Texas is populated by a horde of depraved adventurers and criminals running from the law."

Ross looked at him. He might be testing Ross, but there was no question that there was a lot of acerbity in his words. "I have done business with Texans," Ross said carefully, "and I expect to do business with them again. But I am not a Texan. I do business where I can make a profit."

Conde nodded, but Ross knew the man had reservations. Well, it didn't matter. If Conde didn't like Texans, all right; that was his privilege. Ross was impatient to see Valeria.

She appeared again, and the progress of her movements was marked by a constant succession of small whirlpools of bobbing *mantillas* and high combs in black hair, of creamy shirt fronts and colourfully embroidered coats and silk sashes. Ross walked rapidly towards her, making his way across the stone floor. He reached her just as she turned from the *alcalde*. He stepped up swiftly and said, "*Señorita,* may I borrow your knife?"

She turned and gave him a warm and dazzling smile.

"*Señor* Felip," she said. "How delighted I am to see you!"

He looked down at her and again he wanted to put his hands on her, and he knew she would not mind if he did, but he said, "*Señorita,* it has been ages, and I'm afraid I have been able to think of little else."

"Little else save mules, wagons, *arrieros.*"

"You have inquired about me!"

"Do not be too sure of my interest," she warned him. "I will admit that I have listened when I have heard your name — and I have heard it a good many times recently."

"The expedition leaves two days from to-day," he said. "There are many things to do, many mules to buy."

Her eyes were veiled as she looked into his. "Mules are important, aren't they?"

"It depends on what one wants to do."

"There are other things, then, besides expeditions to the United States?"

"I think so."

"Yes, *señor?*"

"Since I saw you on the balcony," he said, "but more especially since I danced with you at Cordero's."

"That, I believe, is where you compared my ribs to a haunch of mutton."

"You know very well," he said firmly, "that you yourself drew that comparison. I thought I was dancing with an angel."

"*Señor*," she said, "you have been too long in Mexico. You are too handy with words."

"On the contrary," he said, "I expect to be in Mexico a very long time."

He wished they could go outside away from the crowd, but he knew it would be impossible. He had been lucky to have those few minutes alone with her. "*Señorita*," he said, "I would like to ask you a very important question."

"Yes?"

She waited, and it was plain to him that she knew what direction the question would take.

"I would like —" He stopped. That wasn't the way to say it. Where was his facility with words that never had failed him until then? "We are leaving day after to-morrow," he said, trying to get his feet back on the ground, "and if you would —" He floundered again, and her nearness and the fragrance of her hair as she stood so close and looked up at him, took his breath away completely. "*Señorita* —"

"Oh, *Doña* Valeria," came a cooing voice, and Ross restrained his annoyance, for *Señora* Cordero was bearing down on them. *Señora* Cordero was an unusually

153

large woman, probably of Northern European extraction, and she seemed oblivious to Ross as she marched in and planted herself. "Here is a man who has been looking for you all evening," said Mrs. Cordero. "*Señor* Mangum. You know him, I think."

Ross controlled himself. He ignored *Señora* Cordero and took Valeria's warm hand and said, oblivious to the others, "I shall see you again before I leave, *señorita*, if I may."

"Please do, *señor* — and perhaps you can finish the story you were telling me."

"I am going to do it," he promised.

Magoffin looked speculative when Ross stopped before him. They were of a height, these two — both about six feet three. "The Corderos are taking quite an interest in Valeria all of a sudden," he noted. "Undoubtedly that has become a part of Mangum's price for whatever Cordero has hired him to do."

Ross managed a quick, casual glance at Mangum in his formal Mexican attire. "For some reason," Ross said, "the man gives me a queasy feeling in the stomach. He is so plainly not what he is pretending to be."

I confess it's too deep for me," said Magoffin. "I always favoured a man being

154

what he is and not trying to be something else. He reminds me of a man dressed like a woman. I used to know one among the Ropihues."

"Strange she can't see that," said Ross.

"A woman always sees something in a man that nobody else sees." Magoffin chuckled. "If it wasn't so, a lot of us would never get a woman."

"There's Mrs. von Brauch," said Ross. "I haven't seen her since the *baile* at Cordero's."

"She's a fine woman," Magoffin agreed. "Connelly is going over. We might as well too."

She was a very small woman with dark brown hair; she had the great beauty of a young woman and the quiet maturity of an older woman, and now she looked up at them delightedly, and she had a way of making it seem to each one that she was looking at him alone. "This is an honour," she said. "Three such strong, handsome men at one time. If von Brauch could only see me now!"

"Where is your Prussian husband?" asked Connelly.

"A servant girl of Don Mauricio is quite ill, and he went back to make her some medicine."

"I know that one," said Connelly. "His medicine won't help her. She has had the *susto* — the great fright — and she is convinced that she is going to die and it's only a question of time. She's doctored with all the *herbanderas* in the mountains."

"What causes the *susto?*" asked Mrs. von Brauch.

"Anything or nothing. She may really have had a great fright, but more likely she saw the shadow of a buzzard over her left shoulder, or something equally superstitious."

"I am superstitious," she said brightly. "I believe that one who is lucky in love will be lucky at all things he undertakes."

"That is not superstition," said the big Magoffin. "That is just plain good sense. Such a man can whip the world, providing the woman is right for him."

"You are French, aren't you?" asked Ross.

She smiled with quick pleasure. *"Oui."*

"How did you come to Chihuahua?"

"A man," she said. "Herr von Brauch brought me here."

"From France?"

"Oh, no!" She clapped her hands together. "I was a niece of Count de Saligny, who was Ambassador for the

156

French Government. We were all over the world — Turkey, China, South America. Then he was sent to the Republic of Texas, and there I met von Brauch, and uncle had to find a new secretary."

"Yvette!" The guttural voice of von Brauch came from across the room, and Yvette smiled at them. "He still gets excited when he sees me. He's like an over-grown boy."

"I can well understand that he would be," Ross said, and got one last dazzling smile.

"There's Don Mauricio," said Connelly. "Do you intend to talk to him?"

"Yes, I think I will."

"Be careful how you approach him about Andrés."

"Of course."

Ross started to the corner where Don Mauricio, looking tired, was sitting in a deep-bottomed rawhide chair. On the way he caught sight of Valeria, still in Mrs. Cordero's tow, and still followed by Mangum, and he began to feel a childish resentment towards the man. If they had not been surrounded by guests, he thought he would walk up and punch Mangum in the nose. But instead he went over to the corner.

"Don't get up," he told Don Mauricio. "I'll sit beside you. I've had a hard day myself."

A servant came with wine on one end of the tray and brandy on the other. Don Mauricio and Ross took brandy.

"I'm very much interested in obtaining all the assistance I can get on the expedition," Ross said.

"I have heard that you are hiring *arrieros* all over northern Mexico."

"We have mule men and wagon drivers. What we are lacking is men who can take responsibility, so that, for instance, I can send a man off in charge of half a dozen ordinary men, and know that he can be relied on. Sort of an officer without title."

"Captain Esquibel is going, isn't he?"

"He cannot be any help to me with my own men."

Don Mauricio's eyes were narrow. "You are leading to something, *señor.*"

"I am going to request that you allow your son Andrés to go with the expedition."

"And if he gets killed and scalped by the Comanches?"

Ross said levelly, "You know yourself that that can happen right here — either Comanches or Apaches."

"He is my only child," said Don Mauricio.

"Yes — and what an opportunity for him to mature — on a trip of this kind. It will be something he can tell his children about, and his grandchildren."

"You are not being practical, *señor.* You overlook the fact that he might not return."

Ross shrugged. "I might not return myself — but that isn't the most important factor. Where would you be to-day if your forebears had not come over here from Castile?"

Don Mauricio sipped the brandy. "It is quite certain we should not have so much Indian blood in the family."

"No. Perhaps it would be Irish or Turkish. Who knows?" He leaned forward. "I tell you, Don Mauricio, this is an event that will be talked about in Chihuahua for twenty years."

"If it turns out to be a massacre, it will be talked about for a hundred and twenty years."

Ross smiled. "That is not likely." He looked up as Yvette von Brauch spoke to Valeria. "Don Andrés's two friends are going — Apolinar and Hermenijildo."

"Hermenijildo would do better to stay at

home and take care of his family."

"Andrés has no family."

Don Mauricio seemed to withdraw inside himself, to swell up with stubbornness. "Andrés is my only son. He is not going."

Ross drew a deep breath. He had tried to forestall this point, for one did not argue with a Mexican father when he said positively "no."

He got up slowly. "If you change your mind, Don Mauricio, it will not be too late."

Don Mauricio set down his glass. "I shall not change my mind."

Ross looked down at him for a moment. This was the man who complained because the young men were not vigorous enough to suit him. How then did he expect them to be men when they were tied to the family apron strings? But these were things he could not say to a Mexican father. He said, "Of course there is danger, but with such a large party it will not be very great. However, it goes without saying that the decision is yours alone. You will excuse me, *señor?*"

Don Mauricio nodded without looking up. He was as difficult as the most selfish mother.

There was nothing else Ross could do for Andrés. He excused himself and made his way quickly towards Valeria, who, wonder of wonders, for a moment was not surrounded by men.

"*Señorita*," he said, and suddenly lost his breath as she turned on him that warm, intimate smile.

"Yes, *Señor* Felip?"

He guided her to a corner that was, for a moment, secluded, and stood with his back to the room to ward off intruders. "It is not easy to speak to you alone," he said.

"You manage very well when you are not fighting someone."

"A certain amount of fighting has to be done in my profession."

"What is your profession, *señor?*"

He studied the dark eyes but could not decide what was in them. "Fighting," he answered.

"That hardly leaves room in your life for a woman, does it?"

He regarded her gravely. "A man loses his zest for a fight," he said, "when he sees a girl he feels he must have."

"You speak in generalities," she murmured.

"Then let us talk in specific terms," he said, unabashed. "From the moment I saw

161

you, fighting did not seem as important as it had before."

"You have not stopped."

"You can well understand that a man who has lived a vigorous life does not stop fighting abruptly. As a matter of fact, he may never be able to stop entirely, and I did not imply that he could. It is rather that other things seem more important."

"And those other things, as you said —"

"A girl!" he said, suddenly impulsive. "A girl who puts a dagger into a man's hand when he is unarmed."

"*Señor.*" She was unusually serious. "I am, after all, a girl. I am supposed to be skilled in affairs of the heart, and I am accustomed to the deft approaches of my countrymen, but I confess I find myself at a loss when I am confronted by your intensity, for I am not really experienced in these things, *señor.* With us it is always a game, and the winning or losing sometimes does not seem as important as the playing. But with you I feel it is altogether different. You are intent on winning, and your intensity frightens me."

He touched her arm. "Believe me, *señorita,* it is the intensity of a man who does not try to gain things by half-measures."

She studied him with her grave eyes. "I can believe that."

"Unfortunately," he said, "my present circumstances require my full attention. I would not be honest with my employers if I —"

"Ladies and gentlemen!" came the voice of Cordero. "I am happy to announce that we may this night celebrate not one, but two, expeditions that promise glory and honour and profit to Chihuahua."

Ross turned to look at him. The man was smiling, but his eyes were not.

"I offer a toast to *Señor* Mangum, who will, two weeks from to-day, conduct a wagon train to Missouri."

Ross stood rigid. Valeria did not move, but he was aware that she picked up a wine glass at her side. Mangum's heavy shoulders moved in the group, and Mangum sought out Valeria's eyes and smiled.

Ross turned back to her. "It is unlikely that I shall be able to talk to you alone much longer in this room," he noted. "Therefore I must be brief. I am going to ask you to wait for me."

She looked up, her eyes big. "Wait?"

"Until I return."

"I'm afraid I do not understand."

"Don't promise to marry anybody else

163

until I get back!" he blurted.

Her breast swelled with the breath she took. "You honour me, *señor* — but I understand you have not fully made up your mind."

"Well — yes and no," he said uncomfortably.

"It is not an enviable position you put me in," she told him. "You are free to go in whatever direction your fancy dictates."

Ross frowned. He had hardly anticipated a counter-attack.

"I —"

"While you ask me to refrain from a choice until you return — and who knows how long that may be? A few months? Several years?"

He gathered his wits. "I am aware of what you say, *señorita* — but I am not — I cannot —"

She smiled — a very warming smile but a little rueful. "Then you hardly have anything to offer, *señor*, but hope. And a girl should have more pride than to make such a contract on hope alone."

"*Señorita*, I —"

She said earnestly, "It grieves me to say these things, *señor*, because you have a great appeal for me, but I must tell you that many *anglo* adventurers come down the Trail or up from Acapulco or over from Vera Cruz, and all have the same story: wait for me. They never come back, *señor*." She shook her head sadly. "I myself have not had my heart broken by these false promises, but I know others who have, and since there is no one to look out for me, I must myself be very careful. If you were to say 'marry me,' I probably would be so foolish as to give you my promise, for you have taken my eye from the first. But you are saying to me only, "Perhaps some day I shall be back, and if I am, perhaps I shall talk of this matter again." She set down the wine glass. "I think you will agree, *señor*, that I could make such a promise only at the loss of my pride."

He looked around and saw Mangum watching them. Mangum observed his motion and turned away quickly. Ross said to Valeria, "Has *Señor* Mangum asked you to marry him?"

"Yes," she said quietly.

"And you told him —"

"That when he comes back, we shall see."

It was now plain that she was waiting for him to say the important words, that she had evaded Mangum even more than she had him; that, in other words, he was being given first choice. But still he could not say the words. The Mexican country had created strong patterns, and to ask her now would be fatal, for as yet, he had nothing substantial to offer. To turn the conversation he asked: "You like *Señor* Mangum?"

She glanced towards the man, and her brown eyes were troubled. "It is difficult to say. He is so plainly trying to be something he never can be, and he is so awkward and clumsy at it, that one cannot help feeling sorry for him."

"Then the answer to me is no — you will not promise to wait."

She smiled sadly. "I regret, *señor*. If I am still unmarried when you return, I hope you will call on me. If I am not —" She shook her head, seeming unable for the moment to continue.

He took her hand. "You will forgive me, *señorita*, for not saying more now, but you will forgive me too for hoping you will still be here when I return."

He left as Mangum came towards them. He found a dimly lighted side room and Magoffin discussing Josiah Gregg and his operations on the Trail, and the great fight at the *fandango* in Santa Fé when George Frederick Ruxton took part, and the subsequent adoration of the lustrous-eyed

Mexican girls, always generous to the con-
queror. He got a large glass of brandy and
sat back against the wall, thinking about
Mangum.

He had made a serious mistake in not
killing Mangum, and he should have seen
it before. Mangum was one of those persons who would always be crossing his
path and would always be taking pot-shots
at him; with such a person, life was precar-
ious. Sooner or later he might score a vital
hit. The only way to handle him, really,
was to kill him. He had had one chance
but had failed to improve it; would he get
another or would Mangum get him first?

CHAPTER NINE

On 2nd April he took two hundred mules to
the mine to load the silver. Plácido in all the
glory of his ragged pants and bare feet and
his undoubted virility, supervised the packing. A mule's eyes were covered with *tapajos*
(blinders), and a *salea,* a sheepskin softened
by hand, was thrown over its back as a
saddle blanket. Plácido saw to it that all
saleas were smooth and free of wrinkles.
Then a *xerga* or saddle-cloth was laid over
it, and the *aparejo* or pack-saddle put on top
of that. The *aparejo* in this case was in the
nature of a double saddle-bag, since silver is
very heavy and would not require much
space. Plácido also tightened the broad
grass saddle-girths, with one knee on the
mule's belly to hold it in. A grass pack-rope
was thrown over the whole and then under
the mule's belly in some pattern known only
to Plácido himself.

All this was done with remarkable swift-
ness. Plácido, on the mule's near side, finished fastening the last rope and cried,

"*Adiós,*" and his assistant, on the other side, sang out, "*Vaya.*" Plácido tossed the end of the rope over the cargo, cried, "*Anda!*" and the mule, as if it was an experienced *mula de carga,* trotted off to join its companions.

The silver was in bars, and Ross issued strict instructions as to the number of bars to be packed in each *aparejo,* making sure there would be no more than one hundred and fifty pounds to the mule.

These two hundred *mulas de carga* were quartered in and around the *plaza* that afternoon, under guard of Esquibel's fifty dragoons and watched over by Connelly and Magoffin, who rode herd, assisted by Apolinar and Hermenijildo, all night. All four were mounted, and spent their time riding around the area in opposite directions.

The next morning at daybreak Ross found Plácido already rousing up the *arrieros* for the trip to Los Saucillos, and by mid-morning the five hundred mules were loaded with a fortune in gold and silver, and Plácido turned them north.

They were joined in Chihuahua by the first two hundred, in single file. It took almost an hour to cross the little bridge over the irrigation ditch on the road out of

Chihuahua, for the entire caravan was over two miles long. First went half of the dragoons, then three hundred and fifty mules, then the wagons, then the rest of the mules, and finally the rest of the dragoons. They would have to close up ranks as soon as the mules got train-broke, for they were too vulnerable to Indian attack — but that would come later.

Half the town of Chihuahua was there to watch them leave. Girls and women waved to men in the train, *arrieros* and soldiers, and these grinned broadly and shouted back, then turned and followed the mules.

Esquibel with thirty dragoons led the way north towards El Paso del Norte. The dragoons were a fierce-looking set of ruffians with swarthy faces and great moustaches. One in particular was a bigger-than-average Mexican with a badly pock-marked face. Ross suspected they were the kind that marched south-west when the Comanches attacked from the north-east. However, once they got the train beyond reach of Chihuahua, and especially after they crossed the Río Grande, there would be no place for them to retreat, and so it might be expected that they would fight. There was no attempt at uniforms; they wore the usual ragged pants and shirts;

high boots when they could find them, and big hats, though they favoured felt rather than the straw of the *peon,* which was a mark of bondage. Their rifles were most indifferent; all muzzle-loaders, most of them flintlocks, a few converted caplocks; and three of them had only bows and arrows.

"It's quite an army," said Connelly with sarcasm in his voice.

"They give us one advantage," Magoffin pointed out. "The Indians are not likely to attack a train with so many men."

The Tonkawa scouts, bareheaded, wore breech-clouts, buckskin shirts, and leggings of deerskin; they rode their wiry mustangs bareback.

Apolinar was nominally in charge of the seven wagons; each of these was pulled by eight mules hitched to a chain.

Because the wagons held their food and feed, and extra arms and powder and lead, their position was in the middle of the train.

They had an *arriero* for every eight or nine mules, and this would be sufficient, for on the trail each mule would follow the other's tail once they got the orneriness boiled out of them by the sun.

Ross sat the great black gelding alongside Connelly and Magoffin and Don Fidel; Hermenijildo was at his side. Don Mauricio and Andrés, the first looking set, the other sad, sat their horses at a little distance. Connelly was nervous. "If anything happens," he said, "there'll be a lot of us broke for a long time to come. That's a whopping big amount of bullion. Most of us have plenty of money in land or animals, but that much cash is a lot."

"You can be sure of one thing," said Ross. "The Comanches would rather have the mules than the silver."

The long, long train wound up to the pass on the north, where they would go through the mountains which seemed impenetrable from where they watched. The first detachment of Esquibel's troops were far out of sight.

A slender, bare-legged girl burst shrieking from the crowd that lined the street and ran to throw her arms around an *arriero*. Plácido came by and grinned at them; he was riding a big California mule.

"I wonder where Josefina is," said Connelly.

"Probably looking for another lover," Magoffin answered cynically. "Life is too short for Josefina to mourn the departure

172

of anyone — not even Plácido, whose competence must be conceded, I think."

The grey, brown, dun, black, and bay mules plodded on. Ross had rejected all white mules, for they were too easily seen from a long distance.

Plácido's was the best mule of the seven hundred; he had picked it with unerring judgment: a *coyote* dun, a dun with a black stripe down its back. No Mexican ever rejected a *coyote* dun mule.

The line seemed endless, and the sun grew hot while they waited. There was of course no sign of Valeria, but José Cordero came up after a while and reined in his horse. "A great train you have there," he said to Connelly.

"*Gracias,*" said Connelly.

"If you can get them through the Comanche wilderness you will have performed a great accomplishment."

"We expect to," said Ross shortly.

Cordero looked at him. Ross was dressed in buckskin pants and shirt, both laced at the front with rawhide; Comanche-style moccasins; a wide brimmed felt hat; and his two six-shooters were in a wide belt around his waist.

"You seem prepared for the trip," Cordero said, perhaps a little enviously.

"I have been on the Trail before," said Ross.

He jumped down to pull a mule out of the file and tighten its girth-strap, then led it back into line. "We'll lose some *aparejos* the first few days," he told Connelly, "until the mules get tired of fighting them."

"See you don't lose the silver out of them," said Magoffin.

"No chance of that."

Another party came up with Dr. Jennison and Governor Irigoyen. The Governor had a satisfied smile on his thin face. "I am very happy to see them actually under way," he said. "This is a great day for Chihuahua."

The rear guard of the dragoons came into sight, led by Lieutenant Tapia, who was not quite as struttily dressed as Esquibel but nevertheless sat his fine bay gelding very smartly.

"That horse won't last three days in the desert," said Magoffin. "Too thin."

"We've got forty extra mules," said Ross. "He'll be glad to trade before we reach Paso."

"You are going through Paso, *señor?*" asked Irigoyen.

"No, your Excellency," said Ross. "We have talked of going through Paso for the

174

benefit of those who might be interested — but that is not our plan. Colonel Elias at Paso would be forced to ask questions if we took seven hundred mules loaded with silver and gold through his town."

"That is *bueno*," said Irigoyen. "I confess I was disturbed over it."

"We leave the Paso road shortly after we get over the mountains here," said Ross. "Then we follow the Conchas River to the Río Grande and cross near the Presidio del Norte. We may as well make friends with Don Lawreano Paez on the way to Arkansas."

The last mule plodded past them. The twenty dragoons under Tapia pranced past on fine horses; whatever else they lacked they were beautifully mounted.

The crowd, following the end of the train, surged in behind it. Ross turned to Connelly and shook hands.

"Good luck," said Connelly.

Ross grinned. "See you back in Chihuahua in four months."

"Better make it five," said Magoffin, shaking hands.

Irigoyen shook hands also, and patted him on the shoulder.

Ross started for the front of the train, Hermenijildo behind him. At the first cross

street he left the train, motioning Hermenijildo to continue. It was a long chance, he
knew, but he rode back to the square and
past the Sierra house. He looked up and
saw Valeria on the balcony. She must not
have recognised him at once, but he took
off his hat and swept it low before him, and
he heard her golden laugh. *"Buen suerte,
señor,"* she said, and he rode past her
window and galloped back to the train.

"Was she waiting?" asked Hermenijildo.

Ross stared at him.

"I sent word to her," said Hermenijildo.

Ross nodded. "And what of Chonita?"

"We have said our good-byes. She suffers
from the morning sickness and so she did
not come."

"You're really going to be a father?"

Hermenijildo said without changing ex -
pression, "It was to be expected."

When they camped that night there were
a dozen fires.

Some men were guarding the mules;
others cooked deer meat and *tortillas;* some
made coffee. While they were eating, Ross
made the rounds of the camp. Lieutenant
Tapia's men were at one end of the camp
ground; Esquibel's were at the other. Ross
walked through Esquibel's camp and
sensed something wrong. He went back.

Esquibel himself was eating at a fire with Hermenijildo, Apolinar, Tapia, and Ross — an officers' mess.

Ross went and counted Esquibel's men. Then he went to the fire where Esquibel was eating. "You started with thirty soldiers in your detail," he said abruptly.

Esquibel eyed him over a cup of coffee. "*Sí, señor.*"

"And you now have only twenty-five. Where is the big one with the pitted face?"

Esquibel's answer was long enough delayed to be impudent. "I sent a squad of men ahead to Paso," he said, "to notify the commander."

Ross's eyes narrowed. "Who told you to do this?"

Esquibel wiped his moustache. "I used my own judgment," he said.

Ross's eyes narrowed. "You are not in command of this expedition. You are to send out no advance parties unless I order it."

"But, *señor* —"

"That is an order, *capitán!*"

He watched the man's eyes calculate, and he waited for an attack. Finally Esquibel said sulkily, "The Governor has told me to be helpful."

"But he did not tell you to betray us,"

177

Ross said. "There must be an under-
standing between us, *capitán*. Otherwise
you may take your dragoons and return to
Chihuahua in the morning."

"What is the understanding?"

"I am in charge. I want no arguments."

Esquibel's eyes hid his thoughts. Finally
he said, "Very well, *señor* — if you must be
jealous of your position."

Ross left him. Hermenijildo joined him
later in the dark. "The captain is going to
make trouble," he said.

"I know that."

"Is he in the pay of Mangum, do you
think?"

"Or Cordero."

"What did he have to gain by sending a
detachment ahead to Paso?"

"He could alert the commander there
and they would be ready to confiscate the
gold and silver under the law. No doubt
Esquibel, in addition to whatever he's getting from Cordero, would get a percentage
of the contraband."

"It is a grave problem. What are we
going to do?"

"In the morning," said Ross, "we turn
east across the desert to hit the Conchas
River. We'll follow that into Presidio, and
we won't go anywhere near Paso."

Esquibel started to put up an argument when Ross ordered the caravan to turn east, but Ross gave him no satisfaction. "We go this way," he said. "You may go to Paso if you wish, since you apparently have friends there."

The river afforded water on the long desert stretches of sand and cactus. The stream was marked by willows and cottonwoods, and, back away from the water, by beargrass that grew on tall stems and was called *palmas* by the Mexicans. It was a country of much game, black-tailed deer, red deer, antelope out on the prairies, rabbits and quail, wild turkeys sometimes in the trees, and wild hogs in the brush along the stream.

Ross had Apolinar organise a hunting party, for a hundred men required at least two or three antelope or deer every day as meat. The precious stores of flour and corn must he spread as thin as possible in anticipation of delays in the unexplored wilds of north-west Texas — for nobody could be sure what might be encountered there.

The first untoward incident occurred on their fourth day out. The mules were getting broken to the packs; the wagon mules had settled down to work. The fine dust of

179

the desert blew upon them and settled on their hats, in their clothes, in the lines of their faces. It covered the flat-lashed loads in the wagons, for there were no wagon bows and billowing canvas — the wind would have blown it away — but canvas brought down tight over the load and lashed thoroughly with rawhide strips. The long train was beginning to function well, then, and Ross had ridden ahead to pick out a camping place for the night, when he saw, far across the desert, a small funnel of dust. He watched it for a while and saw it coming closer, and he turned the gelding and rode out to the south-west. Hermenijildo joined him silently.

In half an hour they knew it was a rider, alone. Ross galloped towards him. He made out a black horse, and then a rider dressed in Mexican finery.

"Andrés!" he shouted.

Andrés's answer came like a croak. *"Señor!"*

Ross gave him water from his canteen, and watered the horse from his hat. "You should have had a mule for the desert," he said.

Andrés, still handsome in spite of the layer of dust on his features, grinned. "If I had taken a mule, *papá* would have suspected."

"What will he think now?"

"He will know. I left with a small wagon train for Paso, and after we got about even with you — or what I supposed to be even — I told them where I was going, and struck out across the desert."

"It's nice to see you, but I can't sanction your coming. Your *papá* would never forgive me."

"I have told him it is my own doing. Besides, I was twenty-one yesterday."

Ross considered. "I can't send you back; that's a certainty. There is too much danger of Indians. You've run that gauntlet once and come through. I suppose you'd better go on with us for a while."

"Very good, *señor.*" Andrés was all smiles. "You have a job for me, *no?*"

"There are jobs for all. Do you know anything about a team of mules and a wagon?"

"*Sí, señor.*"

"Then for the present you can take charge of the wagons. Watch the harness; inspect it every night and keep it repaired. Examine the wheels every night and see that the spokes are solid in the felloes. Grease every axle once a week. I want no screeching axles to attract the Indians. Inspect the tongues and the trees every evening. Look to the lashings. When a load has to be unlashed, it is your responsibility to see that the canvas is brought down tight and the ropes fastened so they will not come loose during the day. No man is to be allowed to help himself to supplies of any kind. You will get instructions from me, and I will tell you when to give out supplies and how much to apportion. Think you can remember all that?"

"*Sí, señor,*" Andrés said happily.

"If you fail me, I'll send you back under guard."

"*Sí, señor,* I understand."

"Get that horse watered and fed. Give him a quart of shelled corn. It's in the fourth wagon."

Andrés rode away at a gallop.

Hermenijildo nodded knowingly. "His *papá* will be pleased when it is over."

"Yes." But Ross was not so sure; Don Mauricio had all the look of a very stubborn man, and likewise he was a man who never would blame his own son if there was somebody else handy. Therefore Ross stood to take the onus. Not that that worried him very much except as it might affect the expedition. Don Mauricio might have influence with Irigoyen.

He rode on with Hermenijildo, and five

miles farther found a wide bend in the river and a good grassy flat that would graze the mules for one night. There was driftwood for fires, and the river, besides furnishing water, formed a good natural bulwark against attack. He did not anticipate trouble from Indians along the river, but in the wilderness a man did not relax his guard.

The next day Apolinar galloped back from his hunt with a white face. "There is a man around the bend of the river — dead."

Ross looked at him, wondering. A dead man was nothing new to any Mexican. He turned the gelding downstream.

His first impression was of hundreds of repulsive buzzards — some red-headed, some black. They sat on the ground and in a cottonwood tree until the branches were about to break, and on a small sod hut near the river. Ross rode up, striking among them with his short-handled whip. They rose heavily and flapped out of reach. "Don't waste shots on them," said Ross.

He found the body on its back before the hut. An arrow still stuck up from the chest. "Mescalero," said Ross. "See the blood channels between the three feathers."

Most of the *peon*'s face and part of his

chest and bowels had been eaten away. "Bury him," Ross said gruffly. Why a man would come out there into the wilderness to make a home was hard to know.

Ross dismounted and turned the reins over to Hermenijildo. "I'll see what I can find out in the 'dobe," he said.

But first he walked over to look at the body. He had at first been repelled by the grewsome condition of the corpse and he might have missed something. He looked again at what was left of the face, and then he frowned. "Hermenijildo!" he said in a low voice. "Do you see it?"

"*Señor?*"

"The face! The moustache! It's *Bigote Doblado* — black and white. Diego Olivarez!" His voice dropped to a whisper. "He saved my life, Hermenijildo." For a moment he stood, looking down at the fragment of a man's body. The Mexicans coming up with shovels stopped, watching him.

He remembered Diego smiling in the *plaza*, explaining his name, refusing a gratuity. He remembered the man rushing into the duelling place where *peones* well might fear to tread, giving him the warning that had saved his life. Momentarily Ross closed his eyes. This was a man who had

184

wanted freedom — a little piece of land of his own, a place where he could be a man. A few days ago he had been that man, happy and smiling with his Carlota and his *niños* and his few possessions, and now — this torn mass of stinking flesh. A great hardness went through him as he heard the drone of a cloud of big black flies arising suddenly as the shadow of a buzzard crossed the body.

Ross stood up and looked to the north, towards Texas and the Comanches. "God damn those dirty, stinking, redskin sons-of-bitches!"

He stood there for a moment, his jaws hard, and then a hesitant voice asked: "*Señor,* shall we dig now?"

Ross looked down again and drew a deep breath. "Dig!" he said, and turned away.

He went to the hut, expecting to find the bodies of Carlota and the children, but he should have known better. He found evidence of recent occupation — scraps of clothing, a woman's cotton dress, brush-torn, patched with thorns; children too, from the marks of bare feet — four of them. But they were gone. The woman and the children would be captives; the children would be beaten and brutally treated;

if they were too young, and cried, they would be killed. The woman — it was the usual thing when Indians captured a woman. Their phrenetic homicidal energy on a raid seemed to turn into sexual energy as soon as they captured a woman. Ross shook his head grimly.

Carlota. He remembered her well. A smiling, intelligent, friendly face. A proud girl — and a girl to be proud of. And he remembered that Diego *had* been proud. A woman who had little of material things but very much of spiritual things. He thought about that for a moment, and it came to him that this was the thing he wanted — contentment. Somebody like Valeria or Carlota to be his alone. This was what he had wanted when he had seen Valeria in Durango, he realised now — and though Valeria was surrounded by many material things, he knew the same spirit was there. All he had to do was break through that barrier of his pride and Mexican custom, and he knew from that point on material things would be of little moment to Valeria — as they had been to Carlota.

He finished examining the hut. In a corner opposite the fire-place, a cheap coloured lithograph of Christ on the cross

186

had been mounted on the tall stump of a cottonwood tree, about the height of his head, and through it a tomahawk had cut a deep gash diagonally.

Ross went out. "They're gone," he told Hermenijildo.

"What can we do, *señor?*"

"He saved my life," said Ross. "The least we can do is find her and rescue her from the savages. But I do not know how."

He signalled one of his Tonkawas, who had come in silently. The Indian rode up.

"*Hecula?* Who?"

The Tonkawa, with no expression on his dark face but that of watchfulness, said "*Yakokxon-ecewin* — moccasins turned up at toes."

"That's Mescaleros, all right," said Ross. "How many?"

The Tonkawa shrugged and held up both hands, fingers spread.

Ross nodded. "How long ago?"

The Indian pointed at the sun, described an arc back across the sky to the east, where the sun had arisen, then back up again to the zenith.

"Yesterday about noon," Ross said. "From the looks of the body, that's about right."

"We can organise a party to rescue the mother and children," said Hermenijildo.

But Ross shook his head. "We'd never catch them. If it was a small party they would move fast, and by this time they're probably back in Texas a hundred miles away. Second place, we've got our job cut out for us: delivering this train to Arkansas. For all we know this could be a trap to split us up. I don't say it is, but it could be. They might be just waiting for us to divide our men."

"I didn't know," said Apolinar, who had also come up, "that the Indians were capable of such strategy."

"Some are. Old Muke-war-rah of the Penateka Comanches is a very clever chief, and quite capable of such trickery. Likewise, I wouldn't put it past him to make his braves wear Mescalero moccasins just to fool us. I feel sure this is Comanche work."

"What difference would it make?" asked Hermenijildo. "They're both Indians."

"It makes a considerable difference," Ross said. "If we assume it's a small party of Mescaleros, we would expect them to head back home to the hills of New Mexico, and we wouldn't be worried, whereas if they're Comanches they're the most dangerous tribe in Texas, for they are many and they are aggressive. Likewise, it is nothing for them to travel far from home and be gone for months at a time. So if it was Comanches, the desert might be full of them and we'd never know it." He nodded at the Tonkawa, and the Indian turned and went away silently. "Pass the word through the train," he said, "so nobody will get careless."

"I am feel very sad about the woman and children," said Hermenijildo.

Ross watched the men shovelling dirt in on the mangled body of Diego. He said harshly, "We'll get the girl back sometime, somehow. But right now —" He hesitated, then looked up and controlled his voice. "This kind of thing happens every day. You just have to keep a stiff upper lip."

CHAPTER TEN

Presidio del Norte was a miserable hamlet of a hundred or so mud huts clustered around the presidio, a heavily walled fort within which was the inevitable Catholic church. The town itself was on a gravelly hill overlooking the junction of the Conchas and the Río Grande — which latter was called, at that point, the Puercos, because of its muddy waters.

Their long train rolled in to the wide-eyed amazement of men, women, and children. Apolinar had gone ahead to get permission to camp, and he conducted the train through the little town and on to a grassy shelf where they could camp for the night.

Ross, flanked by Hermenijildo and Captain Esquibel, went to call on Lieutenant Oconor, an astonishingly young man who offered them brandy. "It isn't what you are used to," he said, pouring it. "It comes from Paso up the river, however, and is our best native brandy."

"Have you seen Indians around here lately?"

Oconor looked harassed as he nodded. "A couple of weeks ago four hundred braves under Muke-war-rah crossed the Puercos about twenty miles up. They make it very hard on these people. So far they have not attacked us in town, but they drive off the stock and kill and scalp those individualists who prefer to live out from under the wing of the military."

He did not know the Olivarez family but he knew the situation. "There is nothing we can do. The Government doesn't furnish enough troops."

"How many would be enough?" asked Ross.

Oconor looked up. "Thousands, perhaps."

Ross visited *Señor* Don Lawreano Paez, the Mexican customs officer, and advised him they expected to be back in four or five months with goods, and was assured that Don Lawreano had already received a communication from Irigoyen in regard to the matter. Don Lawreano very discreetly manifested no curiosity about the cargo being taken out of the country, and Ross found that up to that time Don Lawreano had never had an opportunity to give a customs certificate for any imported goods.

The second incident occurred late that night. Most of the *arrieros* and drivers had gone into the town to find *pulque* and females and thus celebrate with whatever facilities the town afforded, and so it was late at night when Andrés finally got together a crew to grease the wagon axles. They could have gone a few days more, but this was the seventh day, and Andrés seemed dead set on carrying out his orders, so Ross said nothing against it.

Hermenijildo sought out Ross. "I have seen the big one with the pitted face who went to Paso. Does it mean trouble, *señor?*"

"Nothing else," Ross said grimly.

The first *arrieros* to spend their few *medios* were back soon after dark, not too sober, but Andrés corralled them just the same. He piled up rough-hewn planks and used a spare tongue to pry each wheel off the ground. While two or three men held the end of the lever down, two others took off the wheel, cleaned out the mixture of dirt and grease with their bare hands, and repacked the axle with clean grease.

During this process the repackers were in no hurry, and there was considerable badinage between them and the men holding the lever. "Why did you come back so early?" asked one. "Did you run out of money?"

"I didn't need money," said a man sitting on the lever. "The woman liked me — but her husband came home and found us in bed."

Ross walked closer. The pile of blocking looked wobbly in the centre.

One man was holding the wheel upright while another was scooping out the dirty grease with his fingers and snapping it to the ground. "Why did *you* come home so early?" he asked without looking up.

"I drank up all the *pulque*," said the man on the end of the lever.

Andrés jumped towards him. *"Cuidado!"*

But the *arriero*, demonstrating the fact that he had imbibed copiously, swayed and then actually lost his balance. He sprawled full length on his face in the dirt, and the lever, losing his weight, arose abruptly. Six feet from the ground it spewed the other two in both directions and shot almost vertical. The corner of the wagon came down with a crash, impelled by the weight of 4000 pounds of food.

Andrés shouted, *"Burros! Jumentos!"* and gave them a tongue-lashing in Spanish that would have done credit to any *arriero* in the business. Ross was about to tell him it was enough when he saw tears in the young man's eyes, and refrained. Then he remembered something else that had happened when the wagon-box dropped. A woman's voice had screamed, and a deep, man's voice had growled.

Ross put a hand on Andrés's arm. "Get more blocking," he said. "Get the axle back into the air and there's no harm done. Just see that the dirt is cleaned off."

Relief had never been more apparent on anyone's face than on Andrés's. "*Sí, señor,*" he said fervently, and began to shout orders.

Ross went to the wagon and examined the lashings on the corner that had fallen. He threw back a rope, grasped a corner of the canvas and lifted it high. In the light reflected from the camp fire of mesquite roots he saw the brown face of Plácido, and beside him, on a pile of blankets, was Josefina, wide-eyed and scared.

"*Señorita.*" Ross bowed. "I do not seem to have seen you since a night in the *Nueve Gatos.*"

"No, *señor.*"

He looked at Plácido. "So you've kept her here in this little nest for all this time." He shook his head. "It must have been a difficult trip, *señorita,* under this hot canvas."

She said nothing.

"But then the exhaustion of making love all night possibly closed your eyes in slumber during the day."

Still she did not answer but drew closer to Plácido.

There was quite a crowd around them now, and Josefina shrank still closer to Plácido.

"I have no control over your habits," Ross said to Plácido, "but the teams have had to pull this woman, and you have had to feed her from our supply. I shall take it out of your pay."

Plácido did not seem greatly disturbed by this news. *"Sí, señor,"* he said.

"And she will have to stay in Presidio."

"But *señor* —"

"There will be no argument, *hombre.*"

Plácido muttered, *"Sí, señor."*

"Now get out of there."

"But, *señor* —"

"No matter. Get out!"

Plácido climbed out sullenly. He reached back in and got his straw hat. *"Señor,* if Josefina stays in Presidio, I stay too."

"If you do, you will end up in the *juzgado* at Chihuahua, for you made a deal with me

195

and I have given you money for your family before we left."

Plácido glowered at him and backed away.

"*Señorita*," said Ross, "I shall have to ask you to give up your quarters in the wagon."

She climbed out slowly, making no effort to conceal her bare thighs in the firelight.

"I don't know where you will go," he said, "but I have no doubt you will be able to make your way in Presidio as well as in Chihuahua."

They forded the Río Grande on its limestone bed; the water was not yet deep from the mountain snows in the Santa Fé district, for those snows had not begun to melt. They crossed the range of mountains immediately north of the river and descended into that desolate wilderness of mountains and desert that led to the Pecos.

A more broken country was hard to imagine. Ross had his Tonkawa scouts out far ahead, and he himself rode widely to find camping places and to locate routes by which they would be able to take the wagons. The country was not only mountainous but rugged; many of the canyons were deep gashes cut straight down into the red earth, and he rode on to them suddenly out of a monotonous prairie of spider-like *ocotillo* and dusty greasewood and odoriferous creosote-bush (the Mexicans called this latter *hediondilla*, stinking-bush), and sometimes the gelding would almost step off the edge before it would see the chasm. Most of these canyons were dry at the bottom, and water holes were far apart and hard to find.

The journey to the Pecos was not far but it was arduous. There was little game, but occasionally an eagle soared high in the cloudless sky, and there must have been a few rabbits and rats, and of course there were myriads of rattlesnakes.

Up on top of the mountains were vast towns of prairie dogs, which the Tonkawas called *yacoxana-as,* but these were little help for food, for they were too hard to shoot. Grass too was scarce, and twice on the way to the Pecos Ross doled out feedings of shelled corn in place of forage. The animals began to show the effect of the heat and the lack of feed and water; their ribs became evident, and they were harder to drive and slower to cover a day's journey, while the tempers of the men shortened under the heat of the sun.

They were plagued with small troubles.

A wheel broke against a stone, and Andrés was desolate. A squad of men from Esquibel's detachment, holding back a wagon on a steep hill by means of rawhide ropes, let it get away, the tongue was split and a mule got a broken hip and had to be shot. A doubletree broke ahead of a spanner, and Ross, beginning to suspect these happenings were not all accidents, examined the tree.

Hermenijildo was at his elbow.

"Do you see what I see?" asked Ross.

"The wood was whittled at the bolt," said Hermenijildo gravely.

"There is no longer any doubt that we have a traitor with us," Ross said, "and I know who he is."

"*Señor* — not Captain Esquibel!"

"Why not?"

"He is of the military," said Hermenijildo.

"Military be damned!" said Ross.

"You are speaking of me, *señor?*" asked a suave voice.

Ross turned. Esquibel stood, feet apart, hands loose, his wide belt carrying two seven-shot pistols. Ross said, "I never noticed you were so well armed before."

"A good soldier," said Esquibel, his

black eyes sharp, "always has forces in reserve."

Ross's eyes began to narrow. "Are you ready to commit yourself, then?"

Esquibel shrugged elaborately. "Oh, no, *señor*. I merely came to inquire about the delay."

Ross pointed to the whittled doubletree. "I'm sure you know as much about it as I do. Whose money paid for it — Cordero's or Conde's?"

Esquibel looked very sad. "I am sure I know nothing of what you speak."

"You know enough," Ross said grimly, "and I am going to hear it from you or take you apart with my bare hands."

Esquibel smiled. "I regret to point out, *señor,* that you have only a knife and pistol, while I have two pistols. Perhaps you have overlooked this."

Ross took a step towards him. "And you —"

"*Señor! señor!*" Apolinar galloped up and jerked his horse to a sliding stop. "*Señor,* there are men ahead! They have a paper from Don Lawreano Paez!"

Ross frowned. "What kind of paper?"

"They demand to search the train for contraband gold and silver."

Ross swung into the saddle and galloped

towards the head of the long train. The mules were standing, cropping the scanty grass, switching at flies. Plácido was sitting indolently on the ground in the shade of his *coyote* dun. A group of Mexicans in the usual motley dress of either outlaws or army men was arrayed in a line across the line of march. Ross rode up to them. "Who is the spokesman here?" he demanded.

A *peon* in a big straw hat said timorously but defiantly, "I am the *mayor domo, señor.*"

Ross looked at him. He was the big man with the pitted face. "Are you from Don Lawreano?"

"*Sí, señor,* here is my paper." He handed Ross a small rectangle of heavy rag paper printed on one side. Ross glanced at it. "To search for suspected items carried without legal permit," it said. Ross looked at the man. "Can you read?"

The man moistened his lips. "No, *señor,* I do not read. I am only —"

"Is thees man give you trouble, Juan?"

Ross turned to look into the insolent face of Esquibel. "These are your men?" Ross said quickly.

Esquibel shrugged. "They are under my orders."

"Are they soldiers?"

"Of course, *señor.*"

200

"Very good. Hermenijildo!"

"*Sí, señor.*"

"Take down the names of every man in this group. I want Conde to know what soldiers he has on his payroll."

Juan backed away, his eyes wide. "I do not want to be in the army, *señor.*" He looked pleadingly at Esquibel. "*Capitán —*"

Esquibel was taken aback for a moment. Then he said, "These men are under Don Lawreano. They have an order to search the mules."

Ross turned to Juan and the ragged-looking men behind him. "*Bien, hombres.* Who will be first to open a saddlebag?"

Juan moistened his lips, looked at Ross, and backed away.

Esquibel shouted, "Do your duty! *Adelante!*"

Juan still backed away, shaking his head.

Ross turned to Esquibel. "Captain, your men refuse to search the train. Apparently they believe the cargo is satisfactory."

Esquibel compressed his lips. He looked at the cowering men and then at Ross. "You damn' *yanqui,*" he snarled, and suddenly drew a pistol. "*Arriba!* Put your hands up, *señor,* or I shall blow your head off!"

Ross laughed. "That's the wrong pistol,"

201

he said. "That one isn't loaded."

He saw the faint look of uncertainty in Esquibel's eyes, and that was enough. He plunged forward to his right. Esquibel pulled the trigger but the pistol missed fire. Ross, with his hand on his six-shooter, said, "Will you draw the other one, Captain?"

Esquibel now was caught in his own trap. If he had carried out this bluff and been successful, he could have retired to the Sandwich Islands and lived like a millionaire. But now he might have to go back and face Irigoyen with very little in the way of explanation. He had no way of knowing why the pistol had misfired. Perhaps, as Ross had suggested — he drew the other pistol.

Ross shot him through the point of the breastbone. Esquibel curled up slowly and went down. Ross reloaded his pistol and said to Hermenijildo and Apolinar: "I will ask you to certify that Esquibel said he was in charge of these men who were to search the train, and that he drew first. *Verdad?*"

Hermenijildo nodded.

"We saw it," said Apolinar, staring at the body.

Ross put the search warrant in his pocket and turned to Hermenijildo. "Get this *coyote* buried. Notify Lieutenant Tapia he is in charge of all the dragoons. Give these men some corn and send them back to Presidio."

"*Si, señor.*"

Ross glanced at the dead captain. "That's one level disposed of anyhow," he said, and picked up the two pistols from the ground. He handed them to Apolinar. "Get the train going!" he said. "We've wasted too much time on this *jumento* already. If he'd had half as much brains as he had ambition, we would be dead and he would be on the road to California."

All day long the huge mule train wound up and down over the hills, in and out and across the canyons, through passes, across open sand. The seven hundred mules and seven wagons raised a tower of dust that could be seen for fifty miles, and there was evidence that the Comanches were watching it, for Apolinar failed to find deer for the second day in a row, and instead brought in two *javelinas* or wild hogs. "I have great sorrow, *señor*," he said earnestly, "but I and my men cannot seem to find enough game except for these pigs, which are hard to locate."

"Keep trying," said Ross. "Give your horses a feed of corn every morning, for

203

they've got to keep going."

He looked at the boy and barely restrained a grin, for Apolinar looked like anything but a young Mexican dandy. All the three Mexican young men had adopted buckskin clothing as soon as their own wore out, and now they wore moccasins and felt hats and, with their brown skins, were indistinguishable from Indians at a short distance. And they repeatedly pleased Ross, for they were the best assistants he had ever had. Hermenijildo watched constantly at Ross's elbow, ready to undertake any job; Apolinar had recently been out of camp before daylight and sometimes would not come back until almost midnight; Andrés guarded the seven wagons as carefully as if they had been babies.

A new element tried their patience: the canyons. It began to require too much time to head the canyons, and Ross appointed a squad to cut down the banks and make a way for the wagons. Even then the banks were almost impassably steep, and it required many mules and men to get a wagon across.

The day after Apolinar had reported no game in sight, Ross, riding far ahead and flanked by the Tonkawas at a distance of several miles, saw an antelope start up fully a mile away, circle, and then float off to the west at its unbelievable speed.

He called the Tonkawas in at noon and handed out a sack of tobacco to each of them, heard their grunts in thanks. Ross, squatting on his heels, asked, "How is it ahead?"

The leader, a grizzled Indian called *Xoyco-okic,* The Soft-Shelled Turtle, looked all around them at the vast expanses of brush and the far-distant horizons. "Long time, no rain," he said, "but river not far."

"Is there water in the river?"

"Will be — much water." Xoyco-okic looked to the west with age-old eyes that seemed to peer into infinity. "Rain in mountains — seven suns ago," he said. "River high when we get there."

Ross had been too much around Indians to question a statement like that. How The Soft-Shelled Turtle could tell it was raining several hundred miles away, none but he knew — and possibly not even he, but Ross had no slightest doubt there would be heavy water in the Pecos when they reached it.

One of the younger Tonks grunted something, and The Soft-Shelled Turtle looked at Ross. "You no drink river water

— is bad salty, mules die — like grasshoppers."

"What will they drink?"

"Fresh water — springs. We find."

"One more thing. You see game run from far away — too far to shoot?"

The old Indian nodded.

"That should not be. It says there are Indians just ahead of us."

"Is so." The Soft-Shelled Turtle nodded. "We see sign."

"What kind?"

The Soft-Shelled Turtle held a guttural conference with his companions, then said to Ross, "All *Penetixka* — Comanche. We find sign at water hole. Comanche brave put hands in water, balance on arms, like this" — he demonstrated — "to drink. Leave no sign. Squaw put knees in soft mud. Only squaws have fat knees."

"How do you know it's not Apache?"

"Apaches no take squaws on raiding party. Only Comanches."

Ross got up. "Far ahead?"

"One sun," said The Soft-Shelled Turtle.

"*Bueno*. You watch — more careful. You report me all signs. Every night I give you more *nexpaxkan* — tobacco. *Está bueno?*"

"*Bueno,*" said the Tonkawa.

The Indians camped by themselves,

apart from the Mexicans. Tapia's dragoons had a separate mess; the *arrieros* camped apart from the mule-skinners, and Ross and his three assistants had their own fire. And that afternoon they stopped early after a good day's trip of some three and a half leagues.

Ross had the big stone *metate* unpacked from one of the wagons, and set two men to grinding corn for *tortillas,* for Apolinar had come in at noon, very disgusted, with nothing but a half-grown ocelot for meat.

Ross went over to the Indians' camp about dark. "Do you find sign to-day?" he asked.

The Soft-Shelled Turtle nodded slowly. "The tracks lead to the Pecos — Horsehead Crossing."

Ross was thoughtful. "You believe they will wait there for us?"

"They have make sure you will go to the Horsehead Crossing; now they are going ahead to wait. You have big train, thousands mules. They like."

"The crossing — is that a good place for ambush?"

"Very good," declared The Soft-Shelled Turtle. "You go down in river, they up on banks. They shoot many arrows, very fast;

take many scalps."

"How many Comanches?"

"Probably many — two, three, four hundred."

"Do you think game will be as scarce across the Pecos?"

"You find — buffalo — other side. Much meat. Good meat. Not like prairie dog."

Ross smiled. He himself was getting a little tired of soup made with wheat flour and a few joints of prairie dog. "Then where can we cross below the Horsehead?"

The Soft-Shelled Turtle's eyes narrowed as he looked into the far distance. "Seven leagues — one good day's march with mules."

"Can we go there directly from here?"

"You go *mas allá* — a little farther, around that peak yonder." He pointed. "Then turn right. You find good road in canyon. No water. Good road. Canyon lead to Pecos."

Ross passed out tobacco. "You go that way to-morrow. Find road. We follow."

He went back. The vast emptiness of the semi-desert brushland; the silence, the oppressive silence; the heat, the sameness, the lack of water and meat — all these were beginning to have an effect on the men. The only thing that held them together now was the fact they would be afraid for their lives to strike off in small parties through Comanche country. That was a way to quick suicide.

There were always small individual parties of Indians hanging on the flanks of a big train, watching to cut off stragglers. These Indians were not found in front of a train, because they well knew that every big train sent its best men out ahead; and such parties offered no threat to their change of route, because the main party which wanted to ambush them had drawn off all its warriors to avoid scaring them away from the crossing.

CHAPTER ELEVEN

The grass seemed to grow even poorer on this route. The mules snipped at greasewood and whatever came along. An occasional clump of mesquite trees showed they were nearing a water course, and these were stripped clean of their tiny, symmetrical leaves by the horses.

They watered at a small spring before daylight the next morning. The spring flowed up out of solid rock and filled a hole the size of a barrel. The path down to the water was wide enough for only one at a time, and the narrow canyon below the spring was completely inaccessible, while within a quarter of a mile, at a point where they could get up to the stream-bed, the water had sunk into the sand.

So Ross watched the slow process of watering seven hundred mules, and warned Plácido and Andrés not to lash packs or harness the animals until all were out, for it would be some time. They had a quarter-moon for the task, which made it easier, and Ross kept the dragoons posted all along the way. He told Tapia, "The guides say the Comanches are waiting for us at Horsehead Crossing. It is good to be very watchful. If they have spies out, they may find that we are changing course, and we can look for trouble."

"*Sí, señor*," said Tapia without apparent feeling.

An hour before sun-up the long, long train of mules was watered. "Give them no feed," Ross ordered, "because to-day they will get no water, and an animal without water will go farther on an empty stomach."

Plácido nodded — almost too agreeably, the fleeting thought came to Ross. But he had other things to think about. He saw that the men filled their canteens and cautioned them against using the water before noon. Twenty miles would be a long day's drive with the mules in no better condition than they were.

He rode ahead with the Tonkawas and picked out a route for the wagons. Back in Chihuahua they had tried to figure out a way of transporting everything in pack-saddles, but bulky items and hard-to-lash items could be transported more easily by wagon — and by one third as many mules.

For four miles they followed along the high edge of the escarpment. The canyon below was dry; the sides were precipitous, and the growth was mostly salt cedars and greasewood and some mesquite.

Then they reached the spot where The Soft-Shelled Turtle said they could get into the canyon. Ross looked it over. It was possible and that was about all. He got a party of Tapia's men to clear out brush and small trees and dig a channel just wide enough for the wagons. They could then tie ropes on to the wagon and put fifty or sixty men to hold it back. In this way the seven wagons reached the bottom of the canyon, where it was relatively easy going on the stream-bed, which sometimes was sand, sometimes gravel. Ross had an extra span of mules put on each wagon, for the pull was long and hard, and the sun at the bottom of the canyon was stifling hot.

He delayed the men's use of their canteens as long as possible, but by ten o'clock they were dipping into them, and by noon there was not a swallow of water left except his own, his three assistants', Tapia's, and, oddly enough, Plácido's.

They stopped in the bottom of the canyon for an hour to rest the mules. A few *tules* or rushes were eaten clean within minutes, but Ross would not allow the mules to be fed or any rations to be given the men. At one o'clock they began to relash the packs. Each *arriero* could get a mule ready to travel in about three minutes, and each man was responsible for ten mules, so it took a half-hour to relash. By that time, of course, Andrés had his wagons on the move, and Plácido himself was a demon of energy.

The long train strung out in the bottom of the canyon and moved forward. Ross was uneasy, for it would be suicidal to get caught in there. But the far-ranging Tonkawas reported no Comanches within several miles, and Ross urged the train on down the canyon.

He rode out ahead, and about six o'clock he found the first water-hole. It was another hour before the mules began to arrive, and Ross gave instructions to Plácido to stand there and personally see that every mule drank his fill, for the water in the Pecos, not far away according to the Tonkawas, was so heavily loaded with brine that it could very well be fatal, and the mules might smell the water and head for it instead of waiting their turns at the spring.

Satisfied that the mules were in good

hands, he rode on to the mighty Pecos, where many caravans had come to a tragic end.

It was not a big water, but the sides were steep and in many places vertical, and the red sandstone walls were strewn with boulders. The course of the muddy water was so tortuous that it was difficult to know where to put the train across without actually trying it, so he rode on, watching carefully.

The canyon of the Pecos was, he judged, three to four hundred feet deep at that point, and they might have to turn the wagons downstream to find a way out. But then he saw The Soft-Shelled Turtle sitting his barebacked horse high on the east bank, and rode through the water, which was about belly-deep on the gelding, and found a narrow dry gully which he realised at once could be widened with picks and shovels to permit passage of the wagons. He rode through it and came out on top, and sat his horse there beside The Soft-Shelled Turtle and looked over the vast expanse of land to the west — dry, desolate, almost devoid of living creatures. He snapped his whip at a rattlesnake and broke its back, then tossed it over the cliff. It was likely, he thought, that *javelinas* could be found in the thick brush along the river bottom, because the *javelina* was not poisoned by the snakes and fed on them with glee.

"The rain has not reached here," he said to the Indian.

The Tonkawa said calmly, "You found the river a day soon. But" — he pointed with a mahogany-red forefinger — "do you see that?"

Ross watched. A few small pieces of driftwood floated around the nearest bend, and after them were a few white bubbles. Ross nodded. "It's coming."

"Soon," said The Soft-Shelled Turtle.

Ross rode back down the *arroyada* and galloped the black to the spring.

"Lieutenant," he told Tapia, "I would like thirty men to widen out a road for the wagons."

"It is late," said Tapia. "We will widen the road tomorrow."

"No. To-night."

"*Señor?*"

"The river is rising."

"I have seen no rain clouds."

"*Teniente!*" Ross's voice was sharp. "You are under my orders!"

Tapia looked at him, and Ross saw the light of rebellion start to grow in the officer's eyes. Tapia had felt his responsibility since the death of Esquibel.

"*Teniente*," said Ross, "I have in my care a great many men and a great deal of property, some of which belongs to the Governor. I would not like to report to him that it was lost through the neglect of an officer of the dragoons."

"But, *señor*, my men have not eaten all day, and they are tired."

"I am not going to argue very long with you, Lieutenant, but I will point out one thing: you have not travelled much in the West or you would know it is always good policy to cross a stream when you come to it, for many things can happen at night. In this case the first flood waters are already showing in the river. By morning it will be impassable, and then you will see the spectacle of seven hundred mules and a hundred men trapped in the canyon. It might well be," he said after a pause, "that the Comanches now waiting for us at Horsehead Crossing would find us here."

Tapia's eyes widened. "I did not know of these Comanches."

"You do not know of many things, perhaps. Your business is soldiering, not freighting."

"Very well, *señor.* I will give you your men."

Ross led them across the river and put them to work. By that time the first mules were reaching the river, and he directed the *arrieros* to let them spread out and graze on the sparse vegetation they might find. He went back to the *arroyada* and wielded a pick with the rest of them. Then he heard a shout and looked up in time to see thirty mules racing under full pack for the river. He stared for a moment, hardly believing what he saw. Then he caught up the gelding and put it into the water at a gallop. But the water slowed him down, and the mules splashed into the river and lowered their heads to drink. He shouted, and the *arrieros* ran towards the spot. The first *arriero* reached them before Ross, and they both tried to haze two mules back out of the water, but could not. Ross rode one mule down with the gelding, but it would not get up but went to its knees and then rolled over, the pack still in place.

Ross left it and tried to head off the others. But they were coming in a beeline and they would not be stopped. He saw it was useless. He used his *lazo* and tried to pull one away from the water, but it was

217

heavier with its legs braced than a five-year-old steer.

Within ten minutes all thirty of the mules had filled up on the water, and Ross was hunting Plácido. "I told you to make sure every mule watered at the spring," he thundered.

Plácido looked scared. "*Sí, señor,* I have done as you ordered."

"Then why did those thirty mules head for the river water?"

Plácido backed a step, fearfully. "I do not know, *señor.*"

Ross was angry. "I know damn' well you know, and I'll find out if I have to beat it out of your hide."

He went back. The mule that had fallen to its knees in the water was still there, its head on the bottom, drowned. A second mule was lying on its side on the sand, gasping. Half a dozen others were lying down. He swore violently.

"But, *señor,*" said Hermenijildo, "thirty mules are not so much. The merchants —"

"I don't give a damn what they're worth in cash. I'm concerned with what they're worth to us out here in the middle of the wilderness!"

"I don't understand."

"In Chihuahua we could buy thirty more

mules. Out here there is no place to buy. *Entiende?*"

"*Sí, señor,*" Hermenijildo said humbly.

They lost twenty-two out of the thirty. The other eight would be all right after a day or two. Ross set men to work butchering the dead mules. Their round steaks, he thought, would be safe enough.

By that time the opposite bank was cut away enough to permit passage of the wagons with care. Ross had kept one eye on the river, which by now was definitely turning roily with a stronger flow, red silt in suspension, small parcels of driftwood, and considerable white foam on its surface.

He had thrown the Tonkawa spies out at a distance of several miles to guard against surprise by the Comanches, and now, after measuring the width of the newly opened passage with a long wand of tamarisk, cut off with his skinning knife, he mounted the gelding and went back across the stream.

"Wagons go first," he ordered. "Andrés, hitch twelve mules to a tongue. It's fairly steep over there. You'll have some trouble with one turn, for the pull on the chain, coming from away around the bend in the *arroyada,* will throw the wagon into the wall, but the men are cutting it away as

219

much as they can."

"It will soon be pitch black," Andrés pointed out.

"All the better. The Comanches are not likely to attack in blackness. Get going now. We should be over within an hour. Then we'll be able to unharness and prepare some food."

"I have much hunger," Andrés said soberly.

"You'll be fed," Ross promised. "Apolinar brought in nine turkeys a while ago and they're cleaning them now. Tomorrow, if all goes well, we'll have buffalo hump for supper."

Andrés began to shout orders.

"*Señor,*" said Hermenijildo, "I too have much hunger. Could you not issue orders that Apolinar and his men start cooking the meat now?"

Ross shook his head. "We don't dare to make a fire until we have all the animals and goods across and are ready to defend them. Just be sure of one thing; every man should have a full canteen before he crosses, for we don't know how far it will be to water on the other side."

"*Sí, señor.*"

"Plácido!"

"*Sí, señor,*" Plácido answered, coming

from under a wagon.

"Get your *arrieros* under way. Bring the mules together and prepare to start lashing pack-saddles as soon as the fourth wagon is across. We'll camp on the high ground on the other side to-night."

"*Teniente!*"

Tapia answered "*Sí,*" and appeared out of the blackness, for no fires had been permitted, even the work on the *arroyada* being done by starlight.

"Throw your twenty men out as foragers to guard against a surprise attack from the rear. They will follow the *mulas de carga* across the river."

"*Bien, señor.*"

"And Andrés, as soon as the *metate* gets across, have your men set it up and start grinding corn. The men must have a good meal to-night — plenty to eat."

The water had risen several inches by the time the first wagon lumbered into the current, and the mules were nervous, but Ross had Hermenijildo go back into the *arroyada* and start a small fire where it could be seen by the mules but from no other angle, and this helped them into the water and guided them to the other side.

When the fourth wagon rumbled across the red sandstone bottom and into the current, Plácido began to shout at his *arrieros*, and they in turn shouted at their mules, and in an incredibly short time the entire long string of mules was lined up, each mule finding its own pack and standing there, waiting to be loaded.

The last wagon was no sooner in the water than Plácido's pack mules were ready to follow. The dragoons closed in behind. Normally they would have driven the reserve band of mules, but with the losses from alkali water and the extra animals pulling the wagons, there was no reserve left.

Each wagon struck its side against the wall of the passage at the turn, but they got by, with tremendous scraping of the wheel hubs through the hard red dirt, by the combined pushing and pulling of many men, accompanied by loud and fervent swearing, of which the words were Spanish but the intonations were familiar to teamsters all over the country.

They got the wagons out on fairly level ground east of the river, and arranged them in a semi-circle with the open side towards the river. The mules were turned out to crop the short, curly buffalo grass that now appeared for the first time, and Ross arranged relays of night guards to run two hours apiece, each controlled by Apolinar, Hermenijildo, or Andrés. It was somewhat after ten o'clock, and three shifts would bring them to four o'clock and daylight.

Long before the last pack mule crossed the river, the *metate* was set up, and the sound of its grinding could be heard a quarter of a mile.

Ross went back across the river to call in the dragoons, and rode across the stream with Tapia. He hoped the lieutenant noticed that the water was over their stirrups by that time.

Santiago, who usually acted as cook, cut up the turkeys and handed out pieces for the men to cook as they would; many of them ate the meat raw. He handed out thick steaks cut from the dead mules. The cornmeal was apportioned, one cupful to the man, and some of this was mixed with cold water and sugar and eaten raw by those who were in a hurry. Others built small fires from mesquite branches and found flat rocks to bake corn cakes. Coffee was passed out, and in most cases eight or ten men would go together and boil it in tin buckets, but here and there a man would build a fire all by himself and make his own coffee to suit his taste.

It was almost midnight when Ross finally squatted on his heels to gnaw his leg of half-cooked turkey and to gulp down his chunk of cornbread. He had a tin cup of coffee beside him, made from his own canteen, to wash down the cornbread. Suddenly he felt unutterably weary, and he was conscious of the fact that every man there felt the same way. It had been a long, hard drive — twenty miles that day, without water or food. It was enough to tire anyone. And yet, he knew, there were many more such days ahead of them.

All over the camp, by the small, glowing fires, the men ate in famished silence. The night wind did not cool off as it did in the mountains around Chihuahua, and it was intensely still. Except for an occasional stamp by the mules, and sometimes a squeal as one mule bared its teeth against another there was silence — the silence of the Pecos, land of the twisting river, home of prairie dogs and rattlesnakes.

He lifted his cup and blew on it, set it temporarily on his knee to cool, holding it there by the handle, and then he heard, out of the quiet night, a quick flash-fire of Spanish imprecations:

"Caramba!"
"Qué hombre malo!"
"Jumento!"
"Burro!"

"Tortuga!"

"Cabrón!"

"Hijo de chingada!"

He leaped to his feet at the first words, recognising Plácido's expression of amazement and indignation. His cup went flying, his cornbread dropped in the grass as he ran to the wagon from which came the oaths.

Two men were struggling in the fire-glow, one in bare feet, the other in boots. Knives flashed in the red light, and the men grunted as they strained against each other. Plácido's back was towards Ross, his splendid muscles bunched, and Ross recognised Santiago's face, contorted with animosity.

Ross raced up, seized Plácido by the shoulders and flung him back. He heard Plácido hit the ground and turn like a cat to get back to his feet, and then Santiago, his eyes blazing with that wild gleam of fury, advanced on Ross with his knife held before his stomach.

Ross kicked him in the groin, then, as the man's hands dropped, seized him too by the shoulders and spun him away. Then he stood, tall and imposing in the firelight, legs widespread, watching both ways. "I said there will be no fighting among my men, and I meant it." He heard Santiago getting to his feet. "You got enough,

225

hombre?" he asked.

Santiago muttered. Plácido was putting away his knife. Ross glared at Santiago. The wild light died in the man's eyes; his eyelids dropped; slowly he thrust the knife back in his waistband.

"Now," said Ross, "what's it about — you two?"

Neither answered.

Ross said, "I never saw you fight over but one thing, Plácido — and that was Josefina." He stopped suddenly and looked at Santiago. "You had words over her in Presidio. *Verdad?*"

Still neither answered.

Ross frowned. "But there's nothing to fight about until you get back. We left Josefina in Presidio." He stared for an instant at Plácido's downcast eyes. "Or did we?" he asked suddenly.

He glanced at Santiago, who also looked at the ground. Then he shouted: "Hermenijildo! Apolinar! Andrés!"

They came running — Andrés with food in his hand.

"Search the wagons! Find that little *chingada!*"

She looked pretty bedraggled when she crawled out from under the canvas of the sixth wagon — worn and a little drawn from the long journey, and Ross could hardly understand, as she stood there blinking in the fire-glow, her black hair dishevelled, how she could have endured the last week's travels confined in an almost airless nest among the boxes and crates that contained the meagre reserves of food for the expedition. And yet he was aware, as she stood with her head high and her eyes unashamed, that she was filled with a wild-animal magnetism that somehow was reflected in her posture, her compact build, her bare legs and shoulders, her fearless black eyes.

"Didn't you like it in Presidio, *señorita?*" he asked, kindly enough.

"Plácido was not in Presidio," she said simply.

"So then how does Santiago get into the game?"

She dropped her head.

"Plácido was not enough for you, eh? And yet it was Plácido, wasn't it, who let thirty mules drink bad water while he was getting a canteen of fresh water to you after a long day's travel?"

He looked at Plácido and then at Santiago. "I don't know what to do with you two. Obviously Josefina is not faithful to anybody. Obviously too we cannot now send her back. So it looks as if she will have to go with us to Arkansas."

Plácido looked up, pleased.

"But one thing," Ross said ominously. "If either one of you fights over her, I will break you over my knee." He stood wide-legged before the fire and looked around him at the crowd, now consisting of nearly every man in camp except the guards. "If any doubts that I will do it, let him speak."

One or two moved uneasily, but nobody spoke.

"Feed her," Ross ordered.

One of Tapia's dragoons went eagerly to the fire.

"A woman out here is like a match in a keg of powder," Ross told his assistants, "but we'll have to do the best we can. *Señorita,*" he said.

She looked up.

"You will have to work your way in a fashion you may not be accustomed to. There is that *metate,* and grinding corn is woman's work. I don't know whether you can grind enough for a hundred men, but you are going to try. And if I catch you shirking, there will be trouble. Maybe," he said, "eight hours of grinding will leave you too exhausted for the men to fight over." He added thoughtfully, "Or will it?"

CHAPTER TWELVE

They were under way at daylight the next morning. The packs from the dead mules were redistributed among the reserve mules. But even before they got the wagons rolling, a band of forty-five antelope started up three miles away and circled gracefully, then floated off down the valley.

"*Berendas*," said Apolinar, watching their course.

"*Berendas*, yes — but why did they start up?"

Apolinar's eyes widened. "Something disturbed them."

"Of course it did — Comanches."

"Do you think?"

"There are no coincidences in Indian country," said Ross. "Nothing just happens. Remember that and you will live longer. For to-day I suggest you don't wander far. We still have mule-meat. The Tonks will be out about three miles, and you better stay about half-way between them and the train."

"But, *señor* —"

"Sometimes," Ross said, "you can hear crows cawing in the distance." He listened, his head tipped to the west. "I heard it about half an hour ago."

"What does that mean?" asked Apolinar.

"An Indian camp. The crows follow it to pick up the refuse. It means the camp has moved either last night or early this morning — probably last night, because the Indians are not early risers, contrary to what you may have heard."

"The train will need meat to-morrow."

"And you need your hair to-night when you come in. Now listen: three men must ride together — no less. Don't get out of sight of the train and don't go far under any circumstances. *Entiende?*"

"*Sí, señor.*"

"No later than to-morrow we'll find buffalo. They'll move north, but not all of them. And in a few days we'll be out of the range of this band of Comanches, and nothing to worry about until we hit the Kotsoteka Comanches along the headwaters of the Brazos. All right, go ahead."

Josefina walked by the side of the first wagon. Somebody, probably Plácido, during the night had cut down a pair of spare moccasins to fit her small feet, and now she walked along in the dust of the train

230

and over the rough ground, seeming quite contented. Andrés rode up and said to Ross, "She might as well help drive, hadn't she?"

Ross nodded.

Andrés looked at her thoughtfully. "She may get pretty tired grinding all that corn."

Ross smiled. "Don't worry. She'll have half the men in camp waiting for turns to grind corn."

"*Señor!* Do you theenk so?"

"Knowing Josefina — yes."

Their route was north-east, and the terrain began to straighten out a little. It still wasn't level prairie, but the grass improved, and The Soft-Shelled Turtle reported that there would be fresh water within reach of the wagons.

They stopped before noon to rest the mules and to eat, and almost at once the sound of the grinding pestle in the *metate* arose.

Andrés seemed concerned. "She can't grind much corn in an hour or two," he said.

"Let her go. Our mules carried her for two weeks. It won't hurt her to work a little in return."

"But she's a woman, *señor.*"

Ross grinned. "Never mind. When

you're as old as I am you'll know that women bear up under these conditions better than men."

They moved on soon, for there was no water at their stopping place, and the canteens were empty as soon as they finished eating.

Ross rode ahead. The Tonkawas were fanned out in advance on horseback, but a man never could tell where they were until he stumbled on them. About three o'clock in the afternoon he recognised the peculiarly shaped low hill that The Soft-Shelled Turtle had described as a landmark. They were to swing around to the north-west of the hill, and on the north-east side they would find a small spring. He studied the country for a moment and determined there was no other such hill in the vicinity. He caught sight of Apolinar and two men riding a mile to the east. All this country was open, and it seemed utterly impossible that an Indian could hide behind the scattered clumps of grass. And yet the Tonkawas were out there somewhere with horses.

He leaned forward in the saddle to send the gelding ahead, but then he sat back hard and suddenly, for ahead of him, not over four hundred yards away, on the top of the small hill, stood an Indian.

He wore no feathers. His face was mahogany black and his hair was braided down the side. He was naked from the waist up, and wore breechclout, deerskin leggings, and moccasins. His arms were at his sides, his bow strung over his back.

Ross looked back. He fired a shot from his six-shooter, and then, knowing that Tapia's advance guard had seen him, turned the gelding and rode in a small circle.

The Indian didn't move. Ross rode slowly towards him, watching the skyline with great care — but he saw nothing move.

Apolinar was closing in at a gallop, and, when he was near, Ross went forward at a trot. He stopped the gelding within twenty feet of the Indian and held his right hand up, palm out, about the height of his shoulder; moving it rapidly from side to side, he gradually raised it higher.

The Indian watched this with the insolence typical of the Comanche dealing with whites. Then he said in good Spanish: "I am Ish-a-ro-yeh, second chief to Muke-war-rah."

"Are you alone?"

"I — am — alone."

"You've been watching us for days. What do you want?"

"Muke-war-rah want talk — trade."

"We have no trade goods."

The Comanche waved a short, muscular arm at the train. "You have many, many *mulas*. Must have goods. You do not bring this *mulas* all the way from Chihuahua to eat buffalo grass."

"No goods," Ross repeated firmly. "Some food for ourselves. No goods. White iron only."

Apolinar rode up behind him and stopped.

"The chief Muke-war-rah no believe that story. He has watched this *mulas* many days."

I know," said Ross. "From Presidio del Norte."

Ish-a-ro-yeh looked at him without change of expression, "You know this?"

"We are not men with eyes in the backs of their heads," Ross said scornfully.

"What are you doing in Comanche country?"

This was a point where he had to be careful, for any mention of Texas would infuriate the Comanches. "We are travelling peacefully. We carry the white iron to Arkansas to buy goods. We kill only enough game to eat."

"You are not *Mejicano*."

"No," said Ross. "I am *anglo*." Anything but Texan.

"Muke-war-rah has much to trade."

"We need nothing." Ross waved at the plodding train behind him. "We have clothing."

"You have little *har-ne-wis-ta* — corn."

"True." Ross made it sound deprecating. "But we are hunters."

"You have found little game."

"True. But last night we killed twenty-two mules, and this morning we had a great plenty of meat. And soon we shall be on the buffalo range, and not even the Comanches can scare away all the buffalo."

"Muke-war-rah has much to trade."

Ross said patiently, "We have not come to trade."

"You carry white iron to Arkansas, huh?"

"Muke-war-rah does not want white iron, and he does not have pans and cloth and needles and knives that we shall get in Arkansas."

The Indian said imperturbably, "Muke-war-rah has other things you not get in Arkansas."

"Not whisky?"

The Indian scowled. "Comanches no trade for whisky."

"Then what?"

"Captives."

It hit Ross with a shock. "Captives!"

"Two *to-a-chee* — children." Ish-a-ro-yeh held up two fingers. "One *wy-e-pe* — one woman."

Ross heard an exclamation from Apolinar behind him, but Ross controlled himself and said firmly, "We have nothing to trade for captives."

"You talk — Muke-war-rah."

Ross shook his head. "We are behind schedule now."

Apolinar said in his ear, "*Señor,* he said a woman captive."

"I heard him," said Ross. "But if we act eager we'll never get a chance. Anyway, we are here on business — not to rescue captives."

"You talk — Muke-war-rah?" the Indian repeated.

Ross looked back as if considering it. Finally he said, "We'll talk, but we have not much time."

"I come — after while. Take you see Muke-war-rah, great chief all Comanches."

Ross nodded as if reluctant. "After while."

He turned back. The foremost mules

were within a quarter of a mile, and Plácido had stopped them. He motioned them on and turned back. Ish-a-ro-yeh had disappeared.

"He did it right in front of my eyes," Apolinar said incredulously.

Ross pointed to the left. "See the magpie get up and start scolding. Our friend is going in that direction. He probably has a horse cached down in a draw somewhere."

He led the train to the spring three miles farther on, saw that the animals got watered and the canteens filled, and told the men to go ahead with supper.

In half an hour the slope was dotted with fires, and each fire was surrounded by men holding long strips of mule meat on pointed sticks over the flames.

Ross ate his and wiped his fingers on the grass. "I've eaten a lot worse," he said. "An antelope run to death after you shoot it is tougher and a lot ranker. These mules weren't in the best condition, but they weren't bad."

"To a hungry man," said Plácido from where he sat beside Josefina, "a hatful of grasshoppers can be a good meal."

"I would not eat grasshoppers," said Josefina, who sat with her bare legs discreetly folded under her.

Plácido chuckled. "*Chiquita,* you will eat anything if you get hungry enough. Is it not so, *señor?*"

Ross was staring absently at Josefina. "I have seen many strange things stave off starvation," he said.

And then without warning Ish-a-ro-yeh appeared on the slope. The mules near him snorted and reared and wheeled and ran away.

The Indian, followed by three younger braves — two of them no more than fourteen — stalked majestically to the fire where Ross was still broiling a strip of mule meat. "Stalked majestically" was not exactly the word, Ross noted, for the Indian was short and heavily built and walked as if he were not accustomed to it — almost clumsily. It was a characteristic, Ross knew, of these Indians who of all Indians in America had become horse Indians, and lived and moved and fought and some said loved on horseback. And yet Ish-a-ro-yeh managed to give dignity to his odd walk. He came to the fire with his bow on his back and said, "We go now."

Ross looked around him and saw the tense faces, the hands moving towards rifles. "We go pretty soon," he said. "You like *pa-ha-mo* — tobacco?"

That of course was an unnecessary question, but it gave Ish-a-ro-yeh a chance to nod, and Ross pulled a cloth sack of tobacco from inside his buckskin shirt and handed it to the Indian, who took it gravely. He squatted by the fire, the muscles bulging on his calves and thighs, and set to work to roll a cigarette.

"Coffee?" asked Ross.

"*Hah.*"

Ross said to Plácido, "Get the chief a cup."

But it was Josefina who sprang to her feet, got a clean cup, and poured it full of coffee and handed it to Ish-a-ro-yeh.

He looked at her over the cup as he put it to his lips to see how hot it was, and Josefina, for once abashed by a man's thoroughly frank stare, flushed and turned away.

"You have left your horses?" asked Ross.

Ish-a-ro-yah grunted. "Back yonder."

Ross said in Spanish, "I want you, Hermenijildo, and you, Andrés, to go with me. Apolinar, you will watch the guard over the animals. Be doubly careful. At the least relaxation the Comanches will stampede the entire band and we shall be afoot. Remember — a Comanche can go through the grass with less disturbance

239

than a snake." He made the familiar sign-language motion for "Comanche" — fingers together, hand drawn back and to the right in a wavering motion.

Ish-a-ro-yeh looked up and grinned. He had understood, of course, but it made no difference.

"You see," said Ross, taking the strip of mule meat off of the sharpened stake, "he knows as well as I do what we are talking about. It is a game," he said. "Each of us knows what the other will do if he gets a chance, and we are both looking for that chance. Nevertheless," he warned, "it is a deadly game — for lives are the stakes, and he would murder every one of us as cheerfully as he rolls a cigarette — especially with seven hundred mules as a side bet."

He finished his meat. Ish-a-ro-yeh had smoked the cigarette. Ross got up and went for his horse. He gave instructions to Plácido and Tapia. To Andrés and Hermenijildo he said, "Since he has captives, it's not too risky, for he wants to sell them. We can always pretend to think it over and get out of his camp alive."

Down in a draw the Comanches had mounted. Two of them were on paint ponies, the third on a mule-striped dun, and Ish-a-ro-yeh rode a fine chestnut stallion that most certainly had come from some Mexican ranch. They rode out to the west, and the immediate transformation of the Indians was astonishing. Once on horseback, they almost seemed a part of the horses themselves. The apparent clumsiness or ungainliness completely disappeared.

"That is why," said Ross, "these fellows are so hard to fight."

They rode west for an hour and a half, and Ross saw no sign of an Indian camp, but suddenly they came out on the edge of a great cliff, and down below them was a green valley filled with hundreds of buffalo-hide teepees. Ish-a-ro-yah grunted. "Muke-war-rah camp," he said.

Ish-a-ro-yeh led the way down the cliff on a narrow trail.

"Is Muke-war-rah really chief of all the Comanches?" asked Hermenijildo.

"Chief of the Southern Comanches — as much as any chief, I suppose. The Comanches have a very loose organisation, like all Indians. Nobody is obliged to render loyalty to any chief — let alone whole tribes or divisions."

They came out on a level meadow at the bottom. The valley ran east and west, and the sun still shone, an hour above the horizon. They rode silently through the sprawling camp. Dogs yapped and followed them and snapped at the heels of the horses. Heavy-set squaws and round-eyed children watched them suspiciously while Ish-a-ro-yeh wound his way through the scattered teepees, which were placed without rhyme or reason.

One of the younger watching Comanches turned abruptly on a dog barking at his heels and launched a sudden kick.

The dog's yapping changed instantaneously into a high-pitched broken howling, almost like a sobbing child, and Ross, from the corner of his eye, saw the dog writhing over and over with a broken back. He rode on with his eyes straight ahead.

They stopped before a large teepee with the flap thrown back. In front of the teepee was a smouldering fire and over this, from a tripod of sticks, hung a big brass kettle. Around the fire, smoking pipes, were five Comanches, all with braided hair, all but one naked from the waist up. The sun would soon be down at the west end of the valley, and one, older than the rest, had already pulled a blanket around his shoulders. They looked up without apparent interest as the little caravan stopped.

The one nearest the teepee, however, continued to stare into the fire, puffing his pipe occasionally and seeming to be totally unaware of the arrival. Ish-a-ro-yeh broke out in fast, fluid Comanche. The older man, whose face now showed the seams of many winters of cold wind and snow and many summers of hot sun and blistering wind and driving sand, answered Ish-a-ro-yeh in a low voice. The other three watched and nodded.

Ish-a-ro-yeh asked a question, and the old man nodded. Ish-a-ro-yeh dismounted and gave a curt signal to Ross, who also dismounted.

He said to Hermenijildo, "Andrés and I will get down. You stay on your horse and hold our reins unless they insist on your getting down. In that case, keep your firearms handy. Ish-a-ro-yeh here understands enough Spanish to know what I am saying, but it doesn't make any difference." He was speaking fast so that Ish-a-ro-yeh would have trouble following him. He handed the reins to Hermenijildo and watched Andrés do the same.

Ish-a-ro-yeh said, "My man — take your horses — eat grass."

Ross said firmly, "Our horses are well fed with *har-ne-wis-ta*. They will stay here with us, for they are not used to being pastured." This of course was not true, but he had to say something to keep those horses close and at the same time admit no fear.

Ish-a-ro-yeh grunted. He dropped the *cabestro* that was tied around his horse's under jaw and walked through the group sitting around the fire. He went to the brass kettle, picked up a stick lying on the ground, fished out a piece of boiled meat, and ate it wolfishly with his hand. He looked back at Ross, pointed at the kettle, and grunted.

Ross walked forward. The stench of bodies seldom washed but plentifully smeared with oil or tallow that became rancid within hours, was almost over-whelming. It was distinctive with the Comanches as it was with many tribes that lived in areas where water was scarce. The oil kept their skins from drying out and at the same time collected dirt and dust which could be rubbed off later. But it invariably created a characteristic odour. Ross controlled his first instinctive reaction of distaste and followed Ish-a-ro-yeh to the kettle. He dug a piece of well-boiled meat out of the simmering stew and ate it. Andrés stood back and waited; Hermeni-jildo stayed mounted. The taste was good, and except for the lack of salt he was glad to set his teeth in it. What it was he had no idea — buffalo, wolf, *javelina*. The original meat flavour had all been boiled out.

While he was eating, he estimated the number of teepees, as unobtrusively as possible, at around four hundred. This meant probably two thousand Comanches in the camp, about eight hundred of whom would be warriors. Such a force could overwhelm his train and wipe them all out if they took a notion.

Ish-a-ro-yeh finished his meat, wiped his greasy fingers on his buckskin leggings, and sat down. He pulled out the sack of tobacco and began to roll a cigarette. The man nearest the tent-flap, who had not until then looked up, raised his head and grunted.

Ross reached inside of his shirt, pulled out another sack of tobacco, and handed it to the chief, who took it without looking up. He was a big man even sitting down — outstandingly large for a Comanche, whose height usually was not over five and a half feet.

He began to roll a cigarette. Ross produced four more sacks and handed them to the silent braves around the fire. Some grunted, some said nothing.

Ish-a-ro-yeh jabbed a mahogany-black thumb towards the big man. "Muke-war-rah, great chief of all Comanches," he said.

The big man raised his eyes at last, and Ross felt as if somebody had run a sharp knife-blade down his spine. The face was intelligent but the eyes were evil in their unplumbed depths. Chillingly evil.

Ross stared back at him until he felt the first shock go away, then continued to stare at him, unblinking, until Muke-war-rah reached for a twig to light his cigarette.

Ross felt relieved, he felt he had just looked deep into the most evil eyes he had ever seen. The eyebrows were thin and on the very edge of the bone that formed the eyesocket, and there were deep vertical lines between his eyebrows. But overshadowing all else were those cold, unfeeling eyes.

CHAPTER THIRTEEN

"You have come to ransom our captives," Muke-war-rah said in excellent Spanish.

"No. We have come to visit you, at your request."

Muke-war-rah nodded, a tinge of sarcasm showing in his dark face. "You have much goods."

"As I told your chief, we have no goods for trade. We have only enough for our own use, and the white iron we are going to use for trade."

"White iron is no good to us," said Muke-war-rah insolently. "When we go to the *to-e-titch-e* towns we can get all the goods we want without white iron."

"Then you have no need to trade with us."

Muke-war-rah said, unabashed, "Is not so. We have just returned from a great raid in Mexico, and our horses are all trotted down."

"We have nothing you want," Ross repeated.

"You have corn. My people do not raise corn. We are too busy fighting."

It was a typical Indian gesture. "We have only corn enough for our own use," Ross said.

"You have powder and lead. We need powder and lead, for the new many-shoots guns take much powder and lead."

Ross shook his head firmly. "We have enough only to kill Indians."

Muke-war-rah glanced at him. "You talk like a Comanche."

"We have come far, and shall go farther, and it is no secret that we are well armed and ready to kill Indians at the slightest excuse. If we are allowed to go in peace, we shall keep our rifles in their scabbards, but if we are attacked, we shall fight to kill."

"Big words!" Muke-war-rah said scornfully. "Big words!"

"If Muke-war-rah doubts the fighting ability of the *to-e-titch-e,* he well knows how to test it." Those too were big words, but they had to be used, for if Muke-war-rah ever got the idea they were scared, his braves would overwhelm the entire train.

"You're *Tejano?*"

"Not *Tejano,*" said Ross. "But we have learned many lessons from the Texans."

"You're *Mejicano?*" Muke-war-rah insisted.

"I am not Mexican." He knew the Comanches' contempt for the Mexicans as fighters. He tapped his chest. "I am Godamme." The word was of Apache origin, taken from the familiar curse of the Americans, but it was known to most south-western tribes, and to all it meant the same: a hard-fighting, never-give-up white man who, totally different from all Indians, retreated from no odds whatever.

Muke-war-rah grunted. The grunt might have meant anything or nothing. "You have plenty mules," he said. "I sell you this captive for ten mules."

Ross, to gain time, said, "I have seen no captive."

Muke-war-rah glanced at him again with those evil eyes, and this time there was a sardonic light in them. "The Godamme thinks Muke-war-rah talks to throw his voice to the wind." He stood up suddenly, and Ross almost gasped. The Comanche was huge. He towered over the other Indians by a full head, and he was even taller than Ross. He must have been six feet and a half, and had a torso like a barrel, legs like cottonwood logs.

"Santa María!" Muke-war-rah shouted, his eyes half-hooded.

A whimpering came from the tent

behind him, and Ross realised the Comanche had a Mexican captive who must have repeated the phrase over and over as she prayed for deliverance. Ross began to harden himself for whatever was to appear.

"Santa María!" Muke-war-rah shouted.

The five Comanches sitting around the fire all looked towards the tent-flap.

Muke-war-rah took two big steps and disappeared inside the tent. Suddenly he growled, and there was the sound of a great open hand against flesh, a scream. Muke-war-rah's Comanche phrases sounded vituperative, and again Ross heard the slap, so hard it must almost have caved in the woman's cheekbone. Then Muke-war-rah appeared again in the door, dragging behind him, with no effort on his part, a Mexican woman. She was fighting, but he outweighed her three to one, and he literally dragged her to the fire. She continued to twist and turn and tried to bite his hand, but once again that big hand swung against her face, and this time it knocked her flat in the dust, and she lay there, face down, perhaps momentarily unconscious.

"She is fight plenty hard." Muke-war-rah grinned. "Much spirit. You like."

Ross shrugged, pretending disinterest. He noted the many black marks on the woman's legs and arms and bare shoulders, and it was easy to see that she had been fighting steadily. It was also easy to guess that it had not done her any good, for the Comanches were not inhibited.

Ross shook his head as if to show his disinterest. "She does not belong to us."

"But all *to-e-titch-e* buy all other whites, don't they? Whites don't have much sense that way."

"Perhaps — if they have the goods."

The woman was stirring. Muke-war-rah jabbed a heavy toe in her stomach. "You buy this one. I sell cheap. You take home and put in your teepee."

There were a lot of concepts among the Comanches that the *anglos* or Mexicans didn't have, and that was one. "Her husband would buy her, but her husband is dead," Ross said at a guess.

"We know. We left him for the buzzards. And three children — too little — no good for work. We knocked their brains out on a rock."

The whimpering came again from inside, and Muke-war-rah nodded towards the tent. "That one is next if she doesn't get to work."

The woman on the ground was small and slender, and Ross saw that she was young.

"*Arriba!*" growled Muke-war-rah.

She got up slowly, and, behind Ross, Andrés gasped aloud. Her hair had not been combed since she had been captured, and her face had been pretty, but now it was a mass of purple bruises. Ross shuddered inwardly at what she had been through — the more so because he knew it had been of no avail, for a Comanche was stronger than any woman, and for the Comanches it was as simple as that.

She got on her knees and saw Ross and Andrés, and her eyes darted to Hermenijildo, still on horseback, and she turned back quickly to Ross, a wild light of hope in her eyes. "You have come to rescue me?" she asked.

"*Señora,*" Ross said gently, "we have come to try." He did not dare tell her his limitations. "They outnumber us considerably, and I do not know how we shall get along."

"He's a filthy beast!" She spat on him suddenly, and he slapped her with his huge hand and sent her sprawling fifteen feet away.

"For such a one," he said to Ross, "you

would give much goods, hey?"

Ross watched the girl get up slowly. He tried to keep the horror out of his face. "We might talk," he said carefully. "But if you injure her, the price will go down."

She crawled to her hands and knees, a hideous-looking creature with her black hair over her eyes, her face misshaped and miscoloured, her eyes wild like the eyes of a trapped wolf. But there was a certain familiarity in her posture as she stared up at him that made him look closer.

"*Señora*," he asked suddenly, "did you live on the Conchas?"

"*Sí, señor.*"

"Near Presidio?"

She nodded.

"In a small mud hut on the east bank?"

She nodded, not understanding.

"*Señora.*" His voice was as gentle as if he had been talking to a baby. "Were you in Chihuahua thirty days ago?"

She nodded slowly.

"Your name is Carlota, and you picked up my hat from the street and gave it to me."

She stared at him.

"Your husband saved my life, *señora*, and I have never had a chance to thank either one of you sufficiently. Now listen carefully: be patient and we shall try to get you free. It will not be easy but we shall keep trying. You must remember, *señora,* we will do the best we can. And don't give up hope, whatever happens."

She gazed at him a long time, trying to understand everything he meant. And finally she said, *"Espero, señor,"* and the dullness of her voice indicated more than anything else that she did understand.

Andrés was staring at her with eyes wide in horror and pity, and Muke-war-rah saw that and his shrewd eyes grew calculating.

"Very nice, hey? *Simpática.* You give fifty mules, hey?"

Ross said quickly, "Your chief told me ten mules."

Muke-war-rah looked mockingly sad. "He has a bad memory. I said fifty mules, didn't I?" he demanded of the five braves around the fire.

They all nodded solemnly.

Ross took a deep breath. "The mules do not belong to us," he said.

Muke-war-rah shrugged. "If they're good mules, I don't care who owns them."

To change the subject, Ross asked, "Have you no more captives?"

"Not now," said Muke-war-rah. "We'll have more in another moon, though, when my braves get back from Mexico."

The utter brazenness of the Comanche was infuriating, but there was nothing anyone could do. He looked at Carlota and tried to keep the compassion out of his face because he knew if Muke-war-rah saw any sign of weakness he would be harder to deal with. "Have patience, *señora*," he said in a low voice. "We will do the best we can."

Muke-war-rah lifted her bodily from the ground by one arm, then dropped her to her feet and flung her through the tent opening. She tried hard to keep her feet but finally went over head-first with a force that shook the walls of the tent. He heard her slowly collapse and lie there, breathing hard, trying not to sob.

Ross tried to hold himself in. It would be fatal to show his feelings. Instead, he said as casually as possible, "I will talk it over with the *teniente*. I cannot say what his decision will be."

Muke-war-rah said knowingly, "Who knows? She's a woman. My braves have all tried her and like her. Maybe one of them will give me sixty mules for her tomorrow."

Ross scoffed. "Your braves don't have sixty mules all put together."

Muke-war-rah only grinned scornfully.

Ross turned and took the reins of his black.

"I'll take thirty mules and that horse," said Muke-war-rah.

"I will talk it over," said Ross, and mounted.

Ish-a-ro-yeh said something to Muke-war-rah in Comanche.

Muke-war-rah's eyes widened. "One woman for a hundred men, hey?" A venal smile centred around his straight, cruel mouth. "I give you this woman for yours, *anglo.*"

Ross said harshly, "We do not trade women."

He led the way out of the camp, through the barking dogs, past eyes staring out of the dim corners of the twilight. Hermenijildo and Andrés followed silently. They passed the last teepee and walked their horses across the meadow and up the narrow path. At the top, Ross said, "Keep going until we get away from here. You never know when some brave is going to try for scalps."

They rode a little way and broke into a trot. Andrés pulled up alongside Ross and said bitterly, "*Señor,* did you see how he has abused her?"

"Of course I did, Andrés."

"It is unspeakable — all the other tortures he must have put her through."

"I know," said Ross.

"But, *señor*, we have done nothing."

"There was nothing we *could* do."

"We have six-shooters. We could have rushed them."

"Not there. The Comanche may not like an open fight, but he would not hesitate if attacked in his own village. We would all be killed and the girl would be killed also."

"Better that she should be."

"There's no point in all of us dying, though, unless we accomplish something."

"We can get Lieutenant Tapia and his dragoons and go back and —"

"It is useless. The girl would be killed at the first shot."

"Death is preferable to the life she is living now."

Ross said wisely but not with too much conviction, "Perhaps not. She wants to live, I think." He didn't add that the Comanches, knowing that some women would try to kill themselves, would have taken every precaution against it.

"She could have been Chonita," Hermenijildo said soberly.

"Then let's hurry. We'll get the mules and go back."

"In the first place," said Ross slowly, "we can't spare that many mules. In the second place, if we had a thousand mules we could not go back there to-night."

"But —"

"The mere fact that we were in a hurry would be a warning to Muke-war-rah. He would either put us off till morning anyway, or he would raise the price as fast as we would agree to it. Nor is that all. I have heard of women whose men were in a hurry to release them, who were thrown on the ground and ravished before them — and they were helpless to prevent it. And the Comanches only grinned and assured them the women were the better partners for it. What would you say to that, Andrés?"

"I would kill them! I would murder them! I would hang them up by the *cojones* and burn their tongues out!"

"If you could," Ross reminded him. "Andrés, this is a very bitter pill to swallow, but it is one that has to be taken. They are the strongest and they have the girl. Any move on our part must result in either the girl's liberation or her death. It is well to think several times before one takes a hasty action."

"Is there *nothing* we can do?" cried Andrés.

"In an individual case, no. Some day, of course, the Comanche will be beaten back, and both Mexicans and *anglos* will be able to live on the frontier in safety."

Hermenijildo said helplessly, *"Señor,* isn't there *anything* —"

Ross felt pity for him. This was a far different side of the Mexicans from that which one saw in Chihuahua, where they spent their time riding, flirting, going to bullfights. "Not a thing," he said heavily.

He thought it over, and talked to Tapia when they got back, but Tapia had nothing to offer, as Ross had anticipated. For there was nothing to offer. You paid the fifty mules and hoped for the best, or you went on and left the girl in Muke-war-rah's tent.

"We'll be short of mules," Ross said, "if we give up fifty."

"We can divide the burdens," said Apolinar. "My father will pay for the mules. I pledge it."

Ross shook his head. "We're barely started. We will not be able to buy mules anywhere until we get to Arkansas. In the meantime, overloading the mules we have may be the difference between getting there with the bullion and being stranded out in the middle of the wilderness."

"We should have another wagon," said Hermenijildo.

"We haven't. Of course a mule can transport a lot more in a wagon, but wagons can't go everywhere. We thought it better, not knowing the country, to pack the bullion in packsaddles. Then we won't have to leave any of it in a bed of quicksand or at the edge of a canyon that a wagon could not cross."

"Then —"

"Then," Ross said firmly, "we'll do it anyway. First thing in the morning we'll pick out fifty mules and go back. We'll redistribute the loads the best we can."

Hermenijildo looked grateful; Apolinar was relieved, and Andrés was joyful.

"But not until daylight," Ross cautioned.

Suddenly he felt very tired — tired in the mind and emotions. A fight was one thing, and it only exhilarated him, but this sort of cruelty was almost more than he could bear.

Josefina came up silently with a tin cup of coffee, and he thanked her, and went to sleep before the fire.

Andrés was up early, and Ross told him to get The Soft-Shelled Turtle and take three men besides Hermenijildo and Apolinar, and ride slowly to the Comanche camp. They were to enter it and go to the tent of Muke-war-rah and wait at the fire, saying and doing absolutely nothing no matter what might happen in front of them. "Do you think you can do that, if her life depends on it?" asked Ross.

Andrés said gravely, "*Sí, señor,* I will do it."

"All right. Get going."

Then he took Plácido and spent considerable time looking over the mules and trying to pick out those with hidden faults that had developed on the drive. It took a while, but they got fifty mules, and Plácido and two of his *arrieros,* all armed, went along to drive the animals.

"I hope," said Ross, "to get it over with as soon as possible by sending the boys on ahead. That way we can dispense with some of the rigmarole."

They drove the mules out towards the west, and Plácido said, "*Señor,* a party comes — fast. Several riders."

Ross watched. A faint spiral of dust hung in the early-morning air, and got bigger. He said, "Take the mules back. Warn Tapia."

Plácido asked fearfully, "What do you think it is, *señor?*"

"I don't know," said Ross, watching,

"but we'll soon find out."

He did. Andrés rode up at a furious gallop, foam hanging from his horse's mouth. "*Señor! Señor!* The Comanches have gone! The tents are gone! Everything is gone!"

CHAPTER FOURTEEN

There was of course nothing they could do then. For some reason the Comanches had taken fright and had moved their camp during the night. There was no use chasing them, for even a huge band of Comanches would move faster than a hundred armed men; and even if a hundred armed men caught them — assuming the best of luck — they would be unable to attack them with any success. On occasion, a few determined men had done miraculous things against Indians, but those were only on occasion, and never in the Indians' home territory or against the Indians and their families.

Ross was bitter when he faced it, but he told them it was hopeless. The entire southwest was infested with bands such as Muke-war-rah's, large and small, and all of them had captives sooner or later, and there were so many of them that nobody could do anything about it. The wilderness areas of Texas and New Mexico clear up to the Oregon line were controlled by the savages, with only here and there a group of whites forted up or a retaliatory expedition or a company of beaver trappers or miners to take a stand against them. The total of whites was in the few hundreds at most; the total of Indians was in the many thousands, and Ross forced himself to set his mind towards Arkansas.

Now began the long haul north-eastward through the breaks below the Llano and across the bitter-salted rivers, past quicksand beds and over immense arid prairies. Here they were far beyond the frontier of Texas, for Austin was a long way east; they were nobody knew how many hundreds of miles from Santa Fé, for to the north and west was only the impassable desert of the Llano, that vast expanse of table-flat prairie that few of them had ever seen.

They kept to the north-east and camped in pecan groves or mottes of oak and persimmon, and they fed well on buffalo meat — hump, tongue, and fat intestines — and Josefina spent her days, when they were not travelling, grinding corn in the *metate*, and her nights — Ross did not inquire.

The long miles stretched behind them, and the great distances of Texas stretched ahead, and there never seemed to be an end to it. The Tonkawas identified the

Brazos from its looks and the taste of its water, and then demanded their pay — ten pounds of pressed tobacco — and disappeared, for now the caravan was in the heart of Comanche and Caygüa country, and any Tonkawa taken up there was lucky to be roasted alive, for the Comanches claimed the Tonkawas cooked and ate Comanches and Caygüas. However that might be, it was distinctly poor judgment for any Tonkawa to be very far into this area, and so The Soft-Shelled Turtle and his silent companions faded into the vast wilderness and left the expedition to its own resources.

Ross had been watching the stars, and they turned their route a little to the north, thinking to avoid the Texan outposts for now not only were they running the risk of creating an international dispute; no one knew exactly what would happen if the Texans did find them; it was altogether possible that under the press of internal disturbances, the party in power might — even if they were disposed to wink at this "invasion" of Texas soil — be forced to take some defensive action, and this might end in confiscation of the bullion. Back in Chihuahua they had considered that possibility but it hadn't seemed very important.

Here it had reality, and so, having actually entered the republic and having traversed probably half of it, Ross had an additional worry on his mind.

It was important, therefore, to reach Indian Territory and travel down the north side of the Red River of Natchitoches. Confiscation was only a thing that *might* happen, of course, but with a third of a million dollars in bullion on the backs of those mules, Ross didn't want to take any chances.

The water got worse, and it became necessary to avoid the rivers for drinking, and to find springs. Even some of the springs were impregnated with sulphur and gypsum and copper sulphate until the water was almost undrinkable. On a diet almost solely of buffalo meat, the men developed intermittent diarrhoea, and Ross finally had Josefina steep great pots of tea from the inner bark of cottonwood trees. It was so bitter it was nauseating, but it stopped the diarrhoea.

And so they continued day after day, winding their way along the buffalo trails, over the divides, down into the valleys, across the streams, up through the breaks and over the dry, endless prairies, until they came to a wide river of red water which they were unable to name. Tapia thought it might be the Red River; one of his dragoons said he had been on it and that it was the Brazos.

Ross pointed out that The Soft-Shelled Turtle had already identified the Brazos, but Tapia reasoned that The Soft-Shelled Turtle had not felt comfortable in Comanche country, and so he had identified some other stream as the Brazos — perhaps the Colorado River of Texas — so as to get his pay and go back south. That was a reasonable supposition, and Ross decided they had better go on north to be sure. The country was unmapped and they could identify it only by guess.

They crossed that river, which they now called the Brazos, in shallow water, it being the latter part of June, and lost only one mule in the quicksand. They threw a rope around the mule's neck and tried to pull it out with the horses, but the mule fought furiously to get out and only enmired itself deeper. Ross sent for large branches to lay alongside the mule, and in the meantime he cut the lashing and took off the pack-saddle. The mule continued to struggle, and by the time the branches arrived there was nothing above the surface but its head, and it was impossible to save it. It brayed

267

piteously until it went under.

Then they continued north, through a rather flat country of excellent grass, which began to put the mules in good shape, and occasional shallow breaks grown up with mesquite trees, and once in a while an isolated clump of small oak and blackjack trees.

They reached a shallow stream which they knew could not be the Red, and now for the first time they began to wonder if they had already crossed the Red. But Ross reasoned the only course was north, and they kept on, the prairie growing flatter and the grass more succulent. In some places it was as high as a mule's belly.

"We may hit the Arkansas," said Tapia one day. "I was on that river in 1828, when the Governor of New Mexico sent an expedition to Bent's Fort."

Ross considered. "If we hit it, we'll come in a long way below Bent's Fort, I figure."

Three days later they stopped at the bank of a wide riverbed. There was hardly a foot of water in it, most of the bed being dry sand; the bed was only a few feet below the surface of the prairie, and the sides were sloping so that access was easy. Ross rode into it and up and down the bed for a quarter of a mile each way, and came back and asked Tapia, "Do you think this is it?"

"It is difficult to say. It resembles it — but my memory is the Arkansas had more water in it."

"Of course this river, if it is the Arkansas, has come a long way — several hundred miles across the prairie. It might have dried up."

Tapia agreed, being very plainly at a complete loss.

Plácido lined up the mules on the bank to let them drink, and Josefina almost immediately got out her *metate* and went to work.

Ross took Hermenijildo and rode across the river, watching the sand for signs of sinking. The surface of the sand, where it was dry, was soft like sand in the open desert; where it was wet it formed a compact sort of mat that quivered and gave under the weight of a horse and rider. But Ross was watching for any kind of sand where a horse's hoof would immediately sink in up to the fetlocks, and when he found such a spot he promptly wheeled the gelding and changed his course. He went into the muddy water and let the gelding drink, and he was sitting in the saddle wondering how much farther to go north when Hermenijildo said in a low voice:

"Look up, *señor. Los indios!*"

Ross jerked around and looked at the far bank. On a shelf of sand, not over fifty feet away, three Indians stood watching them. Ross's glance swept the country behind them for signs of others, but he saw nothing but a low semi-circle of sandhills behind them, the hills covered with thick green bushes now red with sandplums. Ross pulled up the gelding's head and rode straight across.

He made the sign for friend, and one of the Indians, black, slight, seamed of face though not old, said, "You 'Merican?"

"American and Mexican," said Ross.

"I'm Si-ki-to-ma-ker — Black Beaver."

Ross smiled. After those long days through Texas, it was good to hear a name he knew. "Black Beaver, the Delaware?"

The Indian nodded. "Delaware. These my friends — Ni-co-man and Jim Linney."

Ni-co-man was a strange sight, for he had a large silver ring in his nose and wore a great turban, wrapped Turkish style, of brightly coloured striped silk. Jim Linney, a well-known Delaware chief, was inconspicuous, wearing white man's pants without a belt, no shirt, and moccasins.

"What are you doing out here?" asked Ross.

"We came to hunt buffalo. No buffalo left yonder." He pointed east.

Ross got down and handed them each a sack of tobacco. They took it eagerly. "You know what river this is?"

"Sure," said Black Beaver. "This Canadian River, all same South Canadian."

"You're sure it isn't the Arkansas?"

"No. Arkansas that way." He pointed north.

"Where's the Red River of Natchitoches?"

"That way." He pointed south.

Ross decided to test him. "Do you know where Santa Fé is?"

"Sure. Him that way." He pointed west. "One long hike, by golly."

Ross laughed. "You've been a guide all over this country, haven't you?"

"Sure," said Black Beaver. "I'm no greenhorn."

"Well," said Ross, "I'm glad we met you."

Black Beaver nodded wisely. "Sure. You lost. You bad lost."

"We weren't sure how much farther to go."

"You been lost eight days now."

"What?"

"We watch. You no see. You too busy being lost. We come after."

271

Ross restrained a smile. "You know where New Orleans is?"

"Sure. Him that way." He pointed southeast. "Long way down river."

Ross said, "I guess you've been everywhere."

"Sure," said Black Beaver. "I been California. Long way. Plenty sand."

"Your friends aren't saying much."

"Sure. They don't know much. I tell them, I talk, they keep still."

Ross grinned at last, and Black Beaver grinned back. "All right," Ross said. "We're lost. You're not. Will you guide us where we want to go?"

"You want to go to Arkansas," said Black Beaver.

Ross looked up. "How'd you know?"

Black Beaver raised his eyebrows. "Indian not so dumb as white man maybe think."

"Can you show us the way?"

"Sure. We guide. Two bits a day to Fort Towson."

"Two bits?"

"Two bits — all three." Black Beaver jabbed a forefinger into each of his companion's chest and then into his own. "Two bits — all three. Cheap. Big bargain."

"We might want to go beyond Fort Towson."

"You no need guide for that. Any fool can find way from Fort Towson."

"All right, you're hired."

"No tobacco," Black Beaver said. "No whisky."

"Most Indians want tobacco at least."

"We buy more tobacco with two bits than you give us. We not ignorant Indians. We learn white man's road. Get the money."

Ross squatted and began to draw a map in the sand. "You show me how to go."

"You pay first."

"Sure." Ross gave him a big silver Mexican dollar.

"Fine. *Peso.* Very good."

"I'll give you the rest at Fort Towson."

"Very good. I draw map."

He drew a crooked line that represented the river. He said, "You here. You lost. Fort Towson here." He made a cross mark two feet away. "Fort Towson not lost."

"All right." Ross stood up. "How far?"

Black Beaver squinted as he counted up. "Two weeks. Not bad unless rain. If rain, very bad. Three weeks. You better off go home."

"In this case," said Ross, "we go ahead

even if it rains every day."

Black Beaver nodded. "Sound like damn' fool white man. Where you come from?"

"Mexico."

"All right. Get mules across. We start out."

They took the wagons across first. The wagons were considerably lighter than they had been at the start, and easier to handle. The long train of mules was well trail broke, and followed each other very well, even across the river.

They followed the river east on its left bank, and Black Beaver showed them where to take short cuts that saved miles, but he always brought them up to fresh water.

They had a week under bright, sunny skies. Then it rained, and the prairie was a sea of mud. Black Beaver advised waiting a few days, for it took twelve mules to pull a wagon, and the wheels after a hundred yards were monstrous things covered with hundreds of pounds of sticky mud.

Ross agreed to wait. The skies cleared and turned to a turquoise blue dome; the grass came out emerald-green on the long slopes, and in twenty-four hours the sun and wind had dried out the gumbo until it was firm footing, and they went ahead.

They pulled into Fort Towson early one afternoon, with the June sun steaming on the mud flats down near the river, buzzards circling in the sky, coyotes watching from the hilltops, and quail running before them and occasionally bursting into a feathered bombshell of flight that caused considerable trouble with the mules.

The fort was composed of many buildings, all of hewed logs, neatly constructed, with brick chimneys and porches at the front of each building. All were whitewashed, and there were separate buildings outside the fort itself for blacksmith's shop, bakery, store, stables, quarters for the laundresses and camp women. And everywhere were nice gardens.

They drew up on the last hill and sat their horses for a moment and looked at it. "The first time in two months," said Ross, "that we have seen anything resembling civilisation."

"This her," said Black Beaver. "You owe us fifteen days — $3.75. You give one dollar already."

"Very good," Ross said. He counted out three pesos. "I'll pay you one extra day for being truthful."

"You no have to pay for that," Black

Beaver said. "Only bad Indians tell un-
truth. But we happy get two-bits anyway.
Thank you."

He left the wagons and mules on the
slope to avoid overrunning the grounds
and went directly to the building which
boasted an American flag. He passed the
guardhouse, and standing on a barrel head
before it was a young soldier with an
empty bottle in each hand and a board
hung from his neck marked "Whisky
Seller." He told them where to find the
commander.

Ross found Major Fauntleroy and
reported the cargo. The major said he saw
no reason why he couldn't go right ahead,
there being no regulation against importa-
tion of bullion; in fact, he thought, the
United States would be right glad to get
ten thousand pounds of gold and silver.

He asked, "Are you with Connelly's
expedition?"

"Yes, sir."

"Doctor Connelly got into Pecan Point,
down the river a few miles, about a week
ago, expecting you, sir."

"Maybe you can tell me where I am,
exactly."

"Look at this map. Here's Fort Towson,
on the Kiamichi River, surrounded by

more Choctaw doggeries than you can shake a stick at."

"Doggeries?"

"Cheap saloons. The soldiers can't buy whisky on the grounds, so the Indians set up these doggeries just outside the reservation. Now then, Doaksville is right here, about a mile from us; that's the capital, so-called, of the Choctaw Nation; big agency there. We're only a couple of miles from the Red."

"The Red River of Natchitoches?"

"Yes, sir. Just below where the Kiamichi runs into the Red is Jonesboro, and just below that is Pecan Point. There's an inn at Pecan Point, that's why Doctor Connelly stayed there."

"That brings up a question: what can I do with my men? I've got about a hundred men and one woman, and they'll be tired of camping out. I've got to do something with them while I go to New Orleans."

"A woman, eh? No trouble there. Women are scarce as hen's teeth out here. But the men." The bewhiskered major shook his head. "There's a problem, I declare. I reckon the best is to scatter 'em up and down the river; the Indians will be glad to put them up for a price; it won't be fancy but it'll be cheap. Some of the people at Doaksville will take in boarders."

"Sounds all right for the men. How about the mules?"

"How many mules?"

"Seven hundred, less twenty-two."

"Hit the quicksand?"

"They drank in the Pecos."

"I heard it was like that. Well, I'd guess you better see Black Beaver. He'll either —"

"The Delaware?"

"Yes. Know him, I see. He'll either pasture 'em for you or put 'em out to pasture with the Choctaws. Absolutely honest; you'll get every head back in fine shape. Never worry about Black Beaver."

"For how much?"

"Oh, say five cents a month per head. Something like that."

He went outside and stood on the porch. His wagons were up on the slope, and his great band of mules was spreading out, some grazing, some lying down with their packs on. All over the grounds of the fort, men in blue uniforms were making their way towards the train. Some were already there, and half a dozen were gathered around Josefina.

Ross stretched. It was wonderful to have arrived. "Pretty soon," he told Hermenijildo, "we'll have a hot bath and sleep in a real bed — maybe even a feather bed."

"I haven't seen my wife in a long time," said Hermenijildo.

"A few more months," said Ross, "and you'll be home. Maybe you'll have a *niño* by that time."

"Oh no *señor*, we won't be gone that long, I'm sure."

"No, I suppose not," Ross said absently. "If we can get our goods at New Orleans and run them back up the river, we should be able to start back right away."

"If this were Mexico," said Hermenijildo, "I would be very sceptical, but this is the United States, and you always do things with great speed, and there are not the innumerable delays that one can encounter in Mexico, when nothing moves and nothing happens."

Ross said, "You sound gloomy. You aren't predicting anything, are you?"

Hermenijildo said, "I don't know, *señor*. It is a feeling I have."

"You can forget it." Ross stepped off the porch and went to his horse. He untied the reins and threw them over the horse's neck. "We'll be back in no time," he promised cheerfully.

Black Beaver and his two Delaware

friends were waiting in front of the guard-house.

"I thought you went home," said Ross.

"I wait. You have many mules. What you do with so many mules? You going back pretty soon, you say. You need somebody feed mules, yes?"

He made an agreement with Black Beaver and Jim Linney and Ni-co-man. They would come for the mules in a couple of hours — sometime before dark. Ross went to Plácido and told him to take the mules down to the boat landing and unload the gold and silver. He gave Tapia instructions to guard the silver until they could get it on a boat, and appointed Hermenijildo, Apolinar, and Andrés to watch the guards, though he noted that Andrés seemed much more interested in Josefina than he did in silver bullion. He remembered briefly that Andrés had once been concerned over Josefina working too hard.

The wagons were largely empty, and he got permission from the major to draw them up on some ground on the reserva-tion, where the major said they would be quite safe.

"This could be a great thing for the United States and Chihuahua too, if you get this route established."

"It looks that way," said Ross.

"No reason why not. It's only half as long as the Santa Fé Trail."

"That's right."

"Well, I'll assign a squad of soldiers to keep an eye on your silver. We look for the boat up from Natchitoches tomorrow."

But the boat from Natchitoches did not come the next day. The Indians said she had run up on a logjam and the receding water had left her stuck there, and there she would be until a rise in the river floated her off — and in the meantime, patience was advised.

Connelly rode in the next day on a big Missouri mule, and Ross heard his roar a quarter of a mile away: "Ross Phillips, where are you?"

Ross was in the officers' cabin which had been loaned to him and the three young Mexicans and Tapia. He ran out as Connelly flung himself from the mule and ran to meet him. Connelly was a bearish man, big, strong, quick. He put an arm around Ross and said, "Fine beard you've got, my boy; wish my hair was brown like yours."

CHAPTER FIFTEEN

Connelly was elated after a week of buying. He had used the storekeepers to beat down prices, even in the face of shortage, for all wanted to get in on the Chihuahua trade, and as a result he had an enormous quantity of goods to take back to Chihuahua. "It damn' near staggers me," he told Ross. "We never hauled any loads like that from Independence."

They stopped for a drink. "There's only one thing bothering me now," said Ross, looking at Connelly across the round table. "We'll get this stuff to Pecan Point, all right. You've got six boats hauling to Natchitoches, and we can swing a handful of gold and charter all the flat-bottoms in Natchitoches to get it on up the river." He tossed down the rum. "But what if we get stuck with all this stuff in Presidio?"

Connelly laughed. "Don't let it worry you. That's my job — and with Irigoyen on our side we'll have no trouble."

"Hope you're right," said Ross.

"I know I'm right." Connelly beamed. "In all my years on the trail I never ran into a gold mine like this." He leaned over. "Do you have any idea how much we can turn this load of goods for?"

"How much?" asked Ross.

"This will stagger you," said Connelly. "We'll clear at least a million dollars on this deal."

Ross looked at him. "My share would be a hundred thousand," he said thoughtfully.

Connelly laughed. "You must have some of your old man's blood, all right. Figures mean something to you when there's a dollar mark in front of them."

"Right now they do," Ross admitted.

He told Connelly good-bye three days later and swung aboard the riverboat *Rover* with his carpet-bag. Her hold was filled with Connelly's goods, and he was literally walking on his own gold.

For now Valeria was on his mind more strongly than ever, and he found himself constantly translating his share of the profit into land and horses or land and cattle. He knew Mangum would return to Chihuahua before he would, but he was counting on Mangum's peculiar bi-nationalistic ideas to give him time — for Mangum undoubtedly would be very leisurely about the entire thing, thinking to do it the Spanish way. That was one point in Ross's favour.

He reached Pecan Point and began to worry about taking care of the goods until the wagons were assembled. He rented storage space from Major Fauntleroy but found he had to build some cheap sheds. Which was all right. They were not expensive — but they did seem to signify delay.

His men now were getting in trouble. Santiago had been in jail three times for fighting. One of Tapia's men killed an American soldier, and there was a to-do with the Mexican Consul in New Orleans. The Mexican teamsters and *arrieros* got into fights with the Choctaws over their women. A Choctaw was killed, and an *arriero* was charged with murder. A teamster was killed and a Choctaw girl was charged with murder.

Ross called a conference of Tapia and his three assistants, but Andrés did not appear. "Where is he?" asked Ross.

"He's rented a house over in Arkansas and is living there with Josefina," said Hermenijildo.

"What does Plácido say about it?"

"He grins," said Tapia, "and says she will come back to him."

Ross said anxiously, "Is he talking of getting married?"

"He's tried already," said Apolinar, "but the priest won't marry them because Josefina is not paid up with the church."

Ross felt a little relief. He pulled the cork out of a bottle of rum. "We've got trouble on our hands, *hombres*. As you observe, we have goods, but mighty few wagons."

"Ten so far," said Hermenijildo.

Ross poured a drink for each. "That leaves us sixty short. How you coming with the mules, Apolinar?"

"I've bought eighty-two," said Apolinar. "The prices have been high, but —" He shrugged.

"Never mind the prices. Get the mules. We can't pull those wagons ourselves. Is Black Beaver taking good care of our own mules?"

"We've lost four," said Apolinar. "The rest are in good shape."

Ross turned to Hermenijildo. "How about teamsters?"

Apolinar shook his head. "The luck is very bad, *señor*. I have engaged eighteen so far."

Ross frowned. "Why is this?"

Hermenijildo was thoughtful. "It is hard

285

to say, *señor*. I have made the rounds of the saloons and public places in this area, and — I don't know —" He shook his head. "They talk very strange."

Ross was alert. "What do they say?"

"They ask strange questions, and they make insinuations. They say that this is a war party for the Mexican Government, and that we are heading into a trap, and the Texans will annihilate us."

"Also," said Apolinar, "they say we will not pay them — that we will turn them over to the Comanches just before we get there to avoid paying."

Ross was astounded. "How did such talk get started?"

"If you ask me," said Major Fauntleroy, "I'd say it is deliberately planted. I've been hearing this stuff from my men, and the stories are so similar and so obviously manufactured that I am sure it is deliberate."

Ross got up. "Do you have any idea who is behind it?"

"Not the slightest," said Fauntleroy.

Ross thought about it. "Has anybody heard about any stranger in the country lately?"

They all shook their heads but Tapia. "*Señor*, I recall a big man who has gotten

286

into fights several times. He is a man of one eye."

"One eye!" Ross exclaimed. "Link Habersham!"

"You know him?" asked Fauntleroy.

Ross nodded slowly. "Rather well. Almost intimately, you might say."

"He's a bad *hombre*," Tapia said soberly.

"Very bad. This means he's spreading lies about the expedition, and the only way to stop him is for me to whip him, and the only way I can whip him is to kill him."

"I hope, after that remark," said Fauntleroy, "that you will not perform this on the reservation."

"I don't imagine he'll ever show up here," said Ross. "However, I don't mean it the way it sounds. I mean that if I ever fight him again I'll be forced to kill him to save my own life."

"It sounds better that way," said Fauntleroy.

Ross nodded. "I'll start looking for him to-night. Hermenijildo, you and Apolinar want to come along to make it a fair fight?"

Both nodded eagerly.

"Very well. As soon as supper is over. And you'd both better drink a pint of olive oil if you have any intention of drinking the poison they serve in the doggeries."

"*Sí, señor.*"

They did not find Habersham that night, although they encountered remarks that indicated he had been there, and they had no difficulty tracing him by the fact that he had only one eye and one ear.

They tried several times later but he was always ahead of them. Then Ross began to worry about wagons, for it was the eighteenth of August.

The grass would be burned already, and if they delayed much longer they ran a risk of northers.

A letter arrived saying that the wagons he had ordered from Pittsburgh would not be shipped for two more months.

That was a blow. He went back to their room and had a drink of rum to think it over. It might be that he could scour the country and get enough wagons second-hand. The real trouble was that not many of those wagons were good enough to make the trip to Chihuahua. He would have bought army wagons, but Fauntleroy had only a dozen or so and he needed those.

Ross got up to pace the floor. He began to speculate on the possibility of carrying everything on pack mules. It would take better than two thousand mules, and it would be hard as hell to graze two thousand mules in one train, for that many mules would have to be spread out over a couple of sections of land and would be prime targets for the Comanches. No, it wouldn't work. They had to have wagons. He thought of sending a note to Connelly, but Connelly had already left New Orleans. Anyway, what could Connelly do that he couldn't do? They had already scoured New Orleans for wagons and had rounded up a scant half-dozen that would do.

Perhaps they could build Mexican ox-carts. With enough of them, pulled by two mules or two oxen — by the great horn spoon, he had an idea there! He poured another drink and then he heard the first soft patter of rain on the roof. He went to the window. It was coming down steadily, and gradually he got the import of it. If this turned out to be a general rain, it would be impossible to take wheeled vehicles back through Texas. Up on the prairies where the grass was matted it might not be too bad, but through heavy black mud such as they had encountered along the Canadian River in Indian country, they could not make three miles a day. He stared at the water dropping from the edge of the roof and falling in little puddles on the ground. The only answer was to wait. . . .

He waited for nine long weeks, from the nineteenth of August to the twenty-first of October. It rained almost every day, and it rained hard. Occasionally in the afternoon the sun would come through for a few hours, but the next morning it would pour again. He rode out on the black gelding to look at the country. There was a quagmire of sticky mud in every direction. The old Indians said there had never been anything like it, but that was small comfort.

Thirty-six wagons came up from New Orleans through Natchitoches, and fourteen came from St. Louis up the Arkansas through Van Buren, which was the nearest regular stop for freight and mail. They had almost enough mules, but now, Ross noted wryly, nothing to do but feed them until spring. He notified all teamsters the expedition would not leave until about 1st April. Some of the Mexican skinners found work around the fort and on freighter lines from Van Buren and Fort Smith to agencies in the Indian Country.

He suggested Hermenijildo go home to

be with Chonita, but the young man refused, saying he was going to go through with it all the way. Apolinar was very popular with the unmarried daughters of officers at the fort. Andrés came in once a week to visit, and professed himself quite happy with Josefina.

By the 1st December the rains had stopped and the ground was reported firm in all directions, but by that time the grass was gone and the mules would have to forage along the way.

Ross fumed and paced the floor but it didn't help. "We're hog-tied; absolutely hog-tied!" he told Major Fauntleroy.

Fauntleroy seemed a little amused. "It is easy to tell you have not spent any considerable time in the army."

Ross glanced sharply at him. "The army is not supposed to be efficient; merchants are."

"And yet," said Fauntleroy, pouring two glasses of rum, "not even a Yankee trader can control the weather. Nor can you make wagons spring up out of the ground."

In January the rest of the wagons arrived. In February Black Beaver went to St. Louis to accompany a party of surveyors going to the western reaches of Kansas Territory. In March Ross called in

Tapia and his three assistants. He was a little shocked at the appearance of Andrés; the young man had grown fat and rather greasy-looking and not too clean. But Ross outlined plans for gathering their men. He told Andrés to check over every wagon and grease every axle, and he made a mental note to double-check behind him, for Andrés did not appear to be the same man he had been on the way north-east.

Ross assigned Apolinar to find some Indian guides, reminding him that on the return trip they would follow the south side of the Red River, in territory unknown to them, until they hit their trail of the previous summer. They would be going through territory inhabited by different tribes: Cherokees, Wacoes, Caddoes, Wichitas — and it was desirable to have Indian guides familiar with the terrain and the natives.

For himself Ross reserved what he anticipated would be the hardest task: that of gathering a crew to drive seventy wagons and 700 pack-mules. He rode the gelding to Van Buren, accompanied by Hermeni-jildo, and it was a rather silent journey. It was March and still too early for the dog-wood to show its gorgeous blossoms, but the first pale green shoots of grass were breaking through the matted carpet of the prairie; following the protracted rain of the previous fall, the grass would undoubtedly be plentiful. But Hermenijildo was wrapped up in his thoughts; Chonita probably had had her baby by now, but so slow were mails from the interior of Mexico that he had had no word.

Ross, on the other hand, was uneasy about Valeria. The winter, in some ways slow, had gone too fast in others. And even assuming great leisureliness in Mangum's suit, Ross faced the fact that almost a year had gone by and he had not spoken his mind. He had thought a number of times of writing her, but on trying it he found it was not easy to put such thoughts on paper; furthermore, he found that he had no knowledge of the proper way to address a young Mexican woman by letter, and he was too self-conscious to reveal this ignorance, especially when he knew it would mean having someone look over his shoulder as he proposed marriage.

And so he had let the matter lie quiescent, imagining all kinds of reasons why nothing final would have been decided in Chihuahua. Impatient he had been, sometimes hard to get along with, and it seemed, as he watched the warm Arkansas sun lay its growing heat on the living things around him, that they could hardly have been gone long enough for a formal marriage to be consummated. Yet as he watched the buds forming on the dogwood he realised it had been like that in Chihuahua when they had left, and indeed a year had elapsed, and while a year on the road might seem short, a year in Chihuahua might seem very long, and he became filled with more and more impatience to be back, and in his mind he saw her as he had seen her at Cordero's, with her glorious golden head tilted to one side and her lilting voice using the melodic Spanish phrases, all bursting with feeling as they could be only when spoken by a girl like Valeria.

CHAPTER SIXTEEN

He and Hermenijildo went up to Van Buren to buy harness and chains, and dropped into the *Freighters' Saloon*. "It may not be very good whisky," said Ross, "but at least it's whisky."

Hermenijildo sighed. "I have tasted some atrocious beverages since we have come here," he agreed.

On their second drink Hermenijildo said quietly, "Do you see the big man in the corner by himself?"

"Hadn't noticed," said Ross. "Anything special?"

"He looks," said Hermenijildo, "like a man in despair."

Ross glanced around. "He does at that." He got up and went over to the big man, who sat alone. "Howdy, mister. Mind if I sit down?"

The man gave him a rueful smile. "Sure don't mind. I'm sorry company, though."

Ross sat down. "Live here?"

"No, came from Kentucky."

"Buy you a drink?" asked Ross.

The man shook his head. "Sorry. I just spent my last two-bit piece. I couldn't buy back."

"That's it, then? You're broke?"

"Bad broke. Name's James Taylor."

"Mine's Ross Phillips."

"Heard of you. Looking for drivers again?"

Ross nodded.

"Maybe I'm your man, Phillips."

"Alone."

"No, my wife is with me. Makes it worse."

"So it does. Look, your glass is dry. Have another while we talk it over."

Taylor nodded. "Brought a circus here — but there just ain't enough people to go to a show out here."

"A circus? You mean performing dogs and trained horses?"

"Yes."

"Who runs it?"

"Me and my wife."

"Where's she now?"

"Packing, I reckon."

"What are you going to do with the animals?"

"Twenty-six dollars feed bill against 'em. Looks like I'll lose 'em."

"All trained?"

The whisky came, and Ross tossed out a silver peso.

"Well trained. I had most of 'em from birth."

Ross was thoughtful. "How do you transport 'em?"

"Got a wagon. The horses are broke to harness, and the dogs ride in crates."

"You ever played in Mexico?" asked Ross.

"Nope. Thought of it, though."

"They don't have much entertainment out a way from Mexico City. I saw a company of Spanish actors in Chihuahua give a play written in English and translated from French, and they drew big crowds. There's mighty little entertainment up there but bullfights and rooster fights. You'd draw big crowds if your show is any good."

"It's a good show," Taylor said. "We just made a mistake coming out here. People have to travel too far to get to town. I jumped here from Little Rock — and where next?" He tossed off his drink. "There's nowhere to go west until you get down into Texas."

"Can your wife drive your wagon?" Ross asked suddenly.

"Sure."

"Then I'll hire you to drive one of mine.

I'll give you protection and guarantee delivery in Chihuahua, furnish food and feed, for half of your net profit for a year after you get there."

"It's a hard bargain, mister."

"You got nothing to bargain with," said Ross. "You got a hotel bill?"

Taylor nodded morosely.

"I'll give you fifty dollars. That pay you up?"

"I need thirty-eight dollars and I'm in the clear."

"A man isn't a man," said Ross, "without a dollar in his pocket." He slapped three gold coins on the table. "There's three doubloons — about $48 U.S. Get yourself in the clear and drive to Fort Towson. We'll rendezvous there. Got any friends who want to drive?"

"Saw a feller in the livery yesterday looking for a job."

"Bring him along." Ross got up.

Taylor took the doubloons and then leaped to his feet. He was an inch taller than Ross and his grip was as hard as a stone-crusher. "You'll find it's a good investment, mister. We put on a good show, we do."

Ross went back to Hermenijildo. Taylor went out, and Ross told Hermenijildo what he had done. Hermenijildo looked puzzled. "This is not like you, *señor*. You do not know this man."

"He looked honest," said Ross. "And down-and-out besides. Anyway, I feel an urge to get into business. My days of roaming are over."

"If the *señor* Mangum stays out of the picture?"

Ross frowned. "I don't like to think about that ugly phiz. Maybe he got drowned in the Seeds-keeder. Maybe the Comanches lifted his hair. Maybe —"

"You dream, *señor*. And dreams are not realities."

"No, but —"

"Are you Ross Phillips?" asked a nasal voice.

Ross looked up. The first thing he saw was a nickel-plated star, and above it a thin face with long, drooping moustaches. "I'm Phillips," he said.

The man held out a paper. "I'm Tillman, deputy sheriff. Got a summons for you."

"For what?"

"Murder."

Ross laughed. "You're joking."

"No joke, mister. You killed a man named Kerlérec in April last year."

"That was in Chihuahua — and it wasn't murder. It was self-defence."

"I ain't the judge, mister."

"What do you propose to do?"

"Put you in jail."

Ross got up, now taut. "You think you can take me?"

"I don't know about that, mister. I'm nearin' sixty and I admit I ain't the fighter I was once. But if I can't, somebody else will, because this is the law you're talkin' to, mister — not John Tillman."

"All right, John, I'll go, but I won't promise to stay."

Hermenijildo had taken it all in, and now he said, "I'll get you a lawyer, no?"

Ross nodded. "Get one *muy coyote*. Something's going on here, and we'll need all the help we can get."

His lawyer was a bearded man named O-sho-nub-bee, a full-blood Cherokee Indian, and they went before the judge in chambers.

"Your honour," said O-sho-nub-bee, "this is a ridiculous pretence of justice. This alleged crime was not committed in the jurisdiction of the United States, even."

"I know," said the judge, who seemed to be trying to think it out rather than apply the statutes, "but the dead man was a resident of Fulton, and he has a lot of friends in Arkansas."

"There is no *corpus delicti*," said the lawyer.

"That might be a problem," admitted the judge.

"And no witnesses."

"Well, now, that isn't strictly true, counsellor. We've got at least one eye-witness to the crime — name of Habersham, Link Habersham."

"Habersham!" Ross repeated.

The judge looked pleased with himself. "Habersham has a lot of friends here too," he noted.

O-sho-nub-bee seemed to sense which way the wind was blowing. "I request your honour put as low a bail as possible on this man, under the circumstances, since it appears quite obvious that a conviction can never be secured — even though Kerlérec and Habersham do have friends in Arkansas."

"Bail set at $3000," the judge snapped. "Cash."

"Cash?" asked Ross.

"I said it plain."

Hermenijildo broke out in rapid Spanish. "*Señor*, I get money from New Orleans. They put you in jail and keep you there for years — as in Mexico."

"It looks like that's just what they're

aiming to do," Ross conceded grimly, "but I'm not contributing $3000 on the say-so of Habersham. Better than that: go to the doggeries around Fort Towson and spread the word that I will be there in person in a day or two to recruit teamsters and helpers. Spread the word but stay out of trouble."

"And you, *señor?*"

"Don't worry about me. Keep an eye out for Habersham."

The jail-keeper was a mixed breed, and Ross gave him a gold half-eagle for a special supper. When it came he intended to get the jail-keeper's pistol, but the man was leery and shoved the food under the door. Ross resigned himself to the hard bench and tried to go to sleep. But around midnight he heard a whisper: "Phillips?"

Ross sat up. "Here."

James Taylor, the circus man, unlocked the barred door. "I gave the keeper whisky with laudanum in it," he said. "We use it sometimes on the animals. It don't take much to put a man to sleep."

Ross thanked him. Taylor said he was ready to pull out. Ross went to the livery and got the gelding and rode out of town at a sedate trot which turned into a hard gallop as soon as he was clear of the settlement.

He followed the military road until he felt sure he was across the state line; then he let the gelding slow down to a steady trot. He rode into Fort Towson at noon the next day, and after he got some antelope steaks under his belt he called in his counsel.

"One thing is sure," he said, "and that is that Habersham's mission is to discredit me personally and make it impossible for us to raise a crew of teamsters. That has been behind the hostility shown towards us everywhere. That was behind the Frenchman's jumping me in the doggery last fall. This country being composed of men who gravitate to the strong, it will never be possible for us to raise a crew until I tackle Habersham and whip him in person. Therefore —" He pounded the bottle on the table. "Spread the word. I will be at the doggeries next Saturday night to recruit teamsters — and this time, we're leaving. If any man in the country has the courage to tackle Texas, let him show up. If he's a coward, let him stay at home and suck eggs. That clear?"

"*Sí, señor*," said Hermenijildo.

They all nodded.

"And," said Ross, "I think we'll draw our

man out of his hole."

On Saturday afternoon he began to make the rounds. It was a beautiful spring day in Indian Territory; the sky was a deep blue and cloudless; the grass had begun to give the hills an emerald green look that meant good grazing. A hawk floated in the sky, and the good earthy smell of growing things in moist, rich soil was like a tonic that made a man want to run and stretch his legs with the young colts on the distant hillside.

But within the dank dimness of the unlighted doggeries all was dark and brooding, and the only looks Ross got were scowls.

He was openly contemptuous of their liquor. He ordered it, paid for it, and let it stay on the boards. "They're sinkholes," he told Hermenijildo, "and since they're determined to be antagonistic to us anyway, I'd as soon give them good reason to be. It will spread our fame faster."

In each place he announced verbally that he wanted competent teamsters for the trip to Chihuahua; he would start within the week, and wages would start as each man signed up.

He got no takers. No one even made inquiry — and by this he knew they had been primed, and were only waiting for the explosion.

It came about ten o'clock Saturday night. It had been dark for two hours, and the night sounds of bullbats and owls and coyotes singing on the hilltops were harbingers of peace and tranquillity, but in the foul depths of the candle-lighted doggeries, saturated with the fumes of turpentine lamps, the rank smell of tobacco, and the sour sweat of unbathed bodies, there was no such indication.

The explosion came in an unusually big place known as *Choctaw Tom's*. He and Hermenijildo and Apolinar descended the dirt steps and walked out into the low room. Ross did not look around but ordered whisky for the three. He paid for it and let it sit, turned his back to the boards that formed a counter, and made his announcement in a loud voice.

For the first time that night he got a response. From a group of men sitting on the floor at the end of the room he heard a voice:

"How are you payin'?"

"Twenty-five dollars a month and found."

"How do we know we'll get it?"

"How do you know you'll need it?"

305

answered Ross. "You may die of a weak heart before you get there."

Silence. No rumble of approval at this sally. No sound whatever — and Ross knew it was coming. He said to Hermenijildo, *"El cuchillo! Pronto!"*

He felt the handle, and took hold of it, turning it within his fingers, behind his back, waiting for the next question.

"They say you're wanted in Arkansas for killing a man."

"They say many thing," Ross answered. "I may be wanted again." He took a step forward. "There may be a reward on my head for all I know. Do you want to claim it?"

"I'll claim it!" said a heavy voice, and Link Habersham sprang to his feet. His head almost touched the sod ceiling, and he came forward on bent knees, a bowie-knife in his right hand.

Ross took a step into the open. "Twice we've met," he said, "and you've lost an eye and an ear. What have you to put up now?"

Silence. Deadly silence as Habersham came clear of the sitting men and moved into the centre of the room. The men behind him got to their feet and crowded back against the wall. He was a ghoulish sight without one ear and with one eye closed, but the open eye burned with a furious fever that could be quenched only by blood.

Ross said aloud, "My friends will shoot any who interfere," and heard the sound of weapons drawn from leather holsters.

Habersham said, "I thought it would be a fair fight."

"It will be fair," said Ross, "if we have to kill all your friends to make it so." He said to Hermenijildo, "Get that bartender out from behind the counter."

Hermenijildo said sharply, *"Andele! Pronto!"* and Ross heard the bartender's shuffling feet.

He looked beyond the circling Habersham and saw the battle-browed, scowling faces of Indians, Negroes, whites, and half-breeds, and he knew their sympathies — such as they were — were with Habersham, perhaps because he had plied them with rotgut on Cordero's money. He turned on one heel, feet apart but well under him.

Habersham was moving deftly from side to side, keeping his distance, waiting for an opening, the blade of his big fourteen-inch knife held low before him.

Ross tried to keep his back in the general

307

direction of the camphene lamp, whose yellow flame made Habersham's dirty skin look scrofulous.

Habersham lunged to Ross's left. Ross, remembering the man's trick in Chihuahua, sidestepped but did not attempt to follow up, standing poised, his knife at the level of his waist. It was well he refrained, for Habersham, seeming about to plunge headfirst into the counter, suddenly whirled in his tracks and chopped hard with his knife at about the height of a man's kidneys.

Ross grinned.

Habersham backed away, now thoroughly aroused. He began to move to the left, and as he faced the light squarely, Ross moved in suddenly and slashed at his neck.

But Habersham had anticipated that. He ducked to one side, and, like Ross, stood for an instant waiting to see what Ross would do.

Ross too had control of his movements, and he stopped short to meet the expected thrust. But Habersham backed away.

Ross now was sweating freely, and that was a good sign, for it meant loosened muscles. For a few seconds he heard the harsh breathing of the men in the room, and the "spat" as somebody propelled tobacco juice into a corner.

Habersham too was sweating and moving easily. His one eye glared with hatred, and that was the only sign of emotion about him. He had dropped his hat as he came out, and his uncombed hair, soiled and matted, showed spots of grizzly grey. He wasn't over thirty-five but he had been long on the trail — long enough to feel no mercy, no compunction.

Ross now was facing the light, and Habersham manœuvring to get it directly behind him. Ross moved, and Habersham growled and rushed straight forward, for a moment tired of fencing and wanting to close.

Ross jumped the other way and was tempted to take a cut at the man but again refrained, and again discovered it had been wise, for Habersham turned just when it seemed he was off balance.

But as he regained his stance, Ross leaped in. He sliced once, hacked, and sliced again. He saw the big blade flash in the yellow light, and strained against it with his left arm. His own knife felt the drag of flesh as he drew it back, and then he was beyond Habersham's reach. His knife blade dripped, and Habersham's left arm and shoulder were bright with blood that looked black in the camphene light.

Habersham roared and rushed. Ross met

him full on. They strained against each other. Ross bowed his back against the greater leverage of Habersham, and felt the man give. He pushed hard, and the man fell backward, seeming to be off balance. Ross was on him like an eagle on a rabbit. Habersham had his left forearm over his face to guard his throat, but Ross tried to get through.

Then he felt Habersham's legs gather under him. Habersham threw him off, stabbing with the knife at the same time. Ross felt the blade go between two ribs but not deeply. He felt himself hurled through the air by the force of Habersham's legs, and knew he had been fooled again.

Habersham was on his feet. He kicked the knife out of Ross's hand and stabbed him through the left shoulder. Ross saw black for a moment, and then Habersham was sitting on his stomach, his back towards Ross's head.

Ross, still thick in the head from the two stabs, felt the point of the knife as Habersham sliced the rawhide thong that laced up his trousers.

He heard the snips, so close together they made almost a single sound, and then he realised with horror what was about to happen. He threw himself up, seized

Habersham's head in both hands, and twisted the man to the floor. He smothered the knife by wrestling Habersham over and over on the dirt floor, and he finally came to the place where his own knife lay against one of the kegs that held the counter. In rolling, he snatched the knife, got it well in his hand, and then drove it deep into Habersham's jugular vein.

He got to his feet, breathing hard, and looked at the scowling faces around him. With the knife still in his hand, he bent over Habersham's head. He seized a handful of the greasy hair and made half a dozen cuts in the scalp, circling an area about the size of a *peso*. Then he braced his knees on the man's chest and gave a mighty yank. He got to his feet with the bloody scalp in his left hand, the knife in his right, and glared at them all. "Anybody — wants to go to Chihuahua — see me — at the fort," he said, and threw the scalp on the dirt floor and walked out.

The night air smelled good, and he took in great draughts of it. He gave the knife back to Hermenijildo. "I'm getting old," he said, "when I can't go through a knife fight without breathing so hard."

"It was a magnificent battle," Apolinar said in awe.

CHAPTER SEVENTEEN

They began to drift in the next day, and by Sunday night he had engaged a hundred and forty-one. James Taylor came in the next day, driving his wagon behind a team of six white horses. The wagon was partly filled with crates containing white and black dogs of various breeds and sizes, and Ross was dubious about taking them through Indian country until Taylor assured him the dogs would not bark unless he gave them a signal to do so.

"This here's my wife," Taylor said, indicating a woman at his side.

Ross took off his hat. "Pleased to meet you, ma'am."

She smiled, obviously not too accustomed to having men remove their hats for her. Her face was a little leathery but her eyes were soft as she smiled, but in a moment she changed, and it was apparent that she was more on the defensive than she was flirtatious — which suited Ross fine, for it meant that she would not have the roosters fighting over her all the way to Chihuahua.

Josefina rode in on a mule that evening, and Ross was relieved, in a way, to see that she showed no apparent change. He had expected some such degeneration as had occurred in Andrés, but Josefina looked exactly the same — no older, no wiser, no different. She was as she was, born with all the instinctive wisdom of a primitive woman. She would never be more, never less. Ross had had it in mind to refuse to allow her to go back with the expedition, but he considered what might come of Andrés and changed his opinion. Whatever else happened — and regardless of the change already made in Andrés — Ross considered it his inescapable duty to deliver Andrés back to Chihuahua. Don Mauricio might be very unhappy at what he would see in his only son — or he might have anticipated it; who could tell? — but Ross felt his own responsibility would be discharged only when Andrés was safely back in Chihuahua.

So he said to Josefina, "*Señora,* you will understand that you will have to grind corn to pay your way?"

She looked at him with those deep, inscrutable black eyes that seemed to contain all the wisdom of Woman down through the ages, and she said meekly, *"Por supuesto, señor* — of course," without taking notice of her change of status in his eyes as shown by his addressing her as *señora.*

This was a thing that had always puzzled him about women: the ability shown by some of them to be completely promiscuous and think nothing of it. Nor was Josefina to be classed with the prostitutes of Mexico, for she was without greed. She demanded nothing and did not worry about the future. She probably never looked beyond the immediate night and the satisfaction of her passions.

The presence of Josefina and Mrs. Taylor brought thoughts of Valeria. He tried to remember exactly how she looked, and his wish to see her again was almost painful in its intensity. It was hard to restrain his impatience to start back.

Actually there had been no news from Chihuahua except what little Connelly had brought the summer before. The mails in Mexico were slow, irregular, and undependable, and so were little used. Anyway, the Mexican attitude was that life went as it went, and what did another year mean anyway? Those who were away would find out the news soon enough when they returned.

He encountered another obstacle thrown up by Habersham: he was not able to hire Indian guides, for Habersham had spread a great deal of talk about the Cherokees in north-east Texas being on the warpath as a result of Lamar's expulsion order, and no Indian wanted to be caught in Texas guiding a party of whites.

He consulted with Major Fauntleroy, who said he doubted that there were any white men who knew the route through Texas, but he advised keeping to the south of the Red until they hit their 1839 trail. This, he said, would assure them water and prevent their getting lost. Tapia thought so too.

And so in April 1840 almost exactly a year from the time they had left Chihuahua, the great caravan of 70 wagons, 850 mules, and 225 men left Fort Towson with 380,000 pounds of trade goods for Chihuahua. In spite of the long delay, the prospects were still bright. The vast quantity of trade goods had been well preserved, and since it had been bought originally with an eye to time spent on the trail, there was no loss except for a few packets of rusted needles. Ross had detected those early in the course of the rain, and had hired soldiers, on their off time, to go over all the metal products and grease them carefully. The cotton goods had been aired and exposed to the sun as much as possible, and there was little or no mildew.

All in all, Ross thought as he sat the black gelding and watched the long, long line of wagons and mules follow the Kiamichi south towards the Red, they had come through the winter in remarkably good shape, and no harm had been done except delay. The cargo still represented a great fortune, and his share would be substantial. There had been considerable unanticipated expense in connection with the long layover, but that would be absorbed easily by the high prices always current in Chihuahua.

He shook hands with Fauntleroy and younger officers of the fort, wheeled the gelding, and galloped after the train. Andrés was still in charge of the wagons, with James Taylor second. Plácido had a mule of his own to ride.

Ross had hired a guide from near Pecan Point to show them the way across the Red, for the river, spread out over the valley by the backing up from the Great Raft, was several miles wide and looked like a vast morass of swamp, with islands of rank vegetation, pools of still brown water, and somewhere, underneath matted entanglements of logs that had themselves become floating islands, flowed the live current of the river — not always following the path cleared by Henry Shreve a few years before.

It required three days for the big caravan to ford the river, and then once again they were on firm ground and the long expedition set its face to the south-west. They rounded the great bend of the Red and turned due west. The sun was warm and bright, and Ross felt invigorated and optimistic for a fast trip. Then it rained.

For weeks they fought the sticky mud, throwing twenty mules on to a wagon and taking them forward a few at a time. The Red rose and overspread its banks, and they were lost in a sea of mud and water and almost impassable fallen timber and brush.

They seldom saw the sun. The leaden skies dripped water incessantly; the stars at night were hidden by clouds. For days at a time they were not sure of their directions, but Ross drove the train forward blindly, relentlessly, every morning hoping for a break, and every night, though exhausted and beaten by the prodigious efforts required to move the train even three miles through the sticky mud, he chafed at the seeming conspiracy of Nature to hold them back.

During the second week they had a rash of squealing axles, and Ross rode back one day to find Andrés.

"We'll never get these wagons across the Pecos without grease on the axles," he said sternly.

Andrés looked up, his neat black moustache now somewhat scraggly and looking somehow in keeping with his fat face. "It might be that I missed it," he admitted.

Ross said sharply, "I have been examining the wheels of every wagon now for some days. There are no fresh finger marks on the spokes."

"I have not felt good," said Andrés.

Ross looked at him, disgusted. With some men it was like that; give them a woman and you had a man with no ambition but to accommodate her. With some it was different. With some a willing woman made them want to work the harder — but with Andrés, no. Andrés had no desire to pull Josefina up to his level, but rather was content to sink down to hers.

Ross got back to the subject of wagons. "This will have to be taken care of, Andrés. We will never move this train to Chihuahua without every man doing his job, and I expect you to do yours."

Andrés mumbled, *"Sí, señor,"* and Ross rode off, not at all satisfied but still hopeful.

The rain lifted and the mud dried out. They had two good days, and then they hit the Cross Timbers. Again they were cruelly punished by the lack of guides. Ross rode to the north and forded the river but found no break. He rode a day's journey south and found no break, and there was nothing to do but fight their way blindly west. He ascertained that it was only thirty miles across, but it took them eight days, for the area was rocky, grown up with a thick mat of blackjack and brush, and cut in all directions with great gullies that were impassable until the banks were cut down — and even then a hundred men would have to hold back the wagons with ropes as they descended, and as many as forty mules were used to pull them up the other side.

It was a backbreaking job for giants, and in that time of testing James Taylor proved his right to stand up and be counted with the men. His great strength, his calmness, his quick perceptions, his ability to handle the men — all those qualities made him stand out among men most of whom were putting forth Herculean efforts of their own.

All but Andrés. Mrs. Taylor drove the circus wagon all day long with never a complaint, and even Josefina ground corn at every moment of stopping until Ross had to tell her to take a rest. But Andrés had lapsed into a lethargy which made him useless.

On a particularly hard day they had trouble getting a heavily-loaded wagon up the side of a gully. Taylor had on forty-four mules, and men walked at the sides with ropes to keep the wagon from turning over. And still the wagon seemed to be held back with invisible chains. Ross rode alongside and asked Taylor what he thought.

"You ask me," said Taylor, "I don't think them axles are greased. They act like they're all plugged up with mud and sand." He wiped the sweat from under his hatband. "I know this is a mighty steep grade and a right smart pull." He pointed forward. "You can see the lead chain is digging into the edge of the ground up there. But hell — forty-four mules ought to be able to pull Fort Towson across the Red River."

"How about more mules?"

"Can't gain much. We've got too many now. We get so much chain and gear and it's hard to make them all pull together."

"You think the axles are dry?"

"Only think I know. We broke two doubletrees and a hound on this wagon already, so it ain't the mules' fault."

Ross made a decision. "I don't think it's the load, either. It's a big load, but I've seen bigger ones go over Ratón Pass. Tell the men to tie their ropes to the axles and running gear and fasten the wagon to the trees. We'll jack up a wheel and see what it looks like."

"I should of done it myself before," said Taylor, "but —"

"No need to apologise. Every man here has worked his head off for two weeks — but one," he said grimly.

They got the end of the wagon raised. The wheel was fast on the axle and they had to pry it off, turning and pulling. Ross looked up and saw Andrés at the edge of the crowd, watching. Ross turned hard. "You haven't greased this axle since we left Fort Towson," he said.

"*Señor*, the mud."

"It was your job," Ross said implacably.

Andrés's eyes dropped. "I'm sorry, *señor*."

Ross had a moment of pity for him, then he snapped at Taylor. "You will be in charge of the wagons from now on — both maintenance and moving. Your pay is doubled. We'll try to stop early to-night so you can organise crews and take care of every wagon. There must be no more of this pulling against ourselves."

"All right," said Taylor.

Apolinar was still in charge of hunting, and had become very good at it. Tapia kept scouting parties ahead and behind, for they had come upon abandoned villages and knew that Indians were in the area. Hermenijildo took charge of a party to make a trail through the trees and brush; the growth was so thick there was no way of accomplishing this except by cutting down trees with axes; stones too high to clear the axles of the wagons had to be broken up or moved. Taylor kept the wagons moving, and there were times when he seemed to will them forward. But no longer did they think of progress in terms of miles per day; there were times when a hundred yards was all they could move in half a day.

Then, almost unbelievably, they broke through the western edge of the Cross Timbers and found themselves on a dry,

open prairie, with the sun warmly overhead, the limitless light blue sky stretching
towards infinity in the west, and the soft
spring breeze carrying the scent of the first
wild flowers.

They stopped at a spring for two days,
and James Taylor, who was also a blacksmith, pressed two men into service with
him and set up a forge and went to work
on the running-gear of the wagons; tyres
were tightened, hubs banded, axles
straightened, shoes applied to the leading
mules — for unshod mules had difficulty
with footing on green grass.

The prairies west of the Cross Timbers
were a series of broad shelves, each one
higher than the last. They would mount
one plateau expecting to cross it and
descend on the other side; there would be
good travelling for two or three days; then
they would reach an area of breaks —
rough country, and after traversing that
would find themselves on another plateau
higher than the last one.

Water was a problem, for the streams
were largely brackish, loaded with mineral
salts that made them not only unpalatable
but unhealthful to both men and mules. In
the absence of guides who knew the
springs, Ross himself rode far and wide

every day in connection with Apolinar to spy out springs of fresh water or near-fresh water that would supply enough for the big train.

They came in contact with small bands of Indians occasionally, but these professed total ignorance of the country to the west and south-west except that it was Comanche and Kiowa country — and that in itself was significant of the awe in which all other tribes held the savage and hard-riding Comanches and Kiowas.

Nevertheless their progress was good. The great undulating prairies furnished good footing and excellent grazing; the mesquite grass was now luxuriant, and the mules made as much as thirty miles a day and still fattened.

Then one mid-morning Ross, with Hermenijildo at his side, sat the gelding atop a hill and looked below and saw the well-marked trail made by the train on its way north. Ross looked at Hermenijildo and grinned. *"Hombre,"* he said, "we'll soon be back in Chihuahua, and you can find out whether it's a boy or a girl."

Hermenijildo smiled for the first time in months. "I have hope it will be a boy," he said. "My Chonita before I left decide' to call him Felipe in your honour, *señor.*"

For a moment Ross was embarrassed. "I — well, I'm sure I would be honoured," he said at last.

They turned south and followed their own trail. Ross had hoped to run into their Tonkawa guides — The Soft-Shelled Turtle and his companions — but day after day they crawled along under the blue Texas sky and the ever-warmer sun without any indication of Indians.

Nevertheless Ross was worried. There were plenty of Indians in the country, he knew, and he began to feel they were holding off to let the train get deep into their territory before they made themselves known.

He issued repeated warnings to Tapia's men, and constantly urged none to go out of sight of the main body for any purpose. For all men and the two women, he warned, the demands of modesty must now be subservient to self-preservation. He knew it was inevitable that most of the men would take his warnings lightly, but he hoped, by constant vigilance, to avoid a tragedy.

Andrés was now no more than a fat teamster with a long black moustache and a scraggly beard. He drove his team during the day, cooked his meal at night over a separate fire with Josefina, kept his own counsel. Ross no longer asked him to sit in on discussions, but Andrés did not appear to mind. Nevertheless, as they continued south, a look of thoughtfulness appeared in his black eyes. It turned into worry as the train penetrated farther and farther into Comanche country, reaching for the Río Grande, steadily cutting down the miles to Chihuahua.

They were about three days north of the Pecos when the Comanches struck. It was early evening, and so still the distant bark of prairie dogs was plainly heard throughout the camp. The sound of Josefina grinding corn on the *metate* arose presently, but that unnatural quiet pervaded the countryside to such an extent that Hermenijildo remarked about it.

"I don't doubt the Indians have been here ahead of us, probably driving off the game to force us to hunt them out and trade mules with them," Ross said.

Then, in the brief course of a few seconds, the entire camp was brought to its feet by an electrifying scream. One of Tapia's men rode into camp from his post at a hard gallop. *"Los indios! Los indios!"* he called in a hoarse voice. He was not holding the reins but maintaining his balance somehow miraculously. His horse, with blood streaming down its hip from a lance wound, galloped past Ross; its reins were trailing.

The man's hat was gone; one side of his head was a mass of bright blood, and his face was grey and contorted with pain. His shirt, open at the throat, showed his upper chest covered with blood.

The horse stepped on a rein and went over on its neck, its hind quarters going far into the air from its momentum. At the top of the arc the man fell off suddenly, seeming to collapse. He fell in a huddle, face down and knees under him. An arrow projected from his back.

Shots sounded in the direction from which he had come, and Ross barked at Tapia, who shouted orders at his men and ran for a mule. The soldier's horse was screaming piteously, still on the ground. Ross saw that it had a broken thigh-bone. He put a cap on his pistol, stepped up and shot the horse in the ear.

Tapia's men were beginning to gallop towards the sound of shooting, which now had stopped. Hermenijildo galloped up, leading the black gelding. Ross seized the reins. The soldier on the ground was dead. Ross vaulted into the saddle and sank his spurs into the gelding's flanks. "Watch the train!" he shouted at Taylor, and rode out after Tapia.

They had a surprisingly short distance to go. Andrés and four *arrieros* had gone over the hill with rifles and pistols, probably hunting. The Comanches had caught them not over four hundred yards from camp, and the carnage was frightful. How it had been done in a few seconds Ross did not know, but one of the men was disembowelled; two had their hands cut off; one was almost beheaded; Andrés — poor fat Andrés, who had lost all ambitions but one — was bristling with arrows in his abdomen; his face was criss-crossed with bloody knife-slashes, and his chest was opened and his heart was torn out.

"Shall my men follow them?" asked Tapia.

"No!" thundered Ross. "Stay back and guard the train! There may be another party watching!"

"*Sí, señor.*"

Ross got down and examined the men's firearms. They had all been fired. Ross straightened up. "They fought back," he said, "and undoubtedly they killed a few of the savages." He said to Hermenijildo, "Get a burial detail up here, with at least twenty armed men to guard them."

"*Sí, señor.*" Hermenijildo galloped back to the camp. Ross searched the ground, and by the time Hermenijildo returned, Ross had come to a conclusion. While the men were digging a common grave, Ross got Hermenijildo and Apolinar to one side. "It's probably best this way," he said. "I think Don Mauricio will live more happily in the knowledge that his son died a hero than he would if Andrés had returned home fat and lazy. It may be that Andrés planned it this way — but that must not be repeated to anyone. Do you both understand me?"

They both nodded gravely. Not only Hermenijildo had turned sober during the past year, but Apolinar had acquired an air of maturity that Ross had never expected.

CHAPTER EIGHTEEN

Ross studied them both. "There is other business at hand; perhaps Andrés has opened a way to take care of it. You remember Carlota?"

They both nodded vigorously.

"I owe my life to her and her husband," he said. "That is not, however, reason enough to risk the success of this entire expedition."

They watched him gravely.

"We are almost at the Pecos, and from there it is only a few days to Presidio. I think Plácido and Tapia could get the train there if they had to. The lieutenant shows a good knowledge of the country and the Indians, and certainly Plácido knows mules."

They both agreed.

"We may be able to rescue her. There is danger —"

"*Señor*," Hermenijildo said with feeling, "if there is anything we can do to save anyone from these blood-thirsty savages —"

Ross said thoughtfully, "The Comanches now have two big affairs to celebrate: the taking of scalps and the killing of some of their warriors."

"You think —"

"It's obvious those men didn't die with their hands in their pockets," said Ross. "Andrés's six-shooter had been fired four times."

Hermenijildo nodded.

"The Comanches will not expect us to leave the train and attack them, and I am sure they will give their full attention to celebrating these two events. While they are doing that, they will be highly vulnerable. It may be we can slip into their camp and get the girl without a fight."

Apolinar said grimly, "*Señor*, if a fight is necessary —"

"I'm counting on you — but let's get one thing straight. One man must stay back and hold the horses. Hermenijildo, that will be you."

"*Señor* —"

"No argument. You are married. Also you are very dependable. You won't get excited and do anything foolish. I will expect you to hold the horses. If anything happens to us, you will try to be reasonably sure whether we can reach you. If not,

you are to return to the train at the Pecos
— because the train will keep travelling,
just in case the Comanches should have
out a spy."

"I don't —"

"Your black can outrun any horse the
Comanches may have. It will be your duty
to return."

"But, *señor*, they may torture —"

"It is not likely." Ross took a deep
breath. "The Comanches kill very savagely
sometimes, but generally they don't waste
much time on it. I think you will soon
know."

Apolinar said eagerly, "Then I will go
with you?"

"You — and one more."

He looked up and down the camp
ground. The armed guards were patrolling,
and Lieutenant Tapia was riding a circuit
of the camp, accompanied by a squad of
soldiers.

Ross mounted the gelding and galloped
back along the trail to where James Taylor
was sitting his mule with a rifle in his
hands. "See anything?" asked Ross.

"No sign," said Taylor.

"Where's your wife?"

"Feeding the dogs."

"Come with me."

They rode up to the Taylor wagon, followed by Apolinar and Hermenijildo. Mrs. Taylor had turned the dogs out of their crates and was feeding them scraps of antelope meat.

"They don't bark," Ross said wonderingly.

Taylor shook his head. "They're well trained. They don't bark unless they're told to."

Mrs. Taylor looked up and her eyes narrowed slightly. "There's something in the air," she said.

"Yes, ma'am," said Ross. "There's a gentle little Mexican woman, a prisoner of the Comanches. I think we can rescue her if we could have the help of your husband. It's dangerous but there's a good chance we'll all come out alive."

She took a deep breath and looked down. "Mr. Taylor is a man of great dependability," she said. "I'm sure you will succeed if you take him with you."

Ross, a little astonished, glanced at Taylor, who nodded, watching his wife.

"Thank you, ma'am," said Ross, and rode off to give instructions to Lieutenant Tapia.

"We are going to try to rescue the girl," said Ross. "If we do not come back, you are in charge. If Hermenijildo comes back, he will be in charge. Your duty is to get the train to Presidio by the same trail we made going to Arkansas."

"I will do that, *señor*."

"Doctor Connelly will meet you in Presidio."

Tapia said unexpectedly, "I hope you will return in good health, *señor*."

Ross felt moved. "*Gracias. Bien*, move out in the morning as usual. We'll try to join you at the Pecos to-morrow or next day. But keep moving!"

"*Sí, señor*."

Tapia's acceptance of his charge made Ross feel better. The lieutenant had carried himself well the entire trip, but he had not been tried at all until now. Ross was pleased to note that the sudden responsibility did not seem to go to his head.

Ross saw Taylor loading his rifle, and told the two young Mexicans: "Be sure you've all got rifles, six-shooters fully loaded — five shots anyway, knives and tomahawks with you. If we have to fight we'll fight hard."

"I would not mind killing a few Comanches," said Apolinar, "but if we are engaged in a fight, some of us will be killed too."

"If my plan works," said Ross, "there won't be any fight."

"If it does not," Hermenijildo noted, "you'll end up like Andrés."

"Do you want to change your mind?" asked Ross. "There's no shame if you do. You have a child now." He was trying to make it easy for Hermenijildo.

"No, *señor*," Hermenijildo said fervently.

"Apolinar?"

"I'm going."

"Now, listen carefully — wait, somebody had better tell Josefina what has happened to Andrés."

Apolinar pointed to a camp-fire fifty feet away. "She has already sought solace with Plácido."

Ross stared for a moment, then put his mind to the task. "We'll have two problems — first, to find out if Carlota is still with them and where she is. Second is to rescue her. Now listen carefully. The party that killed Andrés won't expect us to follow them and they won't hurry. They may even stop near the camp for a day to prepare for morning. If the big camp is where it was last year, we can go straight to it and get there before the scalping party and find out whether the girl is still with them. If she is, we'll take it up from there — but

335

remember one thing: we must not be in Muke-war-rah's camp when news of the dead warriors gets there."

Both answered yes, and James Taylor nodded slowly, grave-eyed. Ross was well pleased that Taylor was with them, for the big man was a tower of strength.

"All right —"

"*Señor*," said Plácido, coming up, "you are short men to drive the mules. If you will allow it, I will teach Josefina to be an *arriera*, and then she will not have to grind the corn any more."

Ross looked at the man in the big straw hat. What unexpected small desires rose out of these childish people! "All right," he said, "teach her," and rode on.

They went over the hill and Ross pointed out the course. He set the gelding into a lope, and the others followed. They reached the canyon with the sun shining in the western end as it had a year before. He found the path and led them down it. Dogs barked at them and scurried out of the way. Children ran to hide, and heavily built squaws stared from openings in their teepees.

The four men stayed close together, and none bothered them as they rode through the village, but Ross knew the path behind them was closed until Muke-war-rah should open it. He could not find the chief's tent, but abruptly Ish-a-ro-yeh appeared. "You want something?" he asked.

"We want to see Muke-war-rah."

"Muke-war-rah too busy make useless talk. You come back to-morrow."

"Not to-morrow," Ross said. "We have come to talk. We have goods to trade."

Ish-a-ro-yeh studied him for a moment, and then said, "You follow me. Leave horses."

"We do not leave horses," Ross answered. "We will follow you."

Ish-a-ro-yeh gave no sign that he had heard. He turned and led them, in his awkward walk, to the right. They reached the big teepee with the buffalo painted on it, and there were the same men around the camp-fire, with Muke-war-rah of the big-boned, evil face and the strangely thin eyebrows, his black hair, braided, hanging down his left shoulder. He was sitting in front of his teepee, and he did not look up as the men rode to the fire.

Ross alighted. "Remember, do nothing unless I tell you."

"*Silencio!*" roared Muke-war-rah.

Ross calmly turned his reins over to

337

Apolinar and went to the fire. "Are the great Muke-war-rah's ears so tender that he cannot endure the song of the curlew?" asked Ross.

The great face lifted and the evil eyes looked at him. "I said you leave your horses."

"Do you think I trust your young braves enough to leave my horses?" Ross took five sacks of tobacco out of his shirt and passed them around. Then, remembering Ish-a-ro-yeh, he gave another one to him.

"The Brown Beard," Muke-war-rah said shrewdly, "was here last year about this time. Is it then a custom to violate our hunting grounds?"

"We have not been back home," said Ross. "We are on our way now."

"I know," said Muke-war-rah. "You have many wagons, much goods. Last year you have few wagons, no goods. You would not trade."

"I am sure you know all about us," said Ross.

"We have watched you many days — before you turn south and leave the Red River. What you want now?"

"We want to trade."

Muke-war-rah shook his head. "Is not necessary. My men watch your train. We will get your goods at the Pecos."

"It is not likely," Ross said, squatting before the fire, his rifle on his thighs. "We have more men than last year."

"You tricked us last year," said Muke-war-rah in sudden anger.

Ross laughed. "You could have followed us."

Muke-war-rah scowled, and Ross was amused. He knew why the Comanches had not followed: when they discovered the train had already crossed the Pecos, they had been confused and had turned to the most instinctive thing they knew: flight.

An old Comanche squaw waddled up to the fire with a tow-sack on her back, heavy with its contents. She swung it to the ground, grasped one ear, and up-ended the whole thing over the fire. A bushel of terrapins tumbled out and fell into the live coals, and instantly there was a mad scramble of legs and a frantic stretching of necks as the terrapins felt the heat and made violent efforts to escape.

Muke-war-rah sat there with a stick, and whenever a terrapin escaped from the fire on his side, he calmly put the stick under it and flipped it back into the fire. All the braves around the fire followed his example, and in a few moments there was a crackling and popping as the shells began to burst from the heat.

Ross, to hide his feelings, said, "There must be few buffalo if your people are reduced to eating terrapins."

Muke-war-rah watched the last live terrapin go around in a tight circle and then over and over, trying to escape the torture. Muke-war-rah snorted, then pushed the stick under the terrapin and tossed it back into the fire. "It will not make the price any lower," he said.

"We have goods this time," said Ross. "We can make a deal if you still have the captive."

Muke-war-rah studied him. "We have the woman. The child we had to kill. She whimpered. The woman — I have had to beat her many times with the lance. She is more stubborn than any mule. Maybe I will sell her to you, but the price will be high."

"There's no reason why it should be," said Ross, "if you don't like her any more."

"I like her — but I'm tired of getting my face scratched. I've beaten her until my arms are heavy, but still she fights." Ross had been afraid of that, but now he asked the question which he feared to have answered. "Let us see her."

Muke-war-rah scowled again, and Ross knew his fears were well founded. Muke-war-rah knew he would have to show the captive to make a trade, but he was reluctant to do that, and there could be only one reason: he had abused Carlota so much that even his primitive Indian mind was aware that her value was lower than it should be. "How much you give?" he demanded.

Ross said speculatively, "Two bolts of goods, very pretty; five pounds of tobacco —"

"Rifles!" Muke-war-rah said suddenly. "You give six rifles!"

"No rifles," said Ross. "If your young braves want rifles they can try to take them away from us — but I warn you, many Comanche souls will wander in blackness throughout eternity if they try."

Muke-war-rah grunted suddenly. His eyes were narrow. "You give one bolt of goods for every squaw in camp?"

Ross tried to laugh convincingly. "No squaw is worth that much. Besides, you have not shown her to me yet." He had to know if she was there — and if so, where.

Muke-war-rah arose. As before, his great size was breathtaking. He stamped to the teepee, went inside, and grunted in

Comanche. Ross heard the girl's voice answer, and then the bone-crushing slap of a big hand on her face. She came up screaming at him, and Ross began to understand then why Muke-war-rah would be willing to trade her off. This had been going on for a year, and no matter how brutal he had been to her, she still fought him at every turn. It could get to be annoying to Muke-war-rah. And there was more: Muke-war-rah was losing face with his own men for his inability to tame her. So while he pretended reluctance, Muke-war-rah probably would be glad to get rid of her.

Ross held his breath as the huge Indian dragged her out to the fire. For a moment he thought he would rise up and kill the Indian. The girl was thin to emaciation; they had been trying to starve her into submission. The left side of her face was swollen beyond all recognition, the eye completely closed in. Her arms were tied behind her, and her right leg was twisted, probably from a long scar down the calf, undoubtedly done to keep her from running away. Her hair was uncombed, her skin dirty, her clothes almost non-existent. Only her one good eye showed that she was still alive and still human.

"*Señora*," Ross said gently, "we will try again. Please be patient."

The one eye stared at him and suddenly seemed to open wider, and it came to Ross that she had heard nothing but Comanche for over a year and had almost forgotten her own language. She tried to talk through swollen lips, but the words were distorted and unrecognisable. Muke-war-rah seized her and flung her back into the teepee.

When Ross was sure he could control his voice, he said, shaking his head, "You have beaten her too much. You don't expect a big price for a woman like that."

"She's a Mexican," Muke-war-rah replied. "Her people will give much to get her back."

"She has no people. Your braves killed them all."

Muke-war-rah grinned insolently at him. "You want trade?"

Ross nodded and got up casually. "Three bolts of cloth, three pounds tobacco, beads, vermilion. No more."

He waited, eyes half-closed.

Muke-war-rah said angrily, "I trade. You come back to-morrow."

Ross got up and faced Muke-war-rah. The chief was at least half a head taller than him. "If you beat her more, the price will go down," he warned.

Muke-war-rah growled. Ross turned to his horse, sick at heart. There were times when he wondered exactly what Josefina would have done in a situation like Carlota's. He got on his horse and followed Ish-a-ro-yeh to the edge of the village. He gave him another sack of tobacco and trotted the gelding back up the path. Up on top, he stopped to give the horses a breather. Then he struck out on the return path.

"Que ahora?" "What now?" asked Hermenijildo.

"As soon as we're out of sight," said Ross, "we turn around and approach the canyon from the other side."

"Won't there be lookouts?" asked Taylor.

"Not likely," said Ross. "The Indians aren't as well organised as they're given credit for. Down in that canyon, I doubt they ever post a regular lookout unless they have reason to look for an attack."

"Why don't we trade for Carlota?" asked Apolinar anxiously.

"We won't get a chance. That raiding party will be back before we could deliver the goods, and once the Comanches start their wailing and mourning there'll be no trading of captives for a long time. It's quite possible they'll kill her anyway to vent their spleen. No, my plan is the only one that has a chance, I think."

Ross stopped them. "We've passed the last lookout. They're posted to see that we get started back in the right direction; then they'll forget us and go off hunting. Meantime, we'll go down this *arroyada* here until we can cut across to the west. We'll camp on the other side to-night. At daylight we'll go back to Muke-war-rah's camp."

"Why not earlier?"

"Indians don't get up early unless there's a good reason. But if I guess right, that raiding party will send in a runner to-morrow morning with news of the casualties, and the whole camp will go out to meet the survivors. Then I think we'll have a chance. . . ."

The opportunity came about mid-morning. While the three men were watching from the south rim, with Hermenijildo watching their horses, grazing in a hollow where they were not easily seen, a Comanche warrior came in on a bare-back paint pony and rode through the camp with a wailing howl that brought every resident to the opening of his teepee. Then at different spots in the village arose great wailings and moans of anguish as Comanche women cut off their hair and scarified their arms and legs and abdomens in mourning for lost husbands or sons. Presently a slow exodus began towards the east, and Ross told his companions what to do. "Hermenijildo will stay and hold the horses, for without them we cannot get out of this country alive. You, Apolinar and Taylor, will follow me down that path into the canyon. Leave your hats up here. Single file and on foot, we look enough like Indians not to be noticed for a long time, especially since the Comanches will be thoroughly occupied trying to outdo one another in their demonstrations of grief. Are you ready?"

"Let's go," said Apolinar.

"Lead on," said Taylor.

Ross went down the path, and noted that Apolinar and Taylor followed at ten-yard intervals. He had picked out the chief's teepee by its design, and now they went straight to it, spread out from side to side. The village seemed deserted, but Ross was cautious, he walked quietly around the teepee on his moccasins and found an Indian sitting before the entrance. The Indian looked up; Ish-a-ro-yeh. He opened his mouth to yell, but Ross was on him like a wildcat. He buried his knife in the hollow in Ish-a-ro-yeh's leathery throat, and the warning yell bubbled out through the Indian's blood.

Ross jerked his knife free and stepped inside. "Carlota," he said softly.

He heard no answer, no sound. His eyes began to see in the dimness, and he found her, thoroughly tied and gagged with raw-hide strips and thrown on the bare dirt floor. He bent over her, sliced off the bonds and the gag, stood her on her feet to be sure she was alive, and then took her thin hand and led her outside. She blinked in the sunlight, and he glanced at her to see if she was in condition to walk. "Follow me," he whispered.

They went back the same way — not fast for fear of attracting attention. Apolinar and Taylor were behind him. They found the path and went back up.

Hermenijildo was happy over the fact that a young Comanche brave had tried to steal the horses. Hermenijildo had spotted him first and had waited beside the black. When the Comanche had reached out for the black's reins, Hemenijildo had slipped a knife into his heart. "I tried to scalp him, *señor,* as you did the *señor* Habersham, but I'm afraid I messed it up."

Ross looked down. "You damn near skinned him," he said, "but there's no time now for a lesson. *Señora*," he said to Carlota, "can you ride behind me?"

She nodded. She was unbelievably wild-looking and she had a stench that was repulsive, but none of them mentioned it. The only important thing now was to get her back to civilisation and give her a chance to recover from her year of brutality and terror.

They mounted. "If the Comanches look for us," said Ross, "they will make for our trail. Therefore we'll go straight south from here to the next canyon, and then head south-east to meet the train about the Pecos crossing."

"It seems to me," said Hermenijildo, "that this will bring the whole tribe on our trail."

"Not likely. There's that old factor of the unexpected. The Comanches like to make the surprises, and a surprise going the other way throws them off guard. They won't come for revenge, either. A revenge raid takes some time to work up, and usually it's made against a smaller party. I don't think the Indians will tie into our train at all, especially since they've lost some braves already."

"Won't Muke-war-rah try to get Carlota back?"

"Why should he?" Ross steadied the thin form before him. "He was glad to get rid of her."

They swung around to the east after they had crossed the canyon. They hit the Pecos and followed it down. The water was much too high for fording, and Ross was worried.

At noon of the second day, after hard riding, they found the well-marked trail, and by evening they came upon the camp.

Ross delivered the girl to the care of Mrs. Taylor, who, although horrified at her condition, set about to gather herbs and prepare medicines to help her recover. "And a week of good food will do you a world of good, child," she said.

Ross said solemnly, "She's not altogether a child, Mrs. Taylor. She lost a husband and four children to the Comanches."

"Land's sake! It isn't possible!"

Ross went off to look over the river.

"It's too high to cross," said Lieutenant Tapia, "without ruining the goods."

"We'll cross it anyway. Apolinar!"

"*Sí, señor.*"

"Gather up a dozen water kegs and empty them. Have them here in half an hour."

349

"*Señor*," said Tapia, "surely you are not going to cross to-night."

Ross looked at him. He didn't feel like arguing, so he said the easiest thing he could think of. "With a thousand Comanches over yonder in the canyon, do you think we should loiter, *teniente?*"

Tapia was impressed — more especially when Ross promised him a bonus for having brought the train as far as he had.

By the light of torches they lashed empty kegs, with stopped bungholes, under the wagon-beds. They rolled these into the roily river, with a light on the far side to guide the mules, and men with ropes on the upriver side to be sure the loads did not turn over. When the first wagon load rolled out on the sand at the far side, Ross put men to work unlashing the empty kegs and taking them back across the river. Hermenijildo, meanwhile, had secured more kegs and was preparing the second wagon. Josefina, helping Plácido with the mules, worked like any man.

They were over before the sky began to turn grey above the mesquite and greasewood to the east.

Tapia said, "We rest now, *señor?*"

They could have, but Ross, having crossed the Pecos, now found himself thinking of Valeria and filled with a new and strange driving power that he had not known before. "No, Lieutenant," he said. "It is best we go on. Another day's march will put us out of reach of the Comanches."

That day they drove the mules as only Mexicans could drive them. A mule was not broken in, said the *arrieros*, until his shoulder blades stuck through his skin. Ross would have no part of that kind of treatment, but he allowed Plácido to push the mules to their limit.

A few days later they had slowed to a more reasonable pace, and Ross began to feel victory within his reach. Then, half a day from Presidio del Norte, after he had seen the mud huts of the town from the left bank of the Del Norte, he saw a furious cloud of dust coming up the trail and rode out to meet it.

The square form of Doctor Connelly emerged from the dust cloud, as Ross had half anticipated. He roared a glad welcome, and shook hands hard. "You made it!" he said. "Any trouble?"

"Five men killed by Comanches," said Ross, "including Andrés."

"I am sorry to hear it," said Connelly, and looked past him at the long line of

351

wagons and mules. "It is a great thing you have done, Ross, to bring this huge train across wilderness country with no less than that. But," he said soberly, "there is more trouble ahead."

"What?"

Connelly faced him. "Governor Irigoyen died two months ago. Conde has taken his place, and he has cancelled the agreement we had with Irigoyen on the duties."

CHAPTER NINETEEN

Ross looked at Connelly in dismay. "And Conde has raised the tax?"

"They demand so much in duties that we cannot afford to haul the goods to Chihuahua."

"You can't afford *not* to," said Ross.

"I have a bill of lading for all the goods, and I have tried to talk Conde into some concessions, but at present he is adamant."

"And there is nothing else?" Ross said slowly.

"Not one damn' thing. The moment we take this train past Presidio without customs certificates we are liable to confiscation."

"How much of this is influenced by Cordero?"

Connelly shrugged. "Quite a bit, perhaps — though Conde has never been partial to the idea, as you know."

Ross said slowly, "What will happen to the backers?"

"It's a loss that will hurt — but nobody will go broke."

"And the Merchants' Bank?"

"Partially protected by the bullion they bought from us. They made a neat profit on that. Matter of fact, Ross, you stand to lose more than anybody. You could have been a rich man if our plan had gone through."

Ross said abruptly, "Have you given up?"

"By no means," said Connelly, "though I don't know yet how much of a licking we'll take. We'll get the train into Presidio and keep trying to negotiate with Conde."

"Tell him," said Ross, "that I'll take it back to Arkansas before I'll pay full duties on it."

Connelly began to ride back south with him. "It's a poor bluff and he'll know it, because most of the money was put up by Chihuahua merchants, and they'll have the final say."

Ross was silent a moment. "Hell of a note," he said finally.

Connelly was as glum as he was. They had spent a year, said Connelly, and they had made the trip but they had lost the opportunity. Any way they looked at it, the expedition could not possibly make any money, and it would take years to get together enough money to try it again. "The merchants," said Connelly, "are not concerned with glory of achievement but rather with making a profit."

Ross sighed. "What do we do now?"

"Cross the river and camp near Presidio del Norte, while I dicker with Don Lawreano and make weekly trips to Chihuahua to try to influence Conde."

Ross found out, as they waited at the Río Grande for the train, that the expedition was closer to bankruptcy than Connelly had first told him. High interest rates on the money, plus a soft market in Chihuahua because of heavy traffic on the Santa Fé Trail during the year they had been gone, meant that it was vital to get concessions from Conde just to break even. "We hope," said Connelly, "to have the value of the mules as our profit."

Ross stared at him. "That's nothing."

"It's better than a loss — but it doesn't make much for you."

Ross tried to quell the feeling of bitterness within him. He'd never cared about money before but this time it was important. Before, when it hadn't mattered, he'd made plenty. Now, when he wanted it, he was losing it. He'd wanted enough to buy a

355

ranch, but at best he would get only a few thousand dollars.

Connelly was studying the bills of lading. "Our cost of the goods alone was a little over $300,000, as you know, and Conde insists on assessing it the legal limit, so that actually the customs duties will come to almost $400,000 — and we'll be lucky to sell the entire cargo for that."

"You have one bargaining power," Ross observed. "If you can make him believe you would turn it back into Texas — say Austin or San Antonio — before you would pay the full duty, then perhaps he would settle for half, to get so much cash in the treasury."

"That's what I've been working on. I've asked for half but I don't think I'll get it. Whatever I do get will determine whether we lose money or break even."

"Since it doesn't help me either way," Ross noted, "I shouldn't give a damn how it comes out — but I do. This expedition is not finished until we roll into Chihuahua, and I intend to be at the head of it then."

The first mules came up, and Plácido took them into the Río Grande. It was hardly hock-deep over the limestone bed, and the crossing was easy. Ross sent Hermenijildo and Taylor to locate a camp site and arrange for grazing the animals. "It will cost money to stay here," he warned Connelly.

"I'll do my best. Meantime, try to keep your men out of trouble."

Ross smiled wryly. "After bringing three women and two hundred and twenty-five men across Texas without a fight, you suggest that. Frankly, I have half a notion to let them tear the town apart and help them do it. Maybe Don Lawreano would plead our cause with Conde and get some allowances."

Connelly said, "I know how you feel, Ross. You'll still get your fixed fee and a share of the mules — if that *is* a profit."

"All right," said Ross. "What's the important news from Chihuahua?"

Connelly faced him, his face emotionless, his eyes watchful. "It is said the *Doña* Valeria will marry Mangum in October."

Ross swallowed hard. "She's not yet married?" he asked then.

"No — but Don Fidel has issued his approval, as indeed he was practically forced to do."

Ross said, "I should have written her."

"From what the women say, it would have taken only a word from you to stop it — and perhaps it would do as yet. I would

357

be pleased to take a message."

Ross took a deep breath. "I have my pride," he said. "*Doña* Valeria is a half owner of Los Saucillos, and I had hoped to go to her with money of my own. But now I am to have nothing." He stared towards Chihuahua. "It is hard suddenly to want money so very much and to have none."

"I think we could find backers for a caravan on the Santa Fé Trail."

"Charity!" Ross snorted. "That is hardly necessary."

"It isn't necessary to keep your back so stiff," said Connelly. "The entire state of Chihuahua has tried to dissuade her from marrying the man."

"I can't go to her empty-handed," Ross said stubbornly.

They settled down in camp, and Ross went first to take care of Carlota. He was astonished to see how quickly she had filled out and regained her natural prettiness. She limped a little on the one leg, and she had many small scars on her arms and legs, but she had washed and combed her hair to a glossy black, and her skin was scrubbed until it was dusky only in the hollows, and the light was back in her eyes as he had seen it in Chihuahua.

"*Señora*," he said, "I am tremendously

happy to find you improving."

She smiled. *"Gracias, señor."*

"Do you have parents in Presidio — brothers, sisters? Any relatives?"

"I have a sister who works for Don Fidel at Los Saucillos."

"That's good."

"Perhaps I can get work at the *rancho*. If I could go to Chihuahua with you, *señor* —"

"You certainly may," he said. The thought occurred to him that she was young and pretty and hardly older than Valeria, and she had a tremendous resilience of spirit to have endured the death of all her family and a year's brutality at the hands of Muke-war-rah, and still be able to smile after a few days' time. She had already put on pleasing weight, and he thought she would make a fine wife for somebody. "I'll leave you in Mrs. Taylor's care until we get there."

"Gracias, señor." Her eyes watched his until he turned.

They stayed at Presidio for a month. Ross kept the teamsters on the payroll, thinking constantly that they would be going in a day or two, and not willing to break up the train to save a few hundred dollars.

Connelly was back and forth once a

week, and it was not until the fifth trip that he announced, somewhat ruefully, that they had finally made a deal with Conde. He had compromised at $300,000 — no less, and they had been forced to pay it. With adroit juggling they would be able to break even on the venture.

And so once again the packs were laid in a long line and the mules sent to find their own places and stand until the packs were lashed.

Presently the big train was once again under way. Connelly, with the precious *derechos de arancel* certificates stowed within his shirt, rode alongside Ross.

Ross stopped to watch the entire train pass by, and then he galloped forward to Plácido, near the front. "Where's Josefina?" he asked.

Plácido's big face was sad. "She stay in Presidio with Santiago," he said. "But don' worry — she come back to Plácido."

They crossed the dry, sandy desert of mesquite and *ocotillo* and beargrass and prickly pear. They made their camps without water and went on. Chihuahua came closer every day, and tension began to build in Ross Phillips's chest. It was September the twentieth, and only a few days more and the long trip would be over. . . .

Nothing, thought Ross. His share of the profits was exactly nothing. All he could expect was his flat fee. What of the ranch where he would have his own *peones* to whom he would be a wise and indulgent employer, and what of the golden-haired girl who was to be mistress of this great *rancho?* For a while he thought to speak to her anyway, but after hearing Connelly tell how the entire city felt that Mangum was marrying Valeria to get his hands on half of Los Saucillos, he saw that it would be more difficult than ever to go to her with nothing. Then it would become a question with the townspeople as to which of the two men would win Los Saucillos, and eventually that would reach her ears, and how would she feel then, to think that not she but Los Saucillos had been the object of their campaigns?

Magoffin and Don Fidel met them at the gates, and Hermenijildo's grandfather, and Doctor Jennison — and there was much shaking of hands and embracing in the Mexican fashion.

Ross went on in silence to superintend the unloading of the mules, the placing of the wagons around the *plaza,* the disposition of the mules. To each man he gave a *peso;* they would not be paid off until the

361

wagons were unloaded, and then they would receive their money in full. Meanwhile he had made arrangements for board and room for all who did not live in Chihuahua, and he asked only that they not get so drunk they would be unable to finish the job. There was grumbling at this, but some recognised the justice of it, and all knew it would result in stretching the period of celebration.

They spent three days unloading the wagons and storing the goods in Connelly's and Magoffin's warehouses. Then Connelly took over the wagons and got both them and the mules out to Los Saucillos to await whatever future sale they could work out. That night Connelly, Magoffin, Don Fidel, Apolinar, Don Mauricio and Ross sat down in Don Fidel's *salon* for a glass of brandy. Magoffin watched him pour. "Some new stuff?" he asked.

Don Fidel looked up. "I am ashamed to confess I suspect this was brought down the Trail by Cordero's man. However" — he held up the bottle — "it's real cognac, smooth as silk."

"If its lubrication qualities are what I remember, I will forget that it was brought in by a competitor."

They all settled down. Magoffin sipped the cognac and nodded, a pleased expression on his face. "This is very nearly as good as bourbon, Don Fidel."

Don Fidel glared at him, his great black moustaches bristling. "*Hombre!* You offer insult to the mules that hauled this nectar from St. Louis!"

Magoffin grinned and handed back his glass. "I may change my mind on a second sampling."

Don Mauricio was silent, but after his third glass he said thickly, "I am not blame you, Don Felip, for what happen to Andrés, but you will know it is a hard blow for a man to lose his only son."

"And yet," Connelly said judiciously, "it is better to lose him in the process of being a man — if one has to lose him."

Ross saw Apolinar's eyes on him, and turned away. Both Apolinar and Hermenijildo had thought as did Ross: that Andrés, reapproaching Chihuahua, somehow realised how he had turned and knew that his father would be ashamed, and they therefore, as did Ross, suspected that he had invited disaster at the hands of the Indians, or at least had taken no pains to avoid it. Ross sampled his third glass of cognac. "He died facing the Comanches," he said, "and his six-shooter was empty. He must have fought like a tiger until they struck him down."

Don Mauricio's eyes, sunken a little in his fat face, showed his gratefulness for the words. He finished his fourth glass and got up. "If you gentlemen will excuse me," he said, and bowed and staggered out.

"Will he be able to get home all right?" asked Ross.

Don Fidel nodded. "I suspected this would happen, and I gave my servant orders to accompany him."

None mentioned the tears brimming in Don Mauricio's eyes. It would be a lonesome night for him. . . .

"By God!" said Magoffin a half-hour later. "It's actually one of the greatest accomplishments in trail history." He struck his big knee with a ham-like hand. "In all my time on the Santa Fé Train I never saw anything like it. A third of a million dollars — first through the Comanches as bullion, then back through the Comanches as goods — and you never lost a nickel's worth. Nothing like it was even seen in this country — and yet its memory will be lost to history because it didn't make money."

"If we had made money," Connelly

agreed, "the trail would be swarming with wagons now, and the name of Ross Phillips would be known to our grandchildren. As it is —" He shrugged.

"There's just one thing," said Magoffin. "Damn my soul if I hardly believed you took Habersham's scalp. Did you *have* to lift the poor devil's hair?"

"Did you never take a scalp?" asked Ross suddenly.

"I've taken my share, I suppose — but not a white man's."

"There are several ways of looking at it," said Ross. "The alternative would have required me to soil my hands." He looked up, narrow-eyed. "The man had been after me all winter, determined to stop the expedition, and he was mighty near succeeding. I had to do something startling to convince the teamsters that I wouldn't be leading them to perdition, and I could think of nothing more effective."

"I could," Connelly said darkly, "but as you said, it's an Indian business, and I wouldn't blame you."

"I will concede," Magoffin said, holding out his glass, "that it was a master stroke. You got a good crew and you kept them in hand. Undoubtedly the spectacle of the scalping had a lot to do with it."

Ross got up. "Well, gentlemen, we had our fling — and right now I think I'm beginning to let down. I feel tired for the first time."

"There's no rush," said Don Fidel. "Your room is ready upstairs."

Ross glanced at him. "That's kind of you."

"By the way," said Magoffin, getting up, "your friend Taylor that you brought back with a circus is putting on a performance to-morrow night."

"Matter of fact," said Connelly, "Yvette von Brauch saw it last night and said it was pretty good. She thought she might go again to-night."

"I am going to-morrow night myself," said Magoffin, "and I'll take Mrs. Magoffin. Like to go with us, Ross?"

"No." Ross stared absently at the fire. "No, I don't feel like watching half a dozen white horses and a bunch of dogs do tricks with a hoop."

There was abrupt silence.

"Matter of fact," said Ross, "I have a strong suspicion that I shall go downtown to-morrow night and get howling drunk." He turned towards the door. "I've been sober too long."

There was still silence, as undoubtedly

everybody was thinking the same thing: what did he intend to do about Valeria?

Ross said, *"Buenas noches, hombres."*

There was still complete silence as he passed out of hearing. . . .

He rode around with Don Fidel the next morning, looking absently at the thousands of black horses, sorted into various divisions of the ranch according to age and sex. Don Fidel raised nothing else. Father Ramón was watering his nasturtiums as he had been doing in April of 1839 — it was now late August of 1840 — and he came over to offer congratulations on the success of the expedition.

That afternoon Ross went into town and settled up with Connelly and Magoffin. He got to Magoffin's warehouse to find the grey-haired *alcalde* there. "*Señor,* I am very sad to have done what I did to you," the *alcalde* said.

Ross stared at him, then looked at Connelly and Magoffin. He saw something wrong in their faces. "What is it?" he demanded.

Magoffin drew a deep breath. "We didn't figure on saying anything about it, after the way the expedition turned out and you had only your fixed fee left."

"About what?" demanded Ross.

Connelly said, "The *alcalde* forfeited your bail money while you were in Arkansas — under Cordero's suggestion, no d—"

"Bail money! You mean that $10,000?"

The *alcalde* nodded apologetically. "*Sí, señor,* you left without permission, and I had no choice. It is the law!"

Ross turned on the two *anglos.* "And you men paid it and weren't going to say anything!"

"You earned it," Connelly argued.

"I made a deal," said Ross harshly. "I keep my deals."

"But you won't have a cent left. The bail money matches your fixed fee."

Ross said, "In my language that is charity. I told you I keep my deals and I'll keep this one. Do you think the mules and wagons will show a profit?"

"Not that much," said Magoffin.

"Of course not." Ross moisted his lips. "Keep my fee to cover the bail money, and loan me a hundred dollars against the mules. I am at least going to have a celebration. . . ."

Ross went first to the *Nueve Gatos.* Some of his Arkansas teamsters were there. One borrowed a dollar from him; the others still had money. He bought a round of *pulque* but he did not join in the loud talk and banter and reminiscences of the trail. He sat soberly tasting the *pulque* and for the first time it made him feel like throwing up. "It's not fresh," he told the *propriedor.* "It smells like putrid meat — old putrid meat."

The man threw up his hands in pretended horror. "*Señor!* This fine *pulque* was made only yesterday! I myself have seen the *licor divino* taken from the *maguey. Señor,* I cannot express to you —"

"All right," Ross said, and threw out a *peso.* "Bring me another."

The teamsters went out, inviting him to accompany them, but he declined. He sat at the little table and drank himself into a morose half-stupor, for he had made the trip for but one purpose; to acquire a competence which he might lay at the feet of *Doña* Valeria.

This time was different from all the other times when he had completed a difficult mission. Always before it had been a great and glorious feeling of accomplishment, and in his elation it had seemed appropriate to throw away his money and look for the next challenge. But this one was different: he seemed somehow to have come to the end of something; the accomplishment had been made, and now he was ready to enjoy the fruits — but there were no fruits to look forward to, and he had no desire to go on a fling and throw away the money. Hell of a thing, he told himself.

More of the teamsters drifted in, and Ross greeted them and bought them drinks but took no part in their bucolic joys. For the first time in his life he was drinking himself not into conviviality but into sadness. He knew it but he didn't care.

Then at some time during the night the door opened, the night breeze from the mountains flickered the lamps, and Josefina stepped inside and looked around uncertainly.

One of the teamsters recognised her and called to her. She looked at him but did not answer. Then she saw Ross and smiled shyly. He sat up straight and she came over.

His voice was thick. "How'd you get here?"

"I came by mule train — this evening, *señor.*"

"*Pulque!*" roared Ross. "*Pulque* for Josefina!"

She stood close to him.

"What happened to Santiago?" he asked.

"He got drunk," she said, "and did not come home one night. Another *hombre* came, and I was just talking to him, but there was no light, and —" She shrugged. "He was most jealous. He turns me out in the street, and I have decide' to come back home."

Ross grunted. "Plácido was right, wasn't he?"

Her eyes widened as she put a slim hand on his shoulder. "I have not seen Plácido," she said.

"You will. But in the meantime —"

"Yes, *señor?*"

Her lips were on his. Her arms went around his neck. *"Señor!"* she said in a husky whisper.

"Josefina!"

It was a harsh voice — one that Ross had heard few times, but which, even in his drunkenness, he recognised immediately. He lifted the girl and twisted to stare at the door and the black-browed countenance of Ed Mangum.

Ross got to his feet without touching anything with his hands. His head cleared as he arose. He saw the look of jealousy on Mangum's face, and realised it was a look of utter selfishness, for only a man like Mangum could be more concerned with his egotism than his sex instincts.

After Mangum's first glance at Josefina, his blazing eyes settled on Ross, and Ross knew that Mangum too had been drinking.

Ross had no weapon, but he saw Mangum's hand move towards his coat front. He froze Mangum's movement for an instant with a pointed forefinger. "You had a free shot at me already. Are you taking another?"

Mangum debated for only an instant. Then his thin veneer of Spanish gentility was swept aside completely. He drew the pistol as Ross leaped. The bullet hit Ross on the crown of his shoulder. Then, losing all control of his temper at the man's deliberate attempt to murder him, he closed with Mangum and seized the pistol with both hands. He tore it from Mangum's grasp. Mangum produced a knife, but Ross was already crashing the pistol-barrel on Mangum's head. Again and again and again.

Mangum began to slip but Ross kept pounding, for the knife was still in Mangum's hands. When Mangum finally ceased to move, Ross dropped the pistol and backed away, shaking his head. He felt a hand on his arm, and Magoffin's voice: "Come along with us."

Magoffin took him to Connelly's place, where Dr. Jennison cleaned the wound with alcohol and put a bandage on it.

Ross felt the sting of the alcohol and thought of the many fights he had gone through in a year and a half — all for one purpose: to defeat Cordero. And now he had breached all the levels below Cordero, and there was left only Cordero himself. Perhaps it would be a good thing to go after Cordero and make a clean job of it. . . .

Magoffin was back the next morning. "Mangum died," he said, "but I think you're in the clear. There were several mule skinner witnesses, and they all say he drew on you without warning."

Ross chuckled sourly. "His final bungle," he said. "He'd been bungling things all his life, but this time he over-reached."

"How?"

"In marrying Valeria he was carrying through his assumed role as a Mexican gentleman, and probably also in hanging on to Josefina as his mistress. But he made one mistake: a Mexican *caballero* would have treated Josefina for what she is, and would not have lost control of his feelings. He showed his innate Anglo-Saxon heritage by losing his head."

"Is that so bad?" asked Connelly, puzzled. "Maybe he was true to himself for the first time."

"Andrés did the same thing," said Ross, not thinking.

"Yes — and automatically fell in his own eyes. Perhaps," Magoffin said shrewdly, "that had something to do with his getting scalped."

Ross said nothing.

"It's too deep for me," said Connelly. "Let's have a brandy."

"Suits me fine."

Dr. Jennison came back with James Taylor. "Here's a man been looking for you," he told Ross.

Ross got up from his chair and shook hands.

"Have a brandy?" asked Connelly.

Taylor looked at him, pleased. "Don't mind if I do, Mr. Connelly."

Ross said, "You're playing your circus in Chihuahua."

"Yes, sir." Taylor took the brandy eagerly and said thank you. "That's why I came here, Mr. Phillips. We've played three nights now and cleared over a thousand dollars each night. We're all rich!"

"Congratulations," said Ross. "I'm sure you can play for years in Mexico. They get very little entertainment of a professional variety."

"But —" Taylor looked bewildered.

"You're rich too, Mr Phillips!"

Ross stared at him blankly.

"Don't you remember? You said you'd let me come to Chihuahua with your train, and you'd give me work at regular wages, and for protecting me and my wife and the circus you'd take a half interest for a year."

Ross frowned. "There was something like that, now that I think of it. But I wasn't serious. I just didn't want you to think you were getting something for nothing."

Taylor beamed. "It was a wonderful deal for me, Mr. Phillips, and I'm very happy to turn your half over to you. If it hadn't been for you I would have lost the whole circus."

"Well, that's fine," said Ross. "Pay me off and go your way — with my blessing."

Taylor finished the brandy. "I don't know what kind of man you think I am, Mr. Phillips. You said a partnership, and I agreed. As far as I am concerned that still goes. Anyway, it's a strange country and I need your backing for the rest of the year."

Ross finally smiled. He shook hands with Taylor and then looked around at Connelly and Magoffin. "Strange world, isn't it?"

Connelly poured more brandy.

"There's other good news too," said

Magoffin, "now that you mention it. This morning we talked the *alcalde* into remitting the bail money — since you actually returned after all."

Ross shook his head. "You're trying to give me ten thousand dollars."

"No, we merely threatened to throw our goods on the market at half of Cordero's price, and since he has a train due here in a few days —" He chuckled. "Anyway, you've got your fixed fee back."

Ross grinned. "That's better than nothing."

"Now," said Magoffin, "maybe you can propose to Valeria so my wife will quit pestering me about it."

"There's not the question of money now," Connelly reminded him.

Ross looked at them. "Since my feeling about Valeria seems to be a prime topic of conversation in Chihuahua —"

"You needn't be sarcastic," said Connelly. "This is customary in Mexico."

"Very well, *amigos* — but consider this: am I then to kill her fiancé and immediately propose marriage in his place?"

"My God!" said Connelly. "You certainly got it bad. I never saw such a touchy rooster."

Ross thought about it while he helped to

dispose of the mules and wagons. Ten thousand was hardly enough for what he had in mind.

Adolph Speyer came in from Santa Fé after a bad trip across the desert and bought thirty of their wagons and three hundred mules to make the trip on to Mexico City, and Connelly gave Ross a cheque for $3,800 more. Somehow, it seemed, money was piling up in the bank with no particular effort on his part. James Taylor bought one wagon and some mules and took his circus on south to Guajuquilla. Then Apolinar found him one day quietly having a cognac at the *Nueve Gatos*. It was reasonably safe there, he told Apolinar, for Josefina had attached herself to one of the Arkansas teamsters who had gone on with Speyer's train.

Apolinar sat down and ordered a *pulque*, then changed his mind when he sniffed the cognac. "I never knew Antonio to have anything like this before," he said.

"He didn't," said Ross, "until I cadged a bottle from Connelly and told him to keep it for me."

"*Papá* wishes to see you, *señor*."

Ross downed the cognac. "A reason, I suppose."

"*Sí, señor. Papá* wishes to offer you a

377

partnership in Los Saucillos."

Ross laughed. "You're quizzing me."

"No, *señor*, I am quite serious. The *rancho* is much too big for one man."

"He has you."

"I have told him I would like to have you there."

"But —"

"The *rancho* is very big, *señor*. We do not know how many *varas* — millions, undoubtedly. And we have almost fifty thousand black horses — *fifty thousand, señor!*"

Ross looked at him seriously. "That's a lot of horses," he agreed.

"You will talk about it?" urged Apolinar.

"If it's agreeable with you."

"I would be honoured. Of course you understand, *señor*, that this is not a full partnership. It is in relation to what you can put into it."

"Of course."

"Then let us get out to the *rancho*."

It was a pleasant ride in the warm sun, and overhead a *caracara* — bone-breaker — circled, endlessly, looking for an unwary jackrabbit. "Nice country," said Ross, looking at the mountains.

"*Muy bonito,*" Apolinar agreed.

Don Fidel met them and led them past the barking dogs, past Father Ramón, past the staring black eyes of children.

He asked Peralta if he had found who tampered with the pistol before the duel.

"A girl named Anita, who took care of your room. She was bribed by Mangum. How —" He shrugged. "Anyway, Carlota's sister saw her, and told Carlota and Diego. Then Diego became very excited and borrowed one of my black geldings to gallop to Chihuahua. I found all this out later."

"Where is Anita now?"

"She went up the Trail with Mangum last summer and did not return. There are reports she is working in St. Louis."

"You like my proposition?" Peralta asked Ross after they sat down with a glass of brandy.

"I like it if it isn't a gift."

"It's no gift. As you can well imagine, there is room for a good man at Los Saucillos. This is almost a state in itself."

"My money won't make much of a splash in this pond."

"Quite the contrary," said Don Fidel. "To be frank, I lost heavily on the Arkansas expedition. I'm not — embarrassed, as you say, but I'm a little uncomfortable from lack of cash, and it will be a squeeze to operate the ranch until the colt crop comes along next spring, unless I can sell an interest to somebody with cash. And at the moment, *señor,* you have the only cash in Chihuahua."

"How is that? Surely Cordero —"

"His last train was attacked by Pawnees and many men killed, goods taken. Cordero is now no better off than the rest of us."

Ross said thoughtfully, "It sounds like a chance that does not come very often."

"Next year," Peralta agreed, "it may be much different."

Ross said, "Very well, count me in."

"*Bien, señor! Muy bien!* There is of course my other partner to be consulted, but I do not anticipate any difficulty."

"Your other partner?" asked Ross.

Peralta bowed low. "*Señorita Doña* Valeria Sierra," he said.

Ross was thunderstruck for a moment. "Am I to be —"

Apolinar said softly, "*Señor,* it is time to forget your pride."

Ross stared at him, then smiled. "I guess you're right." He turned to Peralta. "Don Fidel, you are the legal guardian of the *señorita,* aren't you?"

"Yes."

"Then I will observe the proprieties by asking you for the hand of *Doña* Valeria in marriage."

Peralta started to smile but checked it. "Very good, *señor*," he said formally. "I will take it into consideration. . . ."

Before the round of social events got under way they had a small family *tertulia* at which relatives, servants, and even the *peones* were welcomed. "It's an old Peralta custom," Don Fidel told him. And on the evening of the party, Don Fidel put an arm around Ross and another around Valeria and led them to the *patio*. "A present," he said, "from Don José Cordero."

Ross shook his head. "Two beautiful chestnut stallions! How is this possible?"

Don Fidel shrugged. *"Una cosa de Méjico,"* he explained. "It is the way we do business. Cordero tried hard to defeat you, but there was nothing personal involved, and this is his apology to you."

"Well," said Ross, drawing a deep breath, "considering the number of times his men tried to kill me —" He broke off. "All right. No offence!"

He stole a glance at Valeria, and thought she had been covertly watching him. So far their engagement had been extremely formal, and he had not been alone with her even to talk. It seemed the closer he got to that tilting golden head and the lilting voice, the more barrier there was between them.

"We have another surprise," said Don Fidel. "Hermenijildo!"

The tall young Mexican came into the room, and Ross shook hands. "You're going to let the moustache grow, I take it."

"*Sí, señor.*" He stepped aside, and the pretty Chonita had a bundle in her arms. At least, it looked so to Ross. He laughed. "A boy or a girl?"

Chonita smiled and pulled back the blanket. "Felipe," she said proudly.

"A boy?" cried Ross. "Congratulations!" He turned. "Don Fidel!" he cried. "Cigars!"

He shook hands with Hermenijildo but was puzzled at the amusement in the man's eyes. He turned back to Chonita and saw a second round face exactly like the first. "Felipe *Segundo*," she said.

"Two boys!" he exclaimed. "Don Fidel! Brandy — quick!"

But now Hermenijildo's amusement seemed to have deepened, and Ross looked in bewilderment at Chonita. His eyes widened and he could not believe what they told him, for Chonita held three identical babies.

"Felipe *Tercero*," she said.

Finally Ross smiled and asked her, "Is

that all, *señora?*"

She smiled and nodded. Hermenijildo said, "I told you my grandfather was one of three twins, *señor.*"

Ross shouted, "Don Fidel! Cognac and cigars! Hurry before it's too late!"

They danced, and Ross had only one objection: he didn't get a chance to dance with Valeria, for the girls of the ranch were allowed to claim him whenever they wished — and it seemed they wished. Before long he found himself dancing with a very pretty girl who also, like Chonita, watched him as if amused.

"*Señorita,*" he said, "I know it is my evening to be laughed at, but do you mind telling me what is funny?"

She said in a familiar voice, "Don't you know me?"

"Carlota!"

In his pleasure at seeing her well and pretty again he hugged her. She was soft and yet pleasantly firm, like Valeria.

"*Señor* —" Her eyes were searching his face. "Are you about to tell me that I have ribs like a haunch of mutton?"

He stared at her for an instant, then looked up. Every woman in the room was watching him. He caught Valeria's eyes, and knew she had put Carlota up to it.

And for the first time in a year and a half he looked straight into her brown eyes, and slowly, gradually his arm dropped from around Carlota and he turned towards Valeria and started that way, but incredibly his knees suddenly weakened and his eyes dimmed, and he stopped in the centre of the floor.

She came towards him from somewhere near the fireplace. It was twilight now, and the golden shadows of the mountains fell over the plain; the doves went *"Cú, cú, cú,"* and then suddenly the whole world was very quiet and peaceful, and for a moment only the girlish laughter of a child superimposed itself on the universal clapping of brown hands shaping *tortillas* for the evening meal.

Then he was walking towards her again through a bright mist of weakness. He stopped before her. *"Señorita,* I —"

Her arms went around him. He kissed her warm lips. Presently she drew back, her dark eyes on his. *"Señor,* don't you hear? The music has stopped."

He held her a little way from him and shook his head slowly. *"Señorita,"* he said earnestly, "the music has barely begun."